I0612956

Love Is Silent

by

Toni V. Sweeney

This is a work of fiction. Names, characters, places, and incidents are either the product of the author's imagination or are used fictitiously, and any resemblance to actual persons living or dead, business establishments, events, or locales, is entirely coincidental.

Love Is Silent

COPYRIGHT © 2023 by Toni V. Sweeney

All rights reserved. No part of this book may be used or reproduced in any manner whatsoever without written permission of the author or The Wild Rose Press, Inc. except in the case of brief quotations embodied in critical articles or reviews.
Contact Information: info@thewildrosepress.com

Cover Art by *The Wild Rose Press, Inc.*

The Wild Rose Press, Inc.
PO Box 708
Adams Basin, NY 14410-0708
Visit us at www.thewildrosepress.com

Publishing History
First Edition, 2023
Trade Paperback ISBN 978-1-5092-5183-4
Digital ISBN 978-1-5092-5184-1

Published in the United States of America

"David, come in." His sister didn't appear to notice. She raised a hand, beckoning. "Let me introduce you to our guest."

Standing, she took the little slate from the desk, scribbling a few words upon it and holding it out to him. Anna would learn that although she always wrote what she wanted to say, she also spoke to him as if he could hear, for the benefit of anyone else present.

She also noticed Lady Eleanor didn't speak loudly, as most people did to someone deaf. Her voice didn't raise above normal speaking level. Indeed, for all the good actually speaking did her brother, she could've simply *mouthed* the words at him.

He glanced at the slate, then back to Anna, and the scowl deepened. A hand went to his riding pocket, bringing out a miniature slate similar to Lady Eleanor's. A chalk pencil was attached and he pulled it loose, writing a couple of words and turning it so his sister could see.

Anna saw also.

Not maid?

He thinks I'm a servant? Anger sputtered, then died. *I am, aren't I? In a way.*

Shaking her head, Lady Eleanor proceeded to write more. "She's here to teach you the deaf language."

On the slate Anna could see the words, *teach you…deaf language…*

Something she could only call fury flashed across his face. His lips tightened, pursing into a pout. He shook his head, glanced at Anna again and repeated the movement even more violently, making curling strands of hair escape from its club. One hand shook in a decidedly negative gesture, then clenched into a fist.

Praise for Toni V. Sweeney

"The love story is sweet and sensual and deep. The characters are layered and compelling in their goals, motivation and conflict. Beyond those important qualities in any work of fiction, the detailed research is impressive. *Love Is Silent* comes with an added bonus of teaching the reader about the history of education of the hearing impaired. Out of 5 stars, this earns a 6."

~Kat Henry Doran, Wild Women Reviews

~*~

"The challenges and frustrations they both face as David struggles to learn sign language, and the danger and delight of falling in love spurred by the threat of losing everything they have gained, makes *Love Is Silent* a unique, compelling story. 5 Stars."

~Linda Laye Shuler, author of Hidden Shadows

Dedication

For those Who Write Romance Novels
and For Those Who Read Them

Chapter 1

On the Road to Mayfield Manor
England, 1815

...As soon as the Right Honorable Lady Eleanor Woods notified me of her desire to have one of the teachers from McAdam Academy for the Deaf instruct her younger brother in Signing, I thought of you, my dear Anna. You've had so much success with youngsters, I felt you'd be the better choice for this position. Granted, the twenty-seventh Baron Mayfield is very low in the peerage strata but, his position notwithstanding, he is nobility, and to successfully instruct a lord will truly be a feather in our collective cap. In expectation of your accepting the position, I have replied to Lady Eleanor's letter by recommending you. I am enclosing the railway ticket which Her Ladyship sent along with her correspondence. You will arrive at Mayfield Village on 12 May, and from there…

"You've had so much success with youngsters…" Anna Leighton reread that line, then folded the letter and returned it to her reticule.

How many times had she done that since receiving the letter? Too many, because she still couldn't believe it was true, that she was on her way to her first independent employment as a teacher of the deaf.

"'Ere we be, miss." The driver's words broke into

her thoughts.

****

Alighting from the train amid steam and cinders, she'd been met at the railway station by a driver with a pony and trap, a smart-looking conveyance with a trim little dappled gray dozing between the traces.

"Pardon me, miss. Be ya Miss Anna Leighton?"

Since no one else had disembarked, Anna smiled at his question. She didn't ask if her identity should've been obvious, thinking that would be considered rude to say to a stranger at their first meeting. She simply nodded.

"Name's Ogilvie," he explained, tapping two fingers against his cap. "Own the livery stable in Mayfield Village."

Rather homely, though pleasant-faced enough, Ogilvie's manner was reserved but friendly. He was an older man, possibly in his mid-forties, clothes a bit rough, being fashioned of fustian, but Anna supposed they were appropriate for someone working with horses and such. He had such a homespun manner about him, she wondered if he might also be a farmer, perhaps having a second livelihood tilling fields.

"Hired by Lady Eleanor I be, t' bring ya t' Mayfield Manor."

With that, he took her portmanteau, deposited it into the trap, which was very up-to-date, looking fairly new and in good condition. He then assisted her up the single step and inside. Once she was settled, he climbed up beside her, gathered the reins, and whistled to the pony, who raised his head as if he'd been jerked from a deep sleep. Ogilvie shook the reins, and they were off.

He didn't speak as they traveled. Not certain if it would be proper etiquette to engage him in conversation, especially since what she'd want to do was quiz him about her prospective employer, Anna also remained silent. For a bit, she watched the spokes of the trap's wheels as they spun. When she realized the mesmerizing effect of that activity, she turned her attention instead to the countryside speeding past.

The pony was an energetic little beast, taking the highroad at a very quick trot. Anna noted that although his bridle had winkers on it—to prevent an animal from being distracted, her father had told her—as well as an overcheck, Ogilvie held the reins lax, giving the creature its head. She liked that, remembering the few times she'd ridden in a coach, and how the driver kept the reins tight and the overcheck forced the horses to tuck in their chins, making their necks arch. It was a pretty sight, but she was certain it also made pulling the heavy weight of the coach difficult when they couldn't stretch their necks.

It was amazing how quickly the little vehicle got her to where she needed to go, for abruptly, Ogilvie pulled the pony to a halt, and spoke those momentous words.

"'Ere we be, miss."

****

Anna started slightly as she focused again on the present.

Can this really be my destination? She looked around in concern, glancing at the stand of pines bordering the highroad with an occasional oak thrusting out its branches as if demanding more room.

Separating the road from the trees, an energetic creek meandered, spanned by a small wooden footbridge. On the opposite side, brush and shrubbery gave way to farm fencing, horizontal planks held upright at intervals by double posts through which the hand-

3

hewn boards were fastened in place by tied rawhide and wooden nails. Far away in the deep meadow enclosed by the fence, mares and cows, some with foals or calves by their sides, were visible.

Nowhere in close proximity was there a manor house or a dwelling of any kind.

"Where?" She grimaced at that slight quaver entering her voice.

Ogilvie was already sliding down from his seat and opening the trap's door.

Surely he isn't expecting me to get out...in the middle of nowhere?

Apparently, he was, because he reached in, seized the handles of her portmanteau, and pulled it from the trap, setting it on the grass by the side of the road.

"B-but..." She found her voice, protesting, "There's no house..."

"Past yon trees." He nodded over his shoulder at the stand of pines.

"You aren't taking me directly there?" That much was obvious, but she persisted, wanting it stated plainly.

"Can't. Yon bridge be too narrow for th' trap...as ya can see."

"Do all visitors have to walk from here?"

"Nay...access t' Mayfield Manor carriage road's a full five mile ahead. Awkward 'avin' it so far out o' the way, but..." He shrugged as if saying, *What can one do?* "I weren't paid t' go that far."

Anna didn't answer.

"All ya 'ave t' do is cross th' bridge an' follow th' path," he continued to her silence. "Manor's at th' end o' it." He held out a hand. "Closest t' walk from 'ere."

"What if I get lost?" Anna made no move to place

her own hand in his.

"Can't…iffen ya stay on th' path, an' it's well-trod so's there's no danger o' missin' it." He gestured a bit impatiently.

Reluctantly, Anna allowed herself to be helped from the trap. Once she was standing beside him, he bent and lifted the portmanteau, handing it to her.

"Just stay on th' path, miss."

"There aren't any wild animals? Dogs or anything?" She accepted the piece of luggage and thought how heavy it felt, wondering if she could carry it very far. Believing someone would assist her, she'd stuffed it with probably much more than she'd need. Now she regretted that.

"Lord, bless ya, miss. Nothin' o' that sort. Naught more dangerous than a chipmunk in these parts, an' those little creeturs'll eat out'n your 'ands after a bit." As if he abruptly sensed her reluctance, he smiled, revealing a missing front tooth which somehow made his homely face slightly endearing. "Don't worry, miss. You just stay on th' path an' you'll be there in two shakes o' a lamb's tail."

With that, he again touched fingers to his cap, nodded, and climbed back onto the driver's seat. He didn't drive off immediately, however, but sat waiting. After a moment's hesitation, Anna stepped onto the first plank of the bridge.

It was narrow, barely wide enough for two people to stand side by side. As Ogilvie pointed out, definitely not enough room for something the size of a pony trap to maneuver, although the pony might've on his own, or a man on horseback…if on a very small horse.

Anna's feet made a hollow *tap, tap* as she walked

across, the sound almost drowned in the gurgling of the creek flowing beneath the planking. Ogilvie didn't move until she was safely on the other side, once again standing on thick, weedy grass.

As she looked back, calling, "Goodbye, Mr. Ogilvie, thank you," he again nodded, then snapped the reins over the pony's back.

Turning the trap in a wide circle, he headed it the way they'd come. He didn't look back. Anna stood a moment longer, watching man and pony disappear down the highroad in a cloud of dust. Once they were out of sight, she took a deep breath, looked to the path worn into the grass, and started out.

Chapter 2

Anna had indeed been successful with children who'd lost their hearing and, in a good many cases, also their ability to speak.

At age fourteen, her younger sister was stricken with a bout of red measles, rendering her deaf. Although Maisie retained the ability to speak, being cut off from everything at an age when the world should be opening up to her caused the child to become severely withdrawn.

As a physician, Maisie's father had heard of the McAdam Academy for the Deaf in London and knew the school offered a way for his daughter to reconnect with her family. Being a doctor choosing to treat the inhabitants of the small farming community of Little Riversreach instead of a higher class of citizen as did his Harley Street associates, he was unable to afford the tuition and fees the school required, having earlier just that year finished paying the tuition enabling his older daughter to graduate from the Dinsmoore Normal School in preparation for being a secondary studies teacher.

Paying for Anna's education prevented her younger sister from getting the instruction she required.

As luck would have it, there was an opening at the Academy for an assistant instructor. In order to help Maisie and perhaps in atonement for taking away funds her sibling required, eighteen-year-old Anna applied for the position, and was accepted. She proved herself an apt and quick pupil, becoming a favorite with teachers and students alike. Within two years, Rupert McAdam, founder of the school, certified her as a teacher, assigning her to the instruction of eight- to ten-year-olds.

The first thing Anna did when she returned home for holidays after her first semester at the school was to begin teaching Maisie to Sign and bring her sister out of the shell of silence in which she was trapped. When she returned to McAdam Academy to begin the second term, Maisie was on her way to communicating again.

****

Teaching those unable to hear and therefore unable to speak was still an innovation in Great Britain.

Though sign language had been known in the country as early as 1570, there were no set methods for teaching those who couldn't hear, other than gestures, pantomime, and body language among family members.

That changed in 1760 when Thomas Braidwood, a teacher from Edinburgh, founded Braidwoods' Academy for the Deaf and Dumb. This was considered a highly-startling endeavor since it was the first school for the deaf in the kingdom. In fact, most people thought it a scandal since a good many families simply accepted the deafness of a child as some type of punishment by God and believed to try and change that was an affront to the Deity.

Braidwood managed to change that opinion by teaching the children of some very influential people. Soon, the Academy was thriving and giving hope to many youngsters and an occasional adult. Several of the people coming there to learn stayed to be trained as teachers and later went back to their homes to open their own schools. One was Joseph Watson, who became the headmaster of the first public school for the deaf.

He also trained Rupert McAdam, who returned to London to open the McAdam Academy. That school was very well known in its own way because it used the method called *Sign-supported Speech*, which incorporated both speaking words aloud while simultaneously Signing them.

****

Whenever she was home, Anna not only tutored Maisie but also several of the townspeople of Little Riversreach, as well. Rallying around the Leighton family, they showed their support for their doctor and his family by asking to be taught how to Sign.

In teaching them, Anna succeeded beyond her wildest dreams, for one of those becoming her pupil was Robert Ellerby, son of a local merchant and a childhood friend of the family. Four years later, he successfully concluded a completely silent but very ardent courting of Anna's little sister. When Anna received Dr. McAdam's letter, she was home for Robert's marriage to Maisie.

Encouraged by Maisie's success in not only prevailing over her deafness but of becoming a wife, Anna accepted the position offered by Lady Eleanor Woods.

Her trip north was filled with excitement and apprehension. Other than traveling to the academy, where she was housed along with the other unmarried female teachers in Dr. McAdam's home and watched over by his wife, she'd never been away from Little Riversreach before.

Her excitement came from that fact, as well as taking on the responsibility of teaching a young person without supervision of another more experienced teacher. Her apprehension was because she feared the child might suffer because of that fact or wouldn't turn out to be one of those who, even with the gift offered him, couldn't readjust to again being able to communicate.

Most youngsters suffering a disability became sullen and withdrawn. A few acted out by transforming into bullies or mannerless louts, almost animals. It was such a joy to see them blossom and respond when they realized they could once more communicate with the world. After that, they became different children, very few continuing their previous chaotic, sometimes violent ways. She hoped this boy would do the same.

Dr. McAdam hadn't given her any information about her future charge except that he was a baron and was younger than his sister. He hadn't even supplied the young nobleman's name.

I hope he won't be difficult.

Chapter 3

Anna was grateful it wasn't yet noon and the sun was shining brightly as befitted a late spring day, though she had to lift her head to peer past the poke of her bonnet to see the sunbeams twinkling through the trees. To have to walk through an unknown forest with the sun dying and the moon soon rising might have been unnerving. If it were darker, the crunch of dirt under her boots would have added a sinister touch. As it was, Anna's progress through the wood was a fairly unharrowing affair.

A faint hum broke the silence…bees, or cicadas, hidden in the trees. Birds flitted about, some lighting on high branches to give a few bright chirps before launching themselves into the air again. Once or twice a crow flew over with a loud cawing.

That made her wonder if there were fields nearby where the scavengers might pilfer some farmer's hard-sown wheat. She remembered the pastures on the other side of the road held both horses and cows. She thought she'd seen two distinct shapes, and where there were such animals, there would surely be farmers growing grains for them as well as providing grist for millers to transform into flour.

Ogilvie spoke truthfully. The path itself was very well-trodden, grass worn away by many feet. It would be very difficult to get lost as long as she stayed sharp and paid attention. Anna glanced around, thinking how evenly-spaced the trees appeared. Surely a man could ride a horse through them after he crossed the bridge, while the sun shone clearly through the branches.

Here and there, berry bushes and a smattering of wildflowers dotted the grass between the trees. Indeed, if she wasn't still a bit anxious at having to walk the final steps to her destination, Anna might've found it a delightful place.

The portmanteau was becoming increasingly heavy as well as unwieldly. It banged uncomfortably against her thigh as she walked.

I'm certain I'll have bruises.

Anna tried swinging it, establishing a rhythm with her gait. That merely threw her off balance and made her stumble. *I hope it isn't much farther.*

As if it had heard her thought, the forest abruptly ended. She found herself in a clearing with neatly trimmed grass and a small hedgerow, on the other side of which stood the building that had to be Mayfield Manor.

She had expected it to be similar to the houses in the estates around Little Riversreach…a stately, elegant, many-storied brick with white Georgian pillars supporting the portico over the front entryway and multiple windows looking down on a graveled drive, with perhaps a widows' walk on its roof. A home in the neoclassical style of architects John Nash or Robert Adam, perhaps. Barring that, something in the Greek Revival tradition of William Wilkins and Robert Smirke. She'd always admired that type of architecture, and— foolish as she knew it to be—dreamed of someday living in such a place.

Mayfield Manor was neither. It was a thick-bricked

gray building with rounded towers at each end, looking like a bastardized miniature Norman castle. Partially covered by ivy crawling up its walls and adding a green shadow to its grayness, it sprawled in front of her, insolent and stark, as if daring her to comment on its difference, defiant somehow. With a thick, ancient oak hugging one wall like a sentinel, the house seemed not so much hiding behind the stand of pines but rather lurking, as if to spring itself upon the unwary traveler walking the path, appearing unexpectedly and startling to those expecting a gracious manor house.

Here I am, it seemed to say. *Not what you expected? Too bad. What you see is what I am.*

Abruptly, Anna shivered. What would people living in such a rebellious-appearing example of architecture be like? What if they weren't as either Dr. McAdam or she expected?

Taking a deep breath, she saw that the path didn't end but continued through the grass. Instead of a turnstile, there was a narrow entrance cut into the hedgerow…hacked through, rather, as if some large animal had forced his way into the bush, tearing it apart and someone later attempted to smooth the broken twigs by trimming them. She hurried through it, lifting her skirt slightly with her free hand, making certain she didn't snag either the hem of her dress or her travelling coat on any brambles along the way.

Once on the other side of the hedge, she found herself standing in the dirt drive leading to the manor. To the right converged the carriage road Ogilvie mentioned, stretching to the horizon and some out-of-the-way and unseen connection to the highroad.

Perhaps taking the footbridge and walking is a

much faster, if slightly unusual, way to get here.

There was nothing else in sight, so Anna hoped she was correct in assuming the stables, barns, and outbuildings were behind the manor somewhere. No sound came from any direction to give a clue where they might be, however. Indeed, the entire scene appeared abandoned.

Hefting the portmanteau, she crossed the courtyard.

The door to the manor was uncovered by a portico or eave of any kind. It was a massive, dark wood affair, aged and weatherworn, though still retaining a high gloss as if even now it was well cared for and polished often. It was fitted with an enormous, ornate brass handle and plate, engraved with curling vines and leaves, the door handle resembling a thick twisted vine. The doorframe itself was also of metal and elaborately decorated.

Stepping onto the square stone stoop, Anna hesitantly touched the handle, imagining for a moment she actually felt the thickness of woody plant instead of metal beneath her fingers.

There appeared to be no knocker.

Setting down the portmanteau, she released the handle, flexing her fingers to get the circulation back into them. Then, she knocked, knuckles tapping against the weathered wood.

Anna waited.

After several moments, when no one appeared and the door remained unopened, she knocked again, reflecting that her feeble raps against the thick lumber probably couldn't be heard inside the house.

Perhaps no one is to home? Surely they wouldn't leave when I was expected. At least, she hoped not.

Then again, would nobility, even a minor baron's

sister, consider a teacher, a would-be employee, important enough to wait for if she was seized by a whim to go for a carriage ride or visit friends?

Once more, Anna knocked, more forcefully this time, to the detriment of stinging knuckles in spite of the protection of her gloves. Again, there was no answer.

What shall I do? She felt a moment of dismay.

Hoofbeats sounded behind her, and Anna looked around.

With an easy lope, a chestnut horse cantered into sight, tossing its head. Snorting, it came to a halt a few feet from her, its rider sliding from its back.

Giving a bare glance and an even barer nod, he turned to the hitching post to the right of the door. Sliding a hand into a hip pocket, he produced a small red ball, feeding it to the horse.

The animal lipped it off his palm, chewing loudly.

"Good morning." Anna said.

She didn't intend to stare, but truly, the man's appearance invited it. He was young, perhaps her age or a bit less, rather tall, and quite handsome in spite of the bristly swathe of dark hair shadowing his jaw. *Decidedly* handsome…there was no other way to describe him. Though he now had his back to her, the brief glimpse of his face burned itself into her memory.

The most remarkable things about him, however, were that he had been riding the horse bareback, no saddle in sight, and he was shirtless, wearing only a pair of buff twilled cotton nankeens with a high fishtail back. These were held up by a pair of cloth braces buttoned with leather loops. They were very tight trousers, so snug-fitting, in fact, they appeared to have been fashioned for someone of a much smaller stature, clinging to his legs in such a way they showed how muscular those legs were. In spite of that, the trousers were well-made, though as worn as his scuffed and dusty boots, having a single welt pocket just over his right hip as well as two riding pockets at the waistband.

Anna drew in her breath sharply, then hoped he hadn't heard. His half-nakedness was a shock. This part of the country was known for its rapid changes in weather, especially at this time of year. Surely, he would be chilled. She also wondered why the Honorable Eleanor allowed one of her servants—for she'd decided the young man must be a groom—to go about in such a state where he might be seen by guests.

He still hadn't answered her salutation. The sun shone on his bare back. She found herself fascinated by the play of muscles in his shoulders as he slid the reins over the horse's head, preparing to lead him away. His skin was burned to a sun-burnished gold, spattered with beads of sweat, unkempt dark hair clinging to his neck in damp strands escaping from a longish and untidy club.

"I knocked," Anna spoke again. "There was no answer. Is Her Ladyship not home? I was expected."

Again, he didn't reply. He didn't even look in her direction. Instead, he wrapped the reins around his hand and pulled on them. He and the horse started toward the far edge of the house.

"You're being very rude." Anna raised her voice slightly. "Why won't you answer me?"

She didn't want to shout. That would be most unladylike, but his continuing to ignore her was definitely very impolite, especially for a servant.

Taking a couple of steps toward him, she caught his arm. "Is Lady Eleanor—"

He spun around so quickly Anna jumped back. He scowled at her.

Did I startle him? He'd certainly startled her. *Why? Because I touched him?*

"I knocked," she began again, then stopped as he switched the reins to his left hand, pointed to his ear with his right forefinger, and shook his head. "Y-you can't hear?"

He didn't answer, merely stared at her and repeated the gesture. His eyes were blue, such a light sky color they were a shocking contrast to his dark hair and tanned skin.

"I knocked." Looking from him to the door, Anna raised her own hand, balling it into a fist. She pantomimed beating it against the wood, then shook her own head, and lifted both shoulders in a shrug, raising her brows questioningly.

He looked from her to the door and back. Without changing expression, he gave an abrupt nod, held up his hand in a halting gesture, then thrust the reins at her. Anna caught at the reins to prevent their falling to the ground.

"Wait, I don't know anything about horses…"

He walked around her, stepping onto the stoop, dodging her portmanteau. He pointed to something hanging against the right side of the doorsill, a round metal ring, looking like nothing more than part of the frame design. Fitted into a leaf-carved base, it was easy to miss.

As she watched, he seized the ring, pulled it from the base, stringing out an attached rounded leather cord, and released it. From somewhere inside, she heard the faint clang of bells.

17

Nodding, he returned to where she stood, retrieved the reins, and gestured at the door, giving a brief little bow. As Anna hurried over to it, he led the horse away. She looked back as he disappeared around the corner of the house.

How odd that Her Ladyship also has a deaf person in her employ. She wondered if Lady Eleanor might want her to tutor the groom also. *I doubt it. If he works with animals, he probably doesn't really need to communicate.*

That was a pity, considering how handsome he was. Not that good looks should be a requisite for helping a person with a disability. Nevertheless, she wondered what thoughts went on inside that beautiful head...how much he knew or comprehended...of the world, other people. Did he feel more of a kinship with the horses he tended than with humans, his thoughts as unformed and instinctive as theirs?

Hearing footsteps inside, she turned back.

The door opened.

Chapter 4

"Yes, miss?" An elderly man stood in the inner gloom of the doorway, giving her an inquiring look.

He was dressed in what she supposed was the Mayfield livery, white knee-breeches and stockings, with a dark blue coat. His cuffs were deep and turned back, their buttonholes looped over six large brass buttons on which she could see a crest was engraved. Matching buttons ran the length of his coat. Beginning at his high turned-down collar and continuing to his waist, the coat was buttoned snugly, the end of a lighter blue waistcoat peeping from beneath.

"I'm Anna Leighton." She gave him a relieved smile as she took in his white hair, tied back in a well-combed club.

"Yes, miss?" His expression didn't change as he repeated his original question.

"The tutor…? I was sent from Dr. McAdam's Academy for the Deaf…to instruct Lord Mayfield…?" *Oh, why am I making each statement into a question?*

"Of course." He stepped back, ushering her inside with a gesture. "Welcome, Miss Leighton. I hope I didn't keep you waiting at the door long?"

Anna picked up her portmanteau and came inside.

"Allow me to take that, miss." He pulled it from her hand and set it beside the door.

"Thank you. I knocked," Anna answered his

question. "Twice…but apparently no one heard."

"I was in the butler's pantry, supervising the polishing of the silver," he replied. "I came as soon as I heard the bell." There was a short deprecating laugh. "I'm afraid I don't move as fast as I used to, and for that I apologize."

"The bell…I admit I didn't notice it at first," Anna answered. "If it hadn't been for the groom, I might be pounding on the door yet."

"The groom?" The butler's white brows slanted slightly.

"Yes. He came riding up as I was standing there wondering what to do. He showed me the bell pull." She decided not to mention his inability to hear. "He'd taken one of the horses out for a run, I believe."

"As far as I know, the horses aren't being exercised today," the old man said. "It's also highly unusual for them to be ridden onto the front lawn. Their hooves can cut up the grass terribly. I wonder why…" Shrugging, he pushed shut the door. "No matter, I'll find out later. If you'll wait here, I'll inform Her Ladyship you've arrived."

"Certainly." Anna hoped she hadn't gotten the young man into difficulties with his employer. He'd been so helpful, and he was so good-looking…as if that mattered where rules of behavior were concerned.

With a nod, the butler turned away, disappearing into the darkness of a nearby hallway. Anna glanced around, trying to get an idea of her new surroundings, but the place was so unlighted and dim, she could barely make out much more than that she stood in a large open foyer.

Goodness, the interior is as foreboding as the

outside.

At one side, behind a large vase of cut flowers, a mirror hung over a low, intricately carved armoire. It reflected a set of double doors and a staircase. Anna looked at the stairs. They curled, clinging to the inner wall, leading to the second story. She wondered if those round towers also held bedchambers. *How would it feel to sleep in a room whose walls curved?*

Everything was so ill-lit she couldn't tell what color the carpet was or the subjects portrayed in the grouping of small paintings on either side of the mirror. She wondered if His Lordship also suffered from eye problems as well as deafness. Sometimes, people who couldn't see well didn't bother with lighting, much to the detriment of others.

The butler returned.

"If you'll come this way, miss?"

Anna bent to pick up her bag.

"Just leave that, miss. The footman will take it up after you speak with Her Ladyship."

At a near trot, she followed the butler down the corridor, not wanting to lose him in the dark.

****

"Miss Leighton, Your Ladyship."

The butler stepped aside, and Anna was ushered through another pair of double doors into what appeared to be a library, if the rows of bookshelves meant anything. She let her gaze sweep quickly over the walls, past the large fireplace over which a landscape hung, and to the woman sitting behind the mahogany desk.

"Thank you, Shelton. Would you have tea brought, please?"

"Yes, ma'am."

21

The doors were quietly pulled shut. Anna glanced back at them then turned around as Lady Eleanor spoke again.

"Miss Leighton...you're much younger than I expected." Her tone was severely disapproving. "From the description in Dr. McAdam's reply to my letter, I'd supposed you would be older. Can you really have had much experience in instructing the deaf?"

She stood as she spoke, coming around the desk and walking over to a chair set before the fireplace. Anna studied her silently. She was a fairly attractive woman, past the bloom of youth, perhaps in her very late twenties, very upright, almost military-stiff in her posture. She was dark-haired, with eyes of a most remarkable shade of pale blue, slender and well-dressed in a flattering morning gown whose color exactly matched her eyes.

Seating herself in the chair, she gestured at its twin across the hearth.

"Please...be seated and tell me a bit about yourself."

"Thank you." Anna obeyed accordingly, smoothing the skirt of her traveling coat.

She felt a bit uncomfortable sitting before Her Ladyship with her bonnet still on and wearing such a dusty garment, but Shelton hadn't offered to take either. She hoped that, along with Lady Eleanor's question, it didn't mean there might be a chance she wouldn't be staying.

"Although it may sound like a bit of bragging," she answered, choosing her words carefully, "I assure you I'm a very good teacher, Your Ladyship. I haven't had many pupils..."

Her Ladyship frowned. Perhaps that was the wrong

thing to say.

"…only eight youngsters in the past two years. However, all graduated from the Academy with flying colors, and each has gone on to be a productive member of society." She decided to brag a bit. "One, a young woman of eighteen, recently married." No need to tell her the young woman was her own sister or that she hadn't been a pupil at the school. She added, "She was my oldest pupil."

"That you've enabled someone to enter into a wedded life is comforting to hear," Lady Eleanor murmured. Her expression changed as Anna spoke, becoming what she could only call *interested.* "Tell me more about your other pupils."

Anna began a recounting of the other children she'd taught, adding a brief description of the severity of each child's disability, but not giving any names, and also how long it took each to respond. As she spoke, Her Ladyship appeared to relax.

"I was certain Dr. McAdam would send me the best teacher he had, but upon seeing you, I'll admit I had some doubt. Now, however, hearing that brief recitation of your *vitæ* and knowing it coincides with the information the doctor sent me, I feel more assured."

There was a knock at the doors.

Calling for whomever it was to enter, Lady Eleanor waited as a young woman in maid's dress, with white pinafore apron and cap, entered, bearing a tray and tea service.

"Put it there, Jane." There was a gesture at a nearby table.

The maid set down the tray. "Shall I pour, ma'am?"

"That's all right, Jane. I'll serve."

The maid curtseyed and disappeared through the doors, closing them after her.

Lady Eleanor poured, asking Anna's preference of sugar or cream.

"One sugar, please," she replied. She wouldn't admit it, but the idea of having tea with a baron's daughter gave her a bit of a thrill. She made certain her hand didn't shake as she took the saucer, raised the cup, and sipped daintily.

"Now then...to business." The preliminaries out of the way and Anna's credentials to her satisfaction, Lady Eleanor immediately launched into a more detailed explanation of why she needed a teacher of the deaf. "When my brother was five, he and my parents were involved in a carriage accident."

Anna lowered her cup, giving Her Ladyship her complete attention.

"For a reason no one has ever been able to ascertain, the horses spooked and the driver was unable to control them. One of the wheels hit a rather large rock protruding from the road. The axle broke and the conveyance overturned. The driver and footman as well as my brother's nanny and our parents were killed, and David...David received a head injury."

She paused.

"How awful." Anna spoke into the silence, saying what she thought was expected. "May I offer my sympathy, Your Ladyship...belated as it is?"

"Thank you. However, it's been many years now, and though I still miss my parents, the grief has been somewhat lessened by the passing of time." Her brief expression of sadness was swept away by a look of determination.

Anna was certain Lady Eleanor still missed her parents. Remembering how she felt when she lost her own mother, Anna imagined that, at night when she was alone Her Ladyship might even give vent to her grief. Surely, her rather cold stating of facts was merely a mask for her pain.

"Your brother…" Anna spoke up as Lady Eleanor paused again. "You say he had a head injury. He isn't…" How to say it without being insulting? "…mentally impaired, is he?"

If David Woods had any sort of brain injury, he might not be a good candidate as a pupil.

"Oh, goodness, no." To her surprise, Her Ladyship actually smiled. It changed her demeanor considerably. "Be assured on that account, Miss Leighton. In spite of his current disability, my brother is as smart as a whip. Being five at the time, he'd already begun learning his letters and sums, and could actually read a bit…to our parents' pride."

She paused to take a sip from her own cup. Anna's went unnoticed in her hands as she listened.

"We communicate mostly through writing…" Lady Eleanor gestured toward the desk.

Looking at it, Anna saw a small slate and chalk pencil lying there.

"…as well as gestures, and we've gotten along fairly well. I've taught my brother a modicum of manners and etiquette as well as I could, and I daresay if necessary he could probably make his way through the edges of Polite Society without causing much of a stir…except for being unable to hear, of course."

Another pause.

This time, Anna didn't answer, being unsure what to

say.

"I suppose you're wondering why, after all this time, I've decided David now needs to learn to communicate with others."

"Well, I would ask…" Anna began.

Lady Eleanor sighed. "After the accident, David had a long convalescence, and when I learned he could no longer hear… I admit I hid him away. Both of us, actually. I wanted to protect him from what I feared Society would say about him, as well as to heal my own grief. Now, however…"

She shook her head, returned her teacup to the tray, and took a deep breath.

Anna tensed, as if bracing for a shock. *What is she going to say?*

"In six months, my brother will reach his majority, Miss Leighton." Lady Eleanor studied her hands, fingers clasping together tightly in her lap. She didn't see Anna stiffen at this revelation.

His majority? He's an adult? I've never taught anyone not a child. In spite of her sister being an adult now, she'd been a child at the time Anna taught her. *I don't know…*

"We have a cousin, Desmond Walters, our father's sister's son. If David should die without heirs, Des will inherit the title and the fortune it entails. A month ago, I was served with notice that he's petitioned the local District Judge of the Magistrate Court to have David declared incompetent, and the title and inheritance default to him as the, to quote from the document, 'mentally viable next in line with the ability to keep the Mayfield name alive.'"

Anna must've gasped or made some sound of

surprise, for Lady Eleanor looked up, smiling sadly.

"I truly never expected something like this to happen. Perhaps I've been living in a fool's paradise, but David was happy and…I thought to leave well enough alone. Now…" She made a helpless little gesture, eyes meeting Anna's. "I've only six months, Miss Leighton—two days before David's birthday, in fact—to enable my brother to become as normal as possible and prove his ability."

One hand clenched itself into a fist.

"Desmond is infamous for being a gambler, and a bad one. He's gone through most of his own inheritance. I don't want our cousin to more or less legally steal my brother's and fritter it away while we're relegated to the gamekeeper's cottage and he moves in here."

"If Dav…I mean, His Lordship can be taught, is there a chance he might actually be able to marry and provide his own heirs for the title?" Anna blushed as she asked, since she considered that a very private, indeed, intimate question, perhaps even impertinent, especially to be asked by a complete stranger. She set down her teacup.

"That pupil of yours notwithstanding, Miss Leighton, can you think of any woman who'd want a man who can't whisper sweet nothings to her…who won't be able to sweep her across the dance floor because he can't hear the music…who doesn't attend concerts or the opera…can never participate in any of those social functions because he's unable to hear them?" She shook her head so vehemently a hairpin actually slid from a curl and fell to the carpet. "I have to be realistic. I don't care if Des gets the title after David dies, I simply don't want it *taken* from him."

She leaned forward, placing a hand over Anna's.

"I suppose I'm asking for a miracle, but do you think you can help him? Help *us*?"

Before Anna could answer, there was a knock at the door. To Lady Eleanor's call, Shelton again appeared.

"Beg pardon, ma'am, Master David's back from his ride and wonders if he may join you?"

"I suppose now's as good a time as any for you to meet your prospective pupil." Lady Eleanor sighed. "Have Master David join us, Shelton."

"Very good, Your Ladyship." The old man bowed and withdrew, leaving the doors open.

In a moment, footsteps came along the corridor.

Lady Eleanor got to her feet. Anna did also.

She looked expectantly at the doors, eager for her first glimpse of the man she was to teach.

It doesn't matter if he's an adult. Perhaps that will work in his favor. He may be easier to instruct than a child. After all, he could once hear, which means he could also once speak...

An image began forming in her mind of a slightly sickly youngster, pale, thin, a little weak perhaps, looking to her for guidance as he did his protective older sister.

David, Lord Mayfield, came through the doorway.

Anna barely stifled her gasp.

Standing there, in dusty nankeen trousers and shabby riding boots, was the bare-chested young groom who had helped her gain admittance to Mayfield Manor.

Chapter 5

There was a distinct falter in his step as he saw Anna. His Lordship's eyes widened and he immediately looked from her to his sister. Dark brows scowled.

"David, come in." His sister didn't appear to notice. She raised a hand, beckoning. "Let me introduce you to our guest."

Standing, she took the little slate from the desk, scribbling a few words upon it and holding it out to him. Anna would learn that although she always wrote what she wanted to say, she also spoke to him as if he could hear, for the benefit of anyone else present.

She also noticed Lady Eleanor didn't speak loudly, as most people did to someone deaf. Her voice didn't raise above normal speaking level. Indeed, for all the good actually speaking did her brother, she could've simply *mouthed* the words at him.

He glanced at the slate, then back to Anna, and the scowl deepened. A hand went to his riding pocket, bringing out a miniature slate similar to Lady Eleanor's. A chalk pencil was attached and he pulled it loose, writing a couple of words and turning it so his sister could see.

Anna saw also.

Not maid?

He thinks I'm a servant? Anger sputtered, then died. *I am, aren't I? In a way.*

29

Shaking her head, Lady Eleanor proceeded to write more. "She's here to teach you the deaf language."

On the slate Anna could see the words, *teach you…deaf language…*

Something she could only call fury flashed across his face. His lips tightened, pursing into a pout. He shook his head, glanced at Anna again and repeated the movement even more violently, making curling strands of hair escape from its club. One hand shook in a decidedly negative gesture, then clenched into a fist.

"There'll be none of that. She's here, and that's all there is to it." Lady Eleanor wrote on the slate and held it up.

He read what was there and…the fist relaxed. Biting his lip, Lord Mayfield forced away his anger with a visible effort. He wrote a single word.

Name?

Miss Anna Layton. Lady Eleanor turned to Anna. "I'm spelling your last name as it sounds. He hasn't been able to grasp the *gh* concept in spelling."

Anna smiled. "I understand. English can be a very difficult language even for those of us with hearing."

Nodding, Her Ladyship added another word. *Manners.*

His Lordship reacted to that by turning to Anna so quickly she nearly jumped. Bowing so deeply his hair fell over his face, he straightened to look her directly in the eye.

"Mizz Ah-nah."

Though deep and quiet, his voice was flat and nasal, with such a lack of inflection Anna barely understood her own name as he spoke it.

"Your Lordship." She bobbed a curtsey and held out

her hand.

He stared at it, making it appear he'd never seen a female hand encased in a white kid glove before. Anna wondered if she should've removed her gloves, but since there had appeared to be some question of her staying, keeping her gloves on as she did her bonnet and coat seemed only proper.

Lord Mayfield solved whatever problem her glove wrought. Replacing the slate into his pocket, he stepped toward Anna, took her hand in his own and bowed over it. His hands were as sun-browned as the rest of him, though they appeared clean. At least there was no dirt under his nails, which also were neatly trimmed and not ragged as might've been expected. There was, however, a definite cloud of stable effluvium surrounding him, and now that he was so near, it was obvious.

Briefly, the scent of horse, dust, and leather was almost overpowering. Anna's nose crinkled. She took a deep breath and held it, fearing she was about to sneeze.

He raised his head, eyes meeting hers. At her quick inhalation, mischief danced in them. The corners of his mouth twitched as if he found her distress amusing.

Releasing her hand, he stepped back. He didn't look away from Anna, however, but immediately raised his hand again balled into a fist. Making a rapping motion as she'd done when they were outside, he moved his hand up and down as if pulling something, then shrugged, copying exactly her own previous gesture, brows going up questioningly.

"David?" Lady Eleanor was watching their exchange rather anxiously.

"When I arrived, I had trouble finding the bell pull," Anna explained. "His Lordship came up on his horse and very kindly rang the bell for me…though I wasn't aware who he was then," she added. "May I use your slate, Your Ladyship?"

Silently, Eleanor relinquished the slate and chalk into Anna's hands. Anna wrote, *Door…Shelton…Thank you…* and turned it so he could see. She waited until he read the last two words, then bobbed another curtsey.

He nodded, started to write a reply, then stopped. Instead, after a lengthy pause in which she thought she saw severe concentration in his expression, he said, "Oo we'cum, Mizz Ah-nah."

There was a sound from Lady Eleanor, a soft inhalation that in someone else might have been a gasp. Lord David didn't react to it, though Anna did, stopping herself before actually turning to stare at her employer. Her attention was pulled back to His Lordship as he did an odd thing. He tapped his chest over his heart, then touched his forehead.

"Oh!" Anna was so startled she couldn't control her reaction.

Lord David smiled, writing a final message to his sister. *Go now…See you…dinner…*

"You're excused, David." She wrote rapidly on her own slate. "Dress for dinner tonight."

That brought another scowl, much as his reaction to the announcement of Anna's identity, as well as a shake of his shaggy head.

"We have a guest." Lady's Eleanor's voice was adamant though he couldn't hear. Anna imagined her handwritten answer was just as firm. "Dress for dinner….shave."

He stared from her to the slate. One hand brushed against his jaw. There was a single jerk of a nod and an equally stiff bow. He spun on his heel and stamped out.

"I apologize for my brother's behavior," Lady Eleanor said quietly. "I've spoiled him, as you can see, and he doesn't like not getting his own way. I'm afraid he doesn't want a teacher."

"I assure you I've had more reluctant pupils," Anna assured her. *He didn't want to dress for dinner, either.* "That little show of temper…"

"I'm afraid that wasn't a show of temper, Miss Leighton—"

Through the still-opened doors came a loud crash, a liquid splashing, and then the sound of someone running up the stairs.

"—*that* was." Lady Eleanor showed no other reaction, except to say, "Drat. I particularly liked that vase. I thought it went perfectly with the décor in the foyer."

"Does he react that way often?" Anna could see endless confrontations and tantrums ahead.

She wondered if David Woods was aware of his good looks and perhaps used them to get his way, also. Remembering her wonder of his thought processes when she believed he was a groom, she now was curious as to the workings of the mind of an undisciplined young man allowed to do as he pleased, possibly running as wild as a horse in the pasture.

"No, thank goodness." Lady Eleanor looked earnest. "I assure you, Miss Leighton, my brother is a gentle soul, even if an indulged one. Generally, I can convince him to do something even if he has objections, but for some reason, when I broached the subject of hiring a teacher, he became immediately opposed. I think he equates a teacher with a physician, and he's seen enough of those.

I've tried to explain the import of our cousin's request to the court, but I'm not certain he fully understands."

"Would it be so very terrible to be relegated to a country cottage?" Anna asked hesitantly, feeling it was an impertinent as well as prying question. "After all, Mayfield Manor *is* a country home, isn't it?"

"If we were to have a full retinue of servants, it might not be so bad," Lady Eleanor admitted. "However, the servants will stay with the manor. The cottage is large enough for two people but we'll be there alone...no servants, and no monies other than whatever stipend Cousin Desmond deigns to allow us."

"That's awful," Anna drew in a deep breath. "Lady Eleanor, I'll do my best to make certain that doesn't happen."

"Thank you, Miss Leighton." Her hands seized Anna's and clasped them tightly before releasing them. Bright spots colored her Ladyship's cheeks as if that brief moment of emotion embarrassed her.

"May I ask you a question, Your Ladyship?"

"Certainly." As if some sort of alliance had been reached, Lady Eleanor became abruptly more forthcoming.

"That gesture your brother made...touching his heart and then his forehead? Why did he do that?"

"That's his way of saying he's sorry. Did he do anything before that might be considered rude?" She sounded a trifle anxious. "We get few visitors here, and as you saw, sometimes David has to be reminded of his manners."

"There was nothing. Perhaps he was apologizing because I had such difficulty getting someone to the door. I didn't see the bell pull."

"That must be it. Why do you ask? I noticed you appeared a bit upset at the time."

"Not *upset*, exactly," Anna replied. "Merely surprised. You see, in Signing, those two gestures mean *I love you*."

Chapter 6

"Oh. I see." Lady Eleanor received that information with aplomb. "How very interesting." She studied her hands a moment, then looked up and smiled. "Why don't we have another cup of tea?"

She returned to her chair, gesturing for Anna to follow. There was an abrupt change in her manner, as if some obstacle had been surmounted and she could now let down her guard. Anna noted that but didn't comment. She took her place again, facing Her Ladyship across the tea table.

"I hope my brother's little fit of pique didn't alarm you too much." Retrieving Anna's cup, she got very busy pouring tea, adding the required lump of sugar before offering it. "It's simply that he doesn't like dressing for dinner, which is a very rare event around here. We're usually very informal since it's only David and myself."

Anna took the teacup and saucer, and Lady Eleanor turned her attention to her own cup.

"Oh, dear…no biscuits," as if she'd just noticed. "I should've asked Shelton to make certain we were served some. Our cook makes the most delicious raisin scones, adds a touch of ginger. Please forgive my carelessness. I was so excited by your arrival."

"That's quite all right," Anna replied. At first glance, she certainly couldn't tell Lady Eleanor was excited. In fact, she hadn't been able to discern a reaction at all. At least Lord David was more obvious. She decided not to comment on that. "It's nearing dinnertime. I wouldn't want to spoil my appetite."

She hoped that wouldn't be taken as a very pointed hint. *Where will I be eating?*

"Quite so." Eleanor apparently approved that remark.

Anna had a sudden wonder about the provisions situation at Mayfield Manor. A cut-back in staff, the fact that Ogilvie hadn't been paid to bring her directly to the Manor's door…*what if their situation is slightly dire?* If Lord David's inheritance had already been threatened? Curtailed, somehow. She wished she dared ask.

"You may have noticed we don't have a large staff."

Did Lady Eleanor read something of my thoughts in my expression? Perhaps she'd best be a little more guarded with them.

"After Mama and Papa were…no longer here…I let most of the servants go. It seemed so useless to have a houseful of servants with only the two of us. Shelton became less of a butler and more a general factotum, while I took over supervising household duties. David doesn't have a manservant and I don't have a maid. That's why we rarely dress for dinner, hence his protest. Occasionally, the footman or the housemaid fills in. though I daresay I've become fairly adept at looping a cravat. David hates tying a neckpiece."

She laughed and placed her fingers to her lips as if to stifle the sound.

"Once, he actually came downstairs with the length of linen wrapped around his head like a turban, as a way of protesting."

"Oh, my! That must have been a sight." Anna was

gratified it was only a neckpiece Lord David misplaced in protest and not something else, such as his trousers.

The thought of him stamping down the stairs completely naked, shaking that disorderly mane, flared into her mind. She took a quick sip of tea to hide her blush behind the teacup.

"My brother has a well-defined sense of humor, Anna, though he generally displays it in the most aggravating ways."

"What do you mean?"

With what could only be described as a slight wiggle, Lady Eleanor leaned back into her chair, as if settling herself for a cozy chat. Anna had the sudden insight that her ladyship was lonely, and her own appearance was an encouragement, if not to share confidences, at least to have a prolonged conversation with someone other than the staff.

"There was a time when I took him to doctors, specialists, and surgeons, hoping one would tell me he had some miraculous cure to restore my brother's hearing. David tired of it long before I, and when I told him I had once more secured an appointment with a renowned surgeon of whom I'd heard wonderful things, he refused to go."

"I hope he didn't break another vase."

"Something much worse…or less, depending on how you choose to look at it."

"In what way?"

"We bickered for several days. If only you could imagine the words passing between us on those little slates. Finally, David appeared resigned, but when we got there, and the physician did his examination…we discovered he had stuffed his ears with cotton wool as his way of stating his opinion of the doctor. I was embarrassed, to say the least, but David laughed all the way home, quite hysterically, judging by the way his body shook. Can you imagine someone laughing without making a sound?"

"I assure you I can," Anna answered. Her ladyship's words brought another vision, of a younger, well-dressed David, body shaking in merriment, eyes crinkling at the corners, though not a sound passed his lips. *The scamp*.

"I suppose we've now gotten a reputation as an overly-protective and possessive spinster and her brother, the dummy lord."

"Oh, your ladyship, please don't…" Had someone actually said that in Lady Eleanor's presence?

"It's when I hear such rude descriptions…" Lady Eleanor's next words confirmed the fact. "I'm grateful we're fairly remote here and don't usually have visitors."

"I suppose it gets lonely," Anna ventured.

"You're very insightful." Eleanor looked as if she were surprised Anna noticed that fact. "It wasn't always that way. When Mama and Papa were alive, there was always a house party, dinner, or a ball at Mayfield Manor…spring festivals, fall bonfires… The house was so noisy then…people chatting, laughing, playing games…music."

She looked pensive, as if once again seeing the manor as it had appeared when her parents were alive and there were guests filling the now-empty rooms.

"When I became old enough, I was allowed to attend. Oh, how I loved to dance." Her hands came together in a sudden clasp. Lady Eleanor glanced down, reddened slightly, and dropped them to her lap. She studied them as she continued, "Occasionally when I went upstairs to bed, I'd find David leaning against the balusters. He'd hide from his nanny and watch the guests arrive, then fall asleep sitting there." She sighed. "After the accident, when he was so ill, I truly didn't want anyone coming around, making unhelpful comments and reminding me all over again what had happened."

"May I ask you a personal question, your ladyship?"

"Only if it isn't *too* personal."

"Then I'll ask it and you may decide whether you wish to answer or not."

"Very well."

"How old were you when his lordship was hurt?"

"That's not too personal. I was eighteen. I'd begun my first season in Society a few months before." She smiled. "I'm afraid my brother was a great surprise to my parents. They'd resigned themselves that I was to be their only child."

Eighteen... That would make her ladyship now thirty-three or about. Anna tried not to let her surprise show, or the accompanying pity she felt. To be eighteen, awhirl in the excitement of making a debut, going to balls and garden parties, meeting and being courted by handsome young men...and then abruptly finding herself orphaned and with a younger brother to care for...a brother who'd always be a burden...

Not if I can help it. Sudden sympathy for her ladyship made Anna determined to change Lady Eleanor's situation as well as her brother's.

"And you became your brother's guardian?"

"It was unusual, I know, but I suppose my father considered me a levelheaded sort. He named me David's guardian in his will, or, in the event I had married and my brother was still in his minority, my husband would take that responsibility."

"You have no husband or betrothed to assist you?" She'd seen no rings on the slender fingers, nor any item of apparel suggesting her ladyship was a widow.

"I'm afraid not. I had thought there was someone, but after he visited a few times and dared suggest I 'put David away,' as he so delicately worded it, I more or less forgot about him. I soon found myself too busy to accept his calls. Very quickly I learned who was and who wasn't a friend." Her expression became sardonic. "There's nothing like a family tragedy to weed out the true from the false." Her voice dropped slightly. "As I said, we have few visitors now."

"Lady Eleanor, I'm so sorry."

"Oh, don't be." Her tone was dismissive. "I've a feeling I escaped a very unhappy fate by turning away that young man, as well as others I've met since. Anyway, living here hasn't been so very bad. Mayfield Manor's forests and fields are very picturesque at all seasons." She looked away a moment. "Nature can be a very fulfilling companion."

The empty cup held idle in Anna's hands caught her attention.

"You've finished your tea?"

Anna nodded. Once again, she replaced the cup upon the tray.

"Well then... I suppose I should have Shelton show you to your room so you can refresh yourself a bit before dinner. I daresay you must be tired after traveling so far."

"It has been a rather exhausting day," Anna agreed.

Hand on her arm, Lady Eleanor escorted her to the doors her brother had left open. Once there, however, she paused, her grip tightening.

"Anna…"

Anna looked up at her, startled by the use of her first name.

"I'm not a very demonstrative person. I suppose one might call me cold. My only excuse is that I've tried to hide my true feelings—my despair, if you will—so David wouldn't sense it. But…" She gave a smile, and it was such a brilliant, carefree one Anna would've sworn she felt warmth spread over her. "Now that you're here…for the first time I truly feel confident things will change for the better."

Chapter 7

"I'll take your bonnet and coat, miss," Shelton said.

Lady Eleanor left her in the butler's care. Explaining he would show Anna to her room, she once again disappeared into the gloom the corridors offered, though into another part of the house.

Noting the destroyed vase and its flowers had been removed—indeed, there was barely a damp spot upon the carpeting—Anna unbuttoned her traveling coat, which was beginning to become a bit uncomfortable since she'd been inside so long. As the butler took it, she untied her bonnet and held it out to him also.

"Oh, my, it's a trifle dusty." He surveyed the coat, then draped it over his arm and asked, "Shall I have it shaken and sponged off a bit before I hang it up, miss?"

"Thank you…uh…Mr. Shelton." Anna told herself she shouldn't be pleased with this thoughtfulness, but nevertheless she was.

"Just Shelton, miss." He turned as he heard footsteps from the direction Anna would learn was the kitchen. "Now here's Jane, to take you to your room."

Wondering if it was a bit unusual for a housemaid to show a guest to her chambers, Anna went with Jane. As they went up the stairs, she studied the maid's ramrod-straight back in its black bombazine dress and starched white apron.

Jane wasn't plain, but she wasn't outstandingly

pretty, a pleasant-faced young woman older than Anna but not near her ladyship's age. Under her maid's housecap, her sandy hair was pulled back in a severe little bun at the nape of her neck. Anna wondered how long she'd been in the Mayfield household.

Was she here when His Lordship lost his parents? Surely she'd have been nearly a child herself, in that case.

The maid took her to a room on the east end of a carpeted corridor lined with tapestries and landscapes. The room was not in one of the rounded towers, however. Through one of the windows, Anna could see the branches of the oak stretching as if to embrace the corner of the house.

Jane offered to help Anna undress. "If you'd like to perhaps take a nap and rest a bit before dinner, miss."

"Thank you," Anna replied.

Briefly, she felt awkward. She'd never had anyone help her dress or undress before. At home, Maisie occasionally assisted with back buttons and such, but otherwise she'd always managed her own *toilette*. She tried not to show how grand that made her feel.

Her thoughts were a little frivolous. *After all, I'm not a peasant. Even if being middle-class isn't nobility, I'm not entirely ignorant of etiquette and how the upper class lives.*

Nevertheless, it gave her a thrill to be waited on, even slightly. She resisted the temptation to ask if Jane was going to be her personal maid. That might be too presumptuous.

Unbuttoning the jacket of her traveling suit, she let Jane pull it from her hand, then proceeded to divest herself of the skirt also. The maid had to help with the *blousette* because it opened in the back. While Anna stood in her underpinnings, Jane hung the clothing she was wearing in the wardrobe.

Anna had chosen the rather severe traveling suit because she thought it made her look very earnest and businesslike. Much good that did, since she hadn't removed her coat. Lady Eleanor never got a chance to see it.

"You're not wearing stays, miss?" The maid sounded disapproving as she shut the wardrobe.

"Of course I am." Anna didn't snap her answer, but she was a little abrupt, mostly in surprise.

She was well aware that with the sheer fabrics fashion now dictated for dresses and gowns, stays became visible quite easily, though anyone with as slender a build as she, or a fairly good figure, could go without them with no recrimination. She, however, felt not wearing such underpinnings was being far too bold.

"Really?" The maid studied Anna's slight body and her white slip.

"It's one of the new style…less boning, and longer," she explained. "It's more comfortable, but I do think I'd like to take it off while I rest." She gestured at the long chemise she was wearing over her stays.

"Certainly," Jane replied.

Stepping behind Anna, she carefully raised the slip and pulled it over her head.

"Excuse me for sounding so disbelieving, miss," Jane went on as she carefully placed the slip on a chair and smoothed the few wrinkles out of the satin. "It's simply that Lady Eleanor still adheres to what I imagine you'd call the old-fashioned corsets." She indicated her own slightly rigid posture. "As do I."

Jane turned her attention to Anna's stays, wider apart than in a conventional corset, and fitting farther down on her hips.

"That does look more comfortable. I imagine it'd be easier to do housework wearing something like that." A sudden spark twinkled in her eyes. "Perhaps you might somehow discreetly manage to turn the conversation to underpinnings and recommend such to her ladyship? If she were to change, then Cook and I could, too. It'd certainly make our chores easier."

"Jane, if I get an opportunity to mention the unmentionables, I promise to do so." Anna met the laughter in the maid's eyes with a smile of her own. *How does one* discreetly *speak of unmentionables?*

"I'd be ever so grateful, miss." Jane bobbed a curtsey. "Now, you turn around and let me loosen those laces."

She began to work open the little corset's strings. It took several moments, as there were a good many eyelets to pull the lacings through. When at last Anna was free of the body-manipulating transformation and standing only in pantalettes consisting of a tiny-strapped batiste upper garment attached to pantaloons buttoning down the front, Jane said, "Now then, is there anything else you might need before I go?"

"I don't believe so." All Anna wanted in that moment was to lie down. Abruptly, she felt very, very tired. Nervous exhaustion setting in, she imagined. Today had been rather nerve-wracking, what with discovering her pupil was an adult...and a heart-shatteringly handsome one, at that.

"I'll come back to help you dress for dinner," the maid told her and went to the door. "If you need anything beforehand, there are bell pulls at the hearth. The red one calls Shelton. I answer the blue."

"Thank you." Anna looked at the indicated items. Two long leather straps hung by the fireplace mantel, disappearing into a wide, metal-rimmed slit cut into the wall. They were similar, both heavily embossed and interwoven with tapestried cloth. "I'm sure I won't need anything, but that's good to know."

With a nod and another bob of a curtsey, Jane was gone, closing the door after her, leaving Anna to survey her surroundings and let all that had happened overwhelm her a little.

She spun, taking in the room in more detail. Besides the wardrobe, lady's vanity, and bench, there was a bed, a sumptuous affair with heavy hangings, set near three mullioned windows. Next to it stood a table holding a fuel lamp with a large milk glass base and chimney. The fireplace and hearth stood between bed and vanity. The hearth was white-painted brick, complementing the mantel and the facing as well as the wainscoting, the upper ceiling trim, and the window casings, which were almost hidden behind draperies matching the bed coverings.

Anna went to the wardrobe and opened it. The dresses she'd brought with her had been unpacked and were hanging inside. Without hesitation, she brought out one, a high-waisted pink muslin chemise, decorated with rose satin appliqués around the neck and hem. It also had a satin sash and low neckline. The dressmaker had called it an *afternoon tea gown*, but Maisie had thought it was elegant enough for evening wear. She'd insisted Anna include it in the portmanteau.

In case there's a ball, she'd said while Anna

laughed and reminded her a teacher wouldn't be invited to a ball.

Draping the gown over a chair, Anna went to a nearby chifferobe, finding her stockings and other set of slip and pantalettes. She selected a pair of white silk stockings, her Sunday ones. Maisie's opinion had been that if she was including the pink afternoon gown, she should include her best stockings also.

That done, she turned to the bed. It looked enormous. With its puffed-up feather mattress and turned-back counterpane, she thought she might need to call Shelton and request a footstool in order to climb into it. After a slight struggle, in which Anna deplored her lack of height, she managed to hoist herself onto the bed where she lay back against the pillows, letting herself slowly sink into the goosedown.

She closed her eyes.

Immediately, they popped open again.

I'm too excited to sleep. Visions of all that had happened, snippets of her conversations with Lady Eleanor, and images from the train trip kept intruding.

Anna thought of what her ladyship had told her…of the young woman on the verge of adult life…and the brave way she accepted caring for her younger brother, with no show of regret. She could've easily agreed with that unnamed suitor, shuffled Lord David off to a well-to-do and very private sanitarium somewhere, and simply forgotten about him, going on with her life…but she hadn't. She'd given up her own prospects to make certain his existence was as comfortable as possible.

Anna wondered if she could've been that brave and sacrificed so much for Maisie if they'd lost their father when they did their mother.

As for Lord David…she thought of that little boy hiding at the top of the stairs…probably wearing a nightshirt, his hair even then a curly, untamed mop, bare toes rubbing against the carpet…staring with wide blue eyes at the beautiful women escorted by handsome men. He'd probably looked forward to the day he would become one of them…guiding some young woman across the dance floor or lounging around the punchbowl with his fellows, talking about his Grand Tour or a hunting party to which he'd been invited…

…and then his future was swept away by the breaking of a carriage axle.

Now there would be no balls…no dancing…not even Mayfield Manor, if she wasn't able to help him. *I wonder how much he's aware of the life he lost?*

A young man of Lord David's age should be finishing his education, not wasting away his life as useless as a stray dog someone took pity on and threw scraps. At twenty, he should be graduating from university, preparing for his expected trip to the capitals of Europe, the culmination of a young gentleman's emergence into adulthood. After his return, he would be ready to enter Society, where he'd be expected to indulge in the drinking, gambling, and hunting pastimes as did his peers. Next, he'd find himself a mistress to fulfill his carnal urges while attending the many parties, balls, and *fêtes* where he could meet and court some heiress and convince her to enter a probably loveless marriage intended to provide heirs for his title.

Since all this was a well-known fact, and indeed an expectation of the nobility, Anna didn't feel she was being bold or scandalous in thinking about those things.

David certainly wouldn't be doing any of that. She

wondered if his lordship even had the same urges as normal young men? Isolated at the manor as he was, would he be aware of the physical interactions between men and women? After all, physically he was twenty, but mentally…

Would he even be curious?

That is definitely not something I should be thinking! Anna told herself, sternly.

She couldn't see Lady Eleanor explaining such facts to him. It was embarrassing enough for a woman to speak of it to another woman. Did her ladyship have Shelton or that as yet unseen footman speak in her place? How did someone communicate such things to a person who couldn't hear and had the reading level of a five-year-old, whatever his mental capacity?

Is it possible he's an innocent, untouched by carnality at all?

Immediately she was shocked at that thought as well as allowing herself to think it. *Surely he has some idea…*

After all, Mayfield Manor was more or less a large farm…across the highroad, there was a meadow filled with mares and cows. Since there were also foals and calves, there had to be stallions and bulls around. Undoubtedly, at one time or another, he might've witnessed the animals mating and eventually associated the same action with humans…

I imagine there's a carefree farm girl or two around who'd give a young man as handsome as his lordship an adventure in a haystack whether he can hear or not. Perhaps that had happened and Lord David was eager for more. *How can I know?*

She wondered if perhaps that was the reason Jane wasn't more attractive, so she wouldn't tempt someone who might have an idea of physical pleasure but no concept of the morality accompanying it. The unashamed way he'd stood before her in the library…shirtless…

Anna shocked herself with that thought as well as the sudden flare of discomfort it engendered. *What am I thinking? Stop it, Anna, this instant! I'm here to help Lord Mayfield retain his title, and nothing more…*

Abruptly, exhaustion overcame her. She was asleep before she finished the thought.

Chapter 8

"Miss, it's dinnertime."

Jane's rapping on the door roused Anna from a pleasant sleep and a dream that rapidly dissolved as she came awake.

What was it about? Something to do with riding, sitting in front of someone on a horse… Strong, warm arms around her… She shook her head and the dream's last memory wisped away.

Anna slid from the bed, pattering on bare feet to the door. She opened it, hand going to her disarranged hair, deciding she probably looked a fright. She seized the door handle, pulling it open.

"Did you sleep, miss?"

"Yes, and very well, too." Anna stifled a yawn. "The bed is quite comfortable."

"You must be a very quiet sleeper. You hardly look as if you've lain down, much less napped for nearly an hour and a half."

"Hour and a…goodness!" *I really slept that long?*

Jane was busy at the wardrobe. "Which gown would you like to wear tonight, miss?" She pulled open the double doors, then saw the dress lying on the chair on top of Anna's slip and stepped over to it. "Oh. I see you've one already laid out. You should've let me."

"Do you think it'll do?" Anna wondered if it were proper to ask a maid's opinion. Hadn't she heard that menservants and personal maids were supposed to have more fashion sense than their masters and mistresses because they were usually the ones selecting what those people wore?

"This is lovely." Jane picked up the dress, studying it. "Those appliqués, what a beautiful touch. It should do nicely." She spun around. "Would you like me to help you with your stockings, miss?"

She held the pair of stockings Anna had placed beside the dress.

"I believe I can do that myself." Anna accordingly sat on the vanity stool and proceeded to pull on the stockings, being careful not to stretch the delicate threads and cause a runner. She was glad she wasn't going to be wearing her everyday cotton ones.

As she finished, Jane tightened her stays. Clad in slip, stays, stockings, and pantalettes, Anna found herself seated on the velvet-covered stool before the vanity, staring at her reflection in the triple mirror as Jane styled her hair.

Making complimentary noises as she did so, the maid combed the long, blonde locks, smoothed, and twisted them into a psyche knot near her crown.

"Tell me, Jane…" Anna decided to satisfy her curiosity about the maid. "How long have you been in service to her ladyship?"

"It seems all my life," the maid answered. With a rat-tailed comb, she coaxed several little ringlets in front of Anna's ears and across the nape of her neck. "I started as a 'tweeney when I were twelve. His lordship were seven at the time, and Lady Eleanor was still struggling with her grief and trying to care for him. Shelton suggested having another young person around might help Lord David adjust somehow."

Jane paused, studying a single recalcitrant wisp of hair that refused to follow the others but insisted on curling in the opposite direction.

"She had him post a notice in the village that she was prepared to hire a young person to assist in the manor. I really think she was expecting one of the boys to apply as a footman. Instead, I was the only one who showed up, the notice in me hand. Would you like me to heat a curling iron and make certain these curls didn't fall, miss? That one wants to make trouble, it seems."

"I don't think that'll be necessary," Anna replied.

She'd tried heat curling once and singed her hair, swearing never to attempt it again. For weeks, until the burned hair grew out enough to be trimmed away, Maisie teased that she looked as if she'd been frightened, the way her hair stick stiffly in all directions.

"Anyway," Jane finished her tale, giving Anna's hair a final pat, "Lady Eleanor said I'd do, and I learned housemaiding, helping her care for his lordship, and being an occasional lady's made to boot."

She picked up the tea gown. While Anna slid her arms into the cap sleeves, Jane deftly fastened the row of tiny buttons from hem to back neckline.

"Do you have jewelry, miss?"

"Oh, yes…" It sounded so much like a prompt, Anna blushed slightly.

She felt as if she were being asked riddles for which the maid already knew the answers. She waved a hand at the little jewelry casque lying on the vanity top.

"In there, there should be some pearl eardrops and a *lavaliere* pearl necklace." Those had been her mother's, presented by their father on their tenth wedding anniversary. He'd given them to Anna on her eighteenth birthday. She adopted a careless tone. "I believe I'll wear those."

"And the bangle, also?" Jane opened the casque, bringing out the items. She did it so quickly, Anna had the feeling she'd already checked what was in the little case. She wondered what Jane would've done if she'd decided on the little jet choker and eardrops instead.

"Um…" Anna pretended to consider that. She'd wondered if wearing the bracelet might make her overdressed. If Jane was suggesting it, however… "I suppose so."

"And your gloves…?"

"Oh, yes, gloves." Drat, she'd forgotten about wearing gloves at dinner. *I forgot to pack any.*

"Would you wish the white or the pink?" Jane was helpfully opening another drawer in the chifferobe and preparing to extract whichever pair Anna decided.

White or pink? Bless Maisie! She must have sneaked in both pair while I wasn't looking. "The pink, I believe."

The pink satin gloves were offered. Anna put them on, working them up her arms and smoothing the fingers. Jane clasped the bracelet over her left wrist. Without asking, she went to the wardrobe and brought out Anna's second pair of shoes, black evening slippers of morocco leather.

Anna blinked. *How did those get here?* She'd certainly not packed dancing slippers. Dancing had been the last thing on her mind. She'd also not thought she'd be eating with the family, either. *Thank you again, Maisie.* Anna decided she really had to let her sister know how she appreciated her foresight.

Stepping into the slippers, she surveyed herself in

the cheval glass. Other than the slightly low cut of the neckline, she found nothing wrong with her image. She couldn't resist whirling around, making her slim skirts billow slightly.

"How do I look, Jane?"

"Perfect, miss." The maid nodded as if proud of her handiwork. "Just perfect. I believe you're ready to join her ladyship and the master for dinner."

For some reason, those words gave Anna the most delicious shiver.

Chapter 9

"Miss Anna, ma'am." Shelton stepped aside so Anna might enter the parlor where Lady Eleanor waited.

Clad in a daffodil-yellow round gown, Lady Eleanor was seated by the fireplace. With her hair drawn back and braided at her crown, with tiny ringlets before her ears that Anna recognized as Jane's handiwork, Eleanor looked much younger and definitely more attractive than the rather severe woman she'd been introduced to earlier in the day.

They might live in the country, but her ladyship looked in the height of fashion. Around her neck she wore a choker of small rubies interspersed with pearls, a single pear-shaped gem hanging from its center. That and the matching eardrops made Anna certain Lady Eleanor's reduction of the staff and her isolation here wasn't because of financial restrictions but due to her withdrawal because of grief, as her ladyship had stated.

The neckline of the gown she wore, pale yellow glazed cotton with an overdress of cream-colored dotted swiss, appeared much more modest than Anna's own, in spite of its understated richness. The unlined full-length sleeves were tightly fitted and because of that, Eleanor wore wrist-length white gloves. Both sleeve cuffs and the ankle-high hem were decorated with a double row of yellow ruffles. Black slippers tied at her ankles with black ribbons.

"Oh, my dear, you look wonderful." Getting to her feet, she rushed to meet Anna enthusiastically. Clasping her hands, she led her to the hearth, then stepped back, spreading Anna's arms and glancing down. "Let me look at you."

The tea gown passed inspection.

"It's lovely…those rose appliqués, what a fashionable touch." She released Anna's hands.

"It's all right, then?" Anna relaxed, though her question was a bit anxious in spite of her ladyship's compliment. "I was worried it might be too…" She hesitated. "…deep-cut in the neckline."

"My dear, it's perfect." Lady Eleanor smiled, though the expression faded quickly as if her face were unaccustomed to wearing such. "Indeed, if someone less…um…blessed, such as I, can wear such a fashion, then a young woman with your…charms…definitely should."

Anna's gaze flicked to her ladyship's slight bosom. Until that moment, she'd never considered herself amply endowed, but compared to Lady Eleanor's small physique, she seemed overly "blessed" as her ladyship termed it.

"You look absolutely lovely…except…" One finger went to Eleanor's chin.

"What is it?" Anna asked anxiously.

Instead of answering, her ladyship reached for the blue bell pull next to the hearth.

In a moment, there was a pattering of feet in the hall. Jane appeared in the open doorway.

"You rang for me, ma'am?"

"Bring my Kashmere shawl, Jane. The rose-colored one."

"Yes, ma'am." Bobbing a curtsey, Jane disappeared again into the hallway.

A shawl? Anna frowned, careful to let it fade as Eleanor turned around. *Why does she need a shawl? She's already wearing one.*

In a remarkably short time, Jane reappeared with the shawl, presenting it to her employer.

Eleanor took the shawl, dismissing Jane. Before Anna realized her intent, the wrap was thrown over her shoulders and tucked around her arms.

"There now." Stepping back, Eleanor surveyed her handiwork as Anna caught at the shawl to prevent it slipping from her shoulders. "The final touch. Just what was needed."

"It's beautiful." Anna's hand came up to stroke the soft wool.

From the moment she heard Kashmere shawls were in fashion, she'd wanted one, but they were expensive, imported from India. Papa had hinted she might receive one for her next birthday, however. He had a patient who was a clothier. She looked up, meeting Eleanor's eyes.

"Your ladyship, I…I don't know what to say." Abruptly, there was a loud, very unladylike rumbling, seeming to emerge from beneath the shawl. "Oh! I beg your pardon." Face reddening, she brushed a hand across her dress-front. "I'm afraid my luncheon and that afternoon tea have long since disappeared. I do apologize, your ladyship."

"One can't argue with one's inner clock," Lady Eleanor brushed her apology aside. "I admit I'm hungry also, and if my brother would make his appearance, we'll go in to dinner."

She glanced at the clock on the mantel. "Five

minutes to the hour. Undoubtedly he'll be late as further protest."

There was the clomp of feet on the stairs, followed by a loud thud, as if someone had leaped down the last three.

Shelton stood in the doorway. "Lord David's here, your ladyship."

David appeared behind him. The old man silently withdrew.

His lordship stalked into the room. He saw his sister and Anna and threw himself into a spin, continued whirling until he stood directly in front of Eleanor. Skidding to a halt, he raised his arms, looking from Eleanor to Anna, as if to say, *Well, Am I presentable?*

His sister surveyed him critically. Anna was enchanted.

The bare-chested, dusty young man she'd mistaken for a rather rude groom was transformed into a fashionable gentleman, beginning with his unruly hair, which had been combed and pulled into a neat club, secured with a dark blue riband.

Without realizing it, Anna nodded approvingly. She didn't like the new style she'd seen on the fathers of some of her pupils, that clipping of the hair at the nape of the neck and combing the rest over the ears and forehead in short spiky curls.

She also noted his face was now devoid of that near-beard, his cheeks appearing quite rosy. There was a faint scent of sandalwood floating about him instead of the previous stable aroma.

She turned her attention to what his lordship was wearing…a royal blue, tailed evening coat, embellished with an embroidered border of interwoven darker blue and gold threads edging the entire garment from the high turned-down collar to its hem. Under the intricate fall of his neckpiece, a paler blue satin waistcoat was also covered with matching embroidery seeming to catch and reflect the light with an iridescent sheen. His trousers…

Oh, my goodness! Anna remembered her speculation that Lord David might show his displeasure at having to dress for dinner by coming downstairs completely naked. *Is this worse?*

He was wearing stovepipe-legged pants. Anna managed to stifle a gasp.

How could he?

Though she'd heard that fashion-setter Master Beau Brummel had dared wear such to evening affairs, Anna had never seen anyone in a pair. There was a rumor the Duke of Wellington himself had been turned away from Almack's for appearing in a pair of the long-legged trousers instead of the more acceptable knee breeches and stockings…yet here was this country lord who'd never go to any club, wearing a scandalous fashion the young bucks of the *ton* were even now struggling to introduce to society.

She had to admit they looked good on him.

"Very acceptable, David." Lady Eleanor apparently agreed. She picked up her slate from its place beside her chair and wrote something, holding it for him to see.

Nice.

He grimaced slightly, evidently desiring more for his obedience than that single terse word. He looked at Anna, eyebrows rising higher. One hand went to his chest. Almost hidden by the folds of his neckpiece, the little slate was suspended around his neck by a chain, the chalk pencil attached. He pulled it free, wrote, and held it toward Anna.

You?

He wants my opinion? Taking the slate from him, she started to write *Magnificent*, then thought better of it. Scratching out the partial word, she wrote instead. *Very nice*.

He saw the scrubbed-out word, frowned, and wrote again.

Mag...? A scowl accompanied that.

"Enough chitchat." Eleanor came to her rescue. "It's eight o'clock. Thank you for being on time, brother." She held up her slate.

On time. Thanks.

He nodded.

Eleanor wrote another word.

Dinner.

David agreed enthusiastically with that. Whirling, he aimed himself for the open door. Eleanor's hand on his arm brought him up short. He glared at her over his shoulder, then at the slate she thrust at him.

Lady. Dinner. She pointed to Anna.

His snort was almost silent. Stalking to her, he thrust out his arm. When Anna didn't respond, he seized her hand, slapped it onto the forearm of his sleeve, then turned. Anna had to run to keep from being dragged into the hallway. As soon as they left the parlor, he slowed his pace, however, but his long-legged stride kept her trotting beside him on tiptoe until they reached the dining room.

Once inside, David released her arm. Pushing her toward a chair, he went to his own place at the head of the table, where he raised a hand, gesturing. Lady Eleanor trailed behind, taking her seat at the foot.

The footman, stationed by the sideboard, hurried over. He slid the chair under Anna. She found herself halfway between his lordship and Lady Eleanor at a table possibly seating twenty people.

"We generally eat here, in the family room," Eleanor explained. "Since we no longer have banquets."

Family room? Anna wondered how many people the banquet table would seat.

Shelton appeared seemingly out of nowhere as the footman again took his place by the buffet. Jane stood opposite him at its other end.

"Shall we serve, ma'am?"

At Lady Eleanor's nod, the meal began.

"Since this is an informal dinner," she went on as Jane and the footman brought dishes from the sideboard and carefully arranged them on the table. "I allow *service à la russe* instead of *à la français*. It makes for a much cozier atmosphere, I feel."

"Oh, I agree," Anna replied, wondering exactly what the difference was.

"Luncheon is generally on the sideboard."

Once the dishes had been transferred to the table, the footman bowed, picked up the first serving tray, and stepped to the left of Anna's chair. Apparently, guests were served first. Bending slightly, he offered it to her.

"Endive-watercress toss, ma'am, lightly sprinkled with blueberry vinaigrette."

"I also did away with those three-course dinners, asking Shelton to have the entire meal served at one time. Except for dessert, of course." Eleanor seemed to feel she had to give detailed explanations, though this was always the way meals had been served in Anna's home.

So we've been eating as the Russians do? Anna tried

not to let this discovery show in her expression.

"I understand." She picked up the two silver serving spoons lying on the tray and transferred a portion to her own plate, managing not to drip any of the dressing. "So much more convenient."

Once she replaced the utensils on the tray, the footman proceeded to serve Lady Eleanor, who took only a small helping, and then Lord David, who made up for his sister's apparent lack of appetite by heaping enough for two people onto his plate.

While the footman was going around the table, Jane offered the next item to Anna, a casserole of creamed beets and parsnips. Anna waited for the serving to end and the signal to begin the meal.

Not David.

He fidgeted, tapping a finger against his fork handle as if impatient to seize it and begin eating. Eleanor shot him a glance and he subsided, dropping both hands out of sight as if that might make them stay still. Once all the dishes had been served and were returned to the linen tablecloth, Eleanor picked up her own fork, saying brightly, "Well, shall we begin?"

David seized his fork and stabbed a beet.

As far as Anna was concerned, the meal was fantastic. She tried not to sound so awe-struck as she marveled over the creamed beets and parsnips, the watercress and endive toss, a sugared carrot-and-grape concoction, and the braised beef tips with carmelized onions and garlic. After all, it was merely food, not garnished with silver and gold, if perhaps tastier than her father's cook prepared.

David's manners were much better than she expected, though he did take his napkin and tuck it into his shirtfront so it completely covered the flowing neckpiece. She ignored that, for her own father also ate that way. He was fairly neat and chewed with his mouth closed, however, occasionally wiping his lips with his napkin. If his lordship wished another helping of something—and he seemed to want seconds of everything—he simply raised a hand, gestured to the desired dish, and it was quickly brought to him by the footman. He did dribble sauce and gravy from serving spoon to plate, however.

It was a rather silent meal, she noted, as she smoothed her own napkin across her lap. Once or twice, David scribbled something on his slate and held it up, turning it so it was visible to Shelton as well as Anna and his sister.

On those occasions, Shelton beamed and nodded at the one-word compliments—*Good…Delicious,* though that one was misspelled as *delyshus…sweet…*

One thing was odd, Anna noted, as Jane went around the table filling their goblets with a clear liquid. Hesitantly tasting, she discovered it was water. She set down her glass.

"Is there something wrong, Anna?" Lady Eleanor was quick to catch her expression. "Is the water not to your liking? We have our own well, and it's pure, I assure you."

"It's not that," Anna answered. "It's very refreshing. I'm simply a bit surprised you don't serve wine…not that I mind, however," she was quick to add.

"My father kept a very fine wine cellar, but I truly feel no need to avail myself of it," Eleanor answered.

Her reply was a bit stiff, Anna thought. As if she were insulted, somehow.

"However, with only the two of us, I discontinued serving wine with meals. My brother has never tasted spirits and since he'll never be going into Society and contact with heavy imbibers, I see no reason for him to become intimately acquainted with the grape."

The emphatic way she said that closed the subject. Anna remained silent, sipping her water. It was several moments before she realized David had been watching his sister as she spoke, his gaze firmly fastened on her lips. His own immediately tightened and he gave his head a bare shake as if deploring something.

****

Unknown to Lady Eleanor, her brother had a very long-standing acquaintance with the grape, as well as another vice acquired by his contemporaries, that of smoking tobacco.

Both began shortly after his fourteenth birthday when he went with his sister into Mayfield Village to have his horse shod. The manor didn't have its own smith, so its horses were taken into the village.

When his father was alive, David had often ridden with the then-Lord Mayfield, seated before him on the pommel of his saddle while the groom rode behind them with the other horses on a lead. Ashley, the smith, had two sons around David's age, and while the horses were being shod, Papa allowed Jem and Albert to play with him.

Mama would always deplore David's dirty face and dusty breeches afterward, but Papa would laugh and say, "Doesn't hurt the lad to get a little good honest soil under his nails, Beatrice. That'll make him better appreciate those who work in it."

After the accident, Eleanor would ride in their

carriage, making an errand day. While the groom went to the smithy, she'd go to the milliners, the seamstress, and also the mercantile where she'd leave a list with the proprietor for goods to be delivered to the manor.

During one of those trips, while Eleanor was allowing herself the brief pleasure of looking at the new selection of fabric swatches and visualizing the gowns that might be fashioned out of them, gowns she'd now never wear, David became bored. As usual, he'd been placed in a chair near the door where she might keep an eye on him while indulging herself. Usually he was quiet and kept entertained by looking through the glass shop front, watching those outside as they went about their tasks. That specific day, he was fidgety and restless.

At last, catching Eleanor's attention, and writing the word *horse* on his slate, he got her permission to leave.

It was a long walk to the edge of town where the smithy was located, but David didn't mind, not if it rescued him from sitting and watching his sister touch those silly bits of cloth glued onto the pages of that book. He hated seeing the glow on her face slowly fade, understanding he was the cause. He vaguely remembered the parties held at the manor, except the ones Eleanor had been allowed to attend…those were specifically embedded in his mind. How pretty she'd looked, like a fairy princess in one of the books Mama read to him at night before Nanny put him to bed.

David now had only a faint recollection of his mother's voice, as well as his own. The few words he could speak he had to dredge from those memories.

That day, as he neared the smithy, he saw Jem and Albert lounging near the hitching post where the groom's horse and his own were tied, almost as if they'd been waiting for him. They greeted him silently with waves of their hands.

Looking around furtively and making certain their father wasn't in sight, Al gestured David over, stopping him from going inside the smithy. With an inquisitive look, David followed the two boys around the side of the building to the back.

Several others awaited them. David recognized each...Roger, the tobacconist's son, Jonathan, whose father owned the mercantile store, and Alfred Ogilvie, whose father ran the livery stable and had once supplied conveyances taking guests to the manor. They greeted him and went back to what they were doing, which was putting odd little white cylinders to their mouths and sucking on them until smoke puffed out.

Cigaritos, Al wrote on David's slate and offered him one from a small tin in Roger's possession, which he'd filched from his father's showcase. David remembered seeing his father smoke cigars, so he was eager to try something his lordship had indulged in, feeling it would briefly bring back his father. With his own *cigarito* dangling from his lip, Al showed him how to hold the thing while he lit it with a sulphur match he'd also brought out of the box. As the match flared, David started slightly, then hesitantly put the *cigarito* to his mouth, copying Al's action.

At first, he didn't like it. The smoke burned his tongue and his nose, making him want to sneeze. His eyes watered, but the other boys seemed to enjoy it, so he bravely puffed and swallowed smoke, letting it trickle out his nose...until the moment he began to feel nauseous and abruptly his smoke-seasoned breakfast came up.

They sympathetically patted his back as he vomited the entire meal into the dirt. With gestures, Al informed him they had all suffered that way at first, encouraging David to try again. Al relit the *cigarito*, and this time, David fared better. He finished smoking it without the least twinge. They celebrated by passing around a small jug of wine, also stolen, this one from Jonathan's father's inventory.

David fared better with that. After the second swallow, however, he felt a bit giggly and warm, and the third swallow made him dizzy. Prudently, Al suggested he not drink any more.

Bidding the others goodbye and returning Al's wink as he read the word on his slate…*secret*…accompanied by a finger to his lips, David nodded to show he'd never tell.

At the smithy's, the groom was preparing to leave, gathering the lead for David's now-shod horse.

Gait slightly wobbly and vision blurred, David walked with the groom back to the seamstress's establishment. His sister was in the carriage, waiting. David climbed in beside her and promptly fell asleep. By the time they arrived at the manor, he'd slept off the whisky's hold on him and was suffering a headache, as well as a severe stomachache.

When he complained to his sister, *Head, Tum hurt, Oh,* she noted his flushed face and put him to bed with a promptly administered spoonful of castor oil. David decided then and there if he ever got any more liquid in a jug, it was best not to mention how bad it made him feel.

It was several visits later before his sister became suspicious of his eagerness to go to the village with her.

That fatal day, ready to come home and missing her brother, she tracked him down behind the smithy where he and the others were well into their cups this time, puffing away. Discovered, the boys scattered before her wrath, while David stood silent and sullen, enduring a tirade he couldn't hear but appreciated nevertheless.

The others were beaten by their fathers. David wasn't—his friends swearing it was his first time experimenting—though he later wished he had been, for he considered his punishment more severe and unfair. Eleanor confined him to his room for a week and refused to let him ride his horse for a month.

When David emerged from his imprisonment, he was a subdued youngster but not a conquered one. From that one incident, he learned subterfuge.

David still smoked and he still drank. Al now supplied him with *cigaritos*, paid for out of the allowance Eleanor gave him. Once a month he met Al at the turn of the highroad, where he exchanged coins for a boxful of *cigaritos* he hid in a hollow tree at the lake. The others he cached behind some books in his room, along with a bottle of his father's finest brandy and a crystal goblet taken from the china cabinet.

Shelton had noticed the goblet's absence and wrongly assumed either Jane or the footman had broken it while dusting. Since both denied being the culprit, he asked Lady Eleanor to dock the price of the glass from their salaries. While David was sorry they were punished for his crime, he didn't regret it enough to confess to his part in its absence.

Though the others were now considered old enough to smoke or drink in public, in deference to David, they still occasionally met behind the smithy for a sip or two and a smoke, to which David brought his own. That allowed Lady Eleanor, in the bliss of her ignorance, to pride herself on the fact that her brother hadn't acquired the vices to which other young men his age were already slaves.

Chapter 10

After dessert, Lady Eleanor laid down her spoon. "This is generally the point where we ladies retire so the gentlemen can enjoy their cigars and brandy, but..." She bestowed a smile on David, who returned it with a limpid blue gaze.

Anna frowned. She'd noticed several times how David watched his sister's lips rather than looking at her face.

"...since my brother neither smokes nor imbibes..."

David's mouth quirked as she said that.

"...I suggest we adjourn to the library and let David show you how well he can read and write so you may evaluate him and decide on a course of study."

David's expression immediately fell into another pout. Anna was startled that such a sullen countenance could make him look so appealing.

With a sigh audible to everyone but himself, he pulled his napkin from his shirtfront, wiped his mouth, then tossed the cloth square at the table. It landed across his plate, cream sauce and beet juice soaking into the snow-white linen.

Anna started slightly, knowing the napkin was ruined. David didn't give it a second look. She supposed she should be grateful he didn't dash his plate to the floor.

Library? he wrote and when Eleanor nodded, he

walked to Anna's side, offering his arm without prompting. After a moment's hesitation, she placed her hand on it. This time, he didn't hurry but strolled at a leisurely pace by her side to the library, where he escorted her to one of the chairs by the fireplace, the one she'd sat in earlier that day.

After that, he simply waited for his sister to speak.

"By the way, I have a gift for you." Eleanor picked up something from the desk, holding it out to Anna.

Anna took it. Another small slate with chalk.

"So you won't have to keep using mine or David's."

"Thank you, your ladyship." *If I have my way, David soon won't need a slate.*

"Now then, what would you like him to do?" Lady Eleanor asked.

Thinking that made David sound like a trained dog about to perform a trick, Anna took a moment in answering. She needed to know his lordship's level of literacy, how well he could read, as well as the extent of his writing ability, and not simply single words upon a slate.

"Your lordship…" She touched his arm, to make certain he was looking at her, and nearly shuddered with pleasure when that sky-blue gaze swung toward her. Managing to suppress the sound, she printed on the slate, *Write your letters.*

He looked from it to her and shook his head.

He's refusing? Anna steeled herself, expecting to be bombarded with vases and perhaps books, but no… He tapped the word "letters," shaking his head again. *He doesn't know that word…*

"Is there paper?"

Lady Eleanor helpfully removed a sheet of foolscap

from a drawer of the desk where she had sat that morning. She placed it on the desktop, indicating the quill and inkwell. Hand on David's arm, Anna walked over to the desk. He didn't move, and she tugged sharply, making him reluctantly accompany her.

Laying down the slate, she dipped the quill into the inkwell and wrote on the paper, "A, B, C…" and under that, "1, 2, 3…" and then handed the quill to him.

He studied the rows of letters and numbers, nodded and, leaning over the desk, began to write. It took him several moments of concentration, teeth nibbling on his lower lip as he laboriously formed the letters, but when he finished, looking up at her triumphantly, there were marks in a remarkably straight line across the paper. There were also several splotches of ink spattering the sheet as well as the top of the desk.

"Tsk." Eleanor pulled another sheet from the drawer and placed it over the ink spots, removing it once they were soaked up. "I'm afraid David has no respect for furniture."

Or anything else. Anna thought of the beet-soaked napkin. She noted several older spots which had apparently missed Eleanor's attention. She decided instilling in her pupil a sense of the value of things might not be a bad idea. Right now, however…

Taking the paper from him, she looked at it. He'd written the entire alphabet. Though printed, the letters were well-formed and recognizable. As for the numbers, one through twelve covered a single line, one after the other.

He pulled the foolscap from her hand. Dropping it to the desktop, he again dipped the quill in the ink and gestured at the paper.

"I think that's enough," she told him and wrote *No* on the slate.

He nodded and replaced the quill on its stand.

"He writes well," she told Lady Eleanor who beamed as if she herself had been praised.

A sound beside her made her glance back. David had picked up the quill again and was scribbling something. She leaned over to see what he'd written.

Beet…red…make pretty mouth.

Anna's hand went to her mouth. She hadn't realized the creamed beets had dyed her lips a rosy pink. David's own lips curved upward in what she could only describe as a grin. She was tempted to become angry, then changed her mind.

Perhaps he means it as a compliment. Or he's merely making a statement of fact. How can I be certain?

She nodded and wrote, *Thank you.*

His own nod was noncommittal. Once more, he laid down the quill.

"What shall I have His Lordship read?" she went on, before Lady Eleanor could ask what he had written.

"David has several books he likes," Eleanor answered. "David, why don't you select one?" On her slate, she wrote, *Book. Read.*

He nodded—a bit reluctantly, Anna thought—and walked to one of the bookcases. One shelf held several very thin chapbooks. Anna recognized them as children's readers. His hand trailed across the spines, then stopped. He selected a small volume whose boards were bound in blue buckram. He held it up for Eleanor to see.

Aesopus Moralisatus.

"Aesop's Fables? Surely he can't read Greek?"

Anna asked before she could stop herself.

"Goodness, no," Lady Eleanor allowed herself a wry smile. "It's an English translation."

David gestured with the book, impatiently.

"Go ahead, dear." She waved her permission.

Opening the book, he flipped through several pages before deciding on one. Then he simply stared at the page before looking at Anna. She nodded.

Clearing his throat with a sound that in another might've been self-consciousness, David glanced at the page and began in a remarkably clear voice, "Dere was…wunz…ah hoose…ov-run…bah mize…" He stopped, looked at Anna, and waited. She nodded and made the same gesture Eleanor had. He bit his lip, then read, "Ah caat bee-gaan tuh…catch…dee…mize…"

"That's enough." Anna touched his arm.

He stopped, head jerking up to stare at her so quickly she was startled. It was the same movement he'd made when she touched him while in the drive.

"He reads fairly well, considering…"

"He does have some trouble with *th*," Lady Eleanor explained. "As well as *gh*, as I said before. He pronounces words with *gh* as *guu*." She sighed and affected a brightness she obviously didn't feel. "So! What do you think, Anna?"

"I think his lordship…" She stopped as David placed a hand over hers resting against the desk. As she looked at him, he wrote something on the sheet.

David.

Warmth flooded her cheeks. Briefly, she wondered if he somehow had learned what Lady Eleanor had told her about being informal.

Nodding, Anna continued, "I think David can not

only read letters, I believe he's also learned to lip read somewhat."

"Lip read?" Lady Eleanor frowned. "What's that?"

"You say something before you write it down," Anna explained. "I believe he knows what you're trying to tell him from reading the words, but he also gets a meaning from the way your lips look when you speak it."

"Really?" Eleanor's fingers went to her mouth. She touched her lips as if they were suddenly a wonder. "Are you certain?"

"Very," Anna answered firmly. "Watch this." Turning to David, she said, "Where is the cat?"

There was a slight scowl. He waited so long Anna was certain she'd been mistaken in her assessment. Then, he looked around, shrugged, and raised his hands as she'd done when standing in the driveway.

"We don't have a cat," Eleanor said.

"Where is the cat?" she repeated, shaking a quieting hand at her ladyship.

He picked up the quill. *No cat. Horses.*

"Yes," she nodded. "There's a cat. Where is the cat?"

Again, he shook his head, then glanced down at the book. There was a quick look at Anna before he picked up *Aesop's Fables*, looked over the line he'd read, and pointed.

"That's right." She nodded again. "The cat's in the book. See?" She turned to Eleanor. "He answered me, without my writing it down."

"Oh, Anna…" Eleanor's voice was so soft it was a mere whisper. Again, her hand went to her mouth, this time to hide a trembling lower lip.

Immediately, David was around the desk, his hand

on her arm. He patted her cheek, then caught her hand and kissed it, looking back at Anna accusingly. Reaching across, he pushed the book so roughly it slid to the edge of the desk.

"It's all right," Anna attempted to reassure him, touching the book to make certain it didn't fall to the floor. "It was good. Your sister's happy."

His expression said he understood *good* and *happy* but didn't believe it. He touched Eleanor's cheek near her left eye, holding up his finger so Anna could see the damp smear.

"Truly, David." Eleanor's hand cupped his chin. "I'm happy."

He nodded, scribbled, *No sad?* on his slate.

"No sad," she repeated.

David retrieved the book. Opening it, he tapped a sentence and held it out to Anna. She took it from him, looking at the moral of the story: *The wise mouse isn't deceived by the innocent cat; those once considered dangerous usually still are.*

Startled, she looked up into the seemingly harmless blue eyes. One lid drooped, then raised so quickly she wasn't certain she'd even seen it. *Did he wink at me?*

There was another scribble on the slate. He held it so both women could see.

Sleep. Good Night. Apparently his lordship had decided there had been enough testing of his abilities for one night.

Not waiting for permission, David swept them both a bow and hurried from the room. A few seconds later, there was the clatter of his heels on the stairs.

"He thought you'd made me unhappy," Eleanor said softly. "In his own way, David's as protective of me as I am of him. I doubt he's ever seen me cry in happiness." She dabbed at her eyes with her fingers. "I daresay I've not had much reason lately."

"At least he didn't smash another vase," Anna murmured.

There was a slight silence and then both broke into laughter.

"If you don't mind, I believe I'll retire also." Anna felt a sudden exhilaration, as well as an eagerness for the next day to begin. "I'll work up a lesson plan before I sleep tonight, and in the morning, we'll begin lessons."

"I thought perhaps after lunch might be the best time," Eleanor suggested with a surprising timidity. "David's rarely around until then. He generally rises early, skips breakfast, and rides most of the morning. He and that horse of his are inseparable."

"Is that the chestnut he was riding this morning?"

"Yes…that's the Horse. I gave it to him for his fourteenth birthday. I remember how happy he was."

"What's its name?" Anna had no trouble remembering the beautiful horse. He and his rider were well-suited, two handsome male animals… *Are their thought processes equal, also?*

"He doesn't have a name." Eleanor looked thoughtful. "I asked David what he was going to name his horse and…do you know what he said?"

Anna shook her head.

"At first, he wouldn't answer me. Finally, he wrote on his slate, *No name. No hear*. I understood, but it saddened me. Why give something a name if its owner will never be able to say it? So we simply call the creature *the Horse*." Not giving Anna time to react to that, she hurried on. "Anna, I've something to tell you…"

"Lady Eleanor, you've done nothing but tell me—" Anna didn't want to be the keeper of any more keys than she had to be.

"I like to feel I have a special relationship with the people in service at Mayfield Manor." Eleanor interrupted. "Shelton has been with my family forever. He was my grandfather's butler before he was Papa's. After the tragedy, when I was so lost and struggling to accept the role foisted upon me, he stepped in and became my advisor, my shield against the outside world…and the shoulder I very often cried upon. In a way, he became a surrogate grandfather, to me and to David. There were several of my father's friends who felt raising David was too much of a chore for someone so young, and Shelton was determined I'd prove them wrong. He encouraged me to become stronger and be the 'lady of the manor.'" Eleanor smiled again as if thinking a very pleasant thought. "You'll notice everyone calls me 'ma'am'?"

Anna nodded.

"Shelton felt it wasn't proper to call me 'Madam,' since I was unmarried, but he felt 'Miss' wasn't quite the term for someone who was now head of the family, so he settled on 'ma'am.' I like to think I lost one family and gained another, though I imagine our so-called peers would be aghast at that thought. And now…"

She returned to the hearth, stopping before Anna.

"You've given me such hope, Anna, I hope you'll become part of our family, too." She took a deep breath as if about to say something momentous. "David has asked you to call him by his given name. Let's dispense with titles… I'd like you to call me 'Eleanor.'"

"Thank you, your la—Eleanor." Anna was shaken by the earnestness with which her ladyship spoke. "I'd be pleased to."

"I suppose we should all be to bed, then." Now Eleanor was brisk and all business, ushering Anna out of the parlor and to the stairs. "I believe tomorrow's going to be a very busy day for all of us."

Chapter 11

The next morning, Anna was awake before Jane's knock. As the maid helped her dress, she felt oddly eager, with the same sense of excitement she used to feel when she was a child and the traveling fair came to Little Riversreach, or the approach of Christmastide. She told herself it was merely the coming challenge David Woods represented.

His Lordship wouldn't be the first difficult case she'd had, but since he was an adult and all her other students had been children, she expected a few problems besides that obvious reluctance he was already displaying. Anna still didn't quite understand his attitude. After all, he knew now she wasn't a physician, or at least she hoped he realized that. Finally, she decided he was merely someone who didn't like change. After all, he'd gotten along fine for fifteen years now, at least to his way of looking at things, and he probably saw no need for anything to be different.

At the ripe old age of twenty, Lord David was set in his ways. *That's it. I'll simply have to convince him otherwise.*

She decided she'd meet the problem head on. At breakfast.

Unfortunately, David didn't cooperate.

As his sister had said, he wasn't at breakfast, his place at the table conspicuously neat because of his absence.

"Shelton tells me he and Horse went galloping out of here around seven this morning," Eleanor told her as she daintily spread a dollop of apple conserve on her toast. She replaced the little knife on the tray next to the bowl holding the concoction. "Thank you, Edward. Would you tell Cook this batch is especially good?"

"Yes, ma'am." Edward bowed and proceeded around her chair, bearing the tray of two bowls of conserve and jam as well as two plates of warm toast, one well-buttered toast, one plain. He offered them to Anna.

Anna didn't comment. She simply declined both and finished her own meal.

"Did you get your lesson plan organized?" Eleanor inquired.

"It took me a bit, but I have it ready." She'd spent nearly an hour before sleeping to work on the course of study. She ate the last spoonful of coddled egg and reached for her napkin.

"I was wondering…would it be permissible for me to sit in on David's first lesson? So I'll have some idea of what's going on?" Eleanor spoke hesitantly as if certain Anna would refuse.

"If David doesn't mind." Anna felt a trifle odd speaking his name without its accompanying title, but he'd asked her to dispense with that, hadn't he? "Family generally comes later because often a pupil feels a bit shy in the beginning. Inhibited, I mean, by the presence of another person, especially if that person's a relative." As Eleanor frowned, Anna hastened to explain, "Sometimes it can give a sense of over-expectation."

"I can appreciate that." Eleanor looked thoughtful,

curiosity to see Anna's teaching methods fighting with not wishing to cause any further dissention with her brother. "Very well, then. When David returns from his ride, I'll ask him if I may be there." She took a bite of toast, quite obviously savored its taste, swallowed, and asked, "What do you plan to do between now and luncheon, my dear?"

"With your permission, I thought I'd take a walk through the woods," Anna replied. "On my way in, I barely gave it a glance because I was so anxious to get here. This morning, I thought to go back for a stroll and really see it."

"That's an excellent idea," Eleanor gave her approval. "However, I'd recommend following the riding path leading behind the manor and not walking back to the highroad. The creek feeds into a lovely little lake a little farther on where ducks and other wildfowl gather. There are wildflowers there, also."

Reaching for her fork, she looked thoughtful. "Papa didn't allow hunting because Mama thought the birds were so beautiful." She smiled. "We'd often picnic there and some of them actually became tame enough for me to feed by hand. I think it must be an indication of how much the villagers like our family that we've never had poachers."

"You make me eager to see it. It sounds idyllic."

"Then be off with you." Eleanor smiled. "And enjoy your walk…oh, perhaps you'd better have Jane get you one of my everyday shawls…it's a bit coolish this morning."

"Please…don't worry. I've a very utilitarian one." Anna placed her napkin by her plate and stood. "I'll be back before luncheon."

"We sit down to table around eleven-thirty." Eleanor replied, adding, "Unless David decides to play another stubborn card." She laughed as she said it, however.

Anna laughed also, hoping Eleanor wasn't making an ominous prediction. As she left the dining room, she heard Her Ladyship say, "I believe I'll have some more of those eggs, Edward. They aren't cold yet, are they?"

****

With directions from Shelton on how to find the riding path and also the assurance that if she stayed on it, she should have no fear of getting lost, Anna set out. The butler's admonition was the same as Ogilvie's, making her immediately wonder what would happen if somehow, she did manage to go astray in the forest.

Her mind immediately wove a scenario.

David would probably inwardly rejoice while his sister became concerned. Anna imagined both of them seated at the dining table, David forging through the meal as if he'd been starved for a week while Eleanor sent anxious glances at Anna's empty chair. Finally, she'd gain her brother's attention and send him and perhaps Edward in search of her.

And where will I be all this time? Seated on a fallen log somewhere, clutching my shawl about me and waiting for rescue as the day begins to wane and I start at every sound coming from the forest. Anna laughed aloud. *That sounds like something from one of those romances Maisie reads. I should never have allowed myself to open one of those novels. Now I'll see a mysterious horseman or a ghostly figure behind every tree.*

Briefly allowed to run free, her imagination supplied

David as the horseman. Indeed, he'd make a lovely hero.

If I were to become lost, there's no one I'd rather have ride to my rescue.

However, knowing David even on such short acquaintance, he'd probably continue with his meal and let her stay in the forest until the next morning.

Truly, she had no idea what he thought. Even when he wrote something on his slate, how could she be certain of its true meaning from one or two words? She thought again of that wink and the moral he'd indicated from the fable.

Was that a warning? Was he telling me he isn't what he seems? Am I being too fanciful?

Wrapping the shawl around her shoulders, she shrugged away such thoughts and started out. Briefly, the feel of the practical, plain wrap Maisie had crocheted for her brought a sense of comfort.

Anna found the path quite easily, though she'd have called it a road. It was a tract about six feet wide, worn smooth with the soil packed hard, no doubt from Horse's hooves traveling over it many times during the years. She could see fresh marks in the dirt, the impressions of a running horse's iron-shod hooves digging in and cutting large crescents.

David and his faithful steed had ridden this way.

Perhaps we'll meet each other.

A sudden breeze blew out of the trees and Anna drew her shawl a little tighter about her shoulders. Eleanor had been right. It was cool, the height of the trees keeping out sunlight and making deep shadows. There would be no real sunlight until that burning orb was directly overhead. When that happened, she'd know it was time to return if she wasn't already on her way back by then.

Best not let myself be distracted. Perhaps it'll give me some mental tranquility. I've a feeling I'm about to meet my greatest challenge after luncheon.

Chapter 12

At the lake, David pulled his horse to a halt and slid from the animal's back.

Contrary to what Eleanor told Anna, he *had* given his horse a name…*Run*…because that was exactly what the chestnut did. For some reason he couldn't explain—even if he'd been able to speak—David didn't want his sister to know Run's name. It was a secret between him and the animal.

Shortly after he received the horse, he had gone to the stable. Making certain they were alone, he seized the halter's cheekpiece, pulling the horse's head down. He'd stared into the big dark eyes and told the animal, mouthing the words, *You are Run. My friend.*

He was certain Run understood, for the horse shook its head and snorted, breath fluttering its nostrils and warming the hand David placed near his muzzle. Run was his best friend, had been for six years now. Run was also the keeper of his secrets, for he took David to his meetings with Al and the others when they met to smoke and drink.

Tying the reins to the lowest branch of the nearest pine, David slipped the bit from the horse's mouth so Run might graze if he cared to, then made his way down the slope to the lake.

Halfway there stood a tree which had fared very badly in a storm several years before. Lightning struck a limb, shearing it off and searing a jagged scar down its center, killing half the tree. Later, a heavy snowfall made a lower limb sag until it touched the ground, finally snapping it off. The absence of the limb left a vaguely circular hole in the trunk.

Remembering how Eleanor had reacted when she caught him and the other boys behind the smithy, David was very careful that his sister didn't learn of his hidden *cigaritos*. He probably could've gotten away with it even if she found out, but only after a few more precious vases were smashed, bringing the inventory of ceramics even lower, or if he performed some other act of childish temper. He realized destruction of those beautiful porcelain creations made Eleanor very unhappy, though it had now happened so often she merely shrugged it off with a sad sigh he couldn't hear.

He always felt guilty afterward because he knew he was destroying another item belonging to his mother and with it a bit more of her memory. He didn't like doing that, but he didn't like not getting his way, either. Whenever that thought came, he'd shake his head and ball his hand into a fist, beating it in the air violently. David didn't know any swear words or vulgarisms. That single movement replaced what he couldn't say.

When David discovered the torn place in the tree, he thought it the best place to hide the most obvious of his vices.

With a knife, he hollowed out the tear, shaping it and smoothing the tree's interior. Taking the little tin box Al had supplied with that first surreptitious purchase, he wrapped it securely in a length of oilcloth and tucked the package inside the hollow. Now, whenever he felt the need of a smoke, or to think, which smoking seemed to assist, he simply saddled Run and rode to the lake, no matter the time of day or night. Everyone in the manor, including his sister, was accustomed to him riding whenever the mood struck, and it wasn't unusual to hear hoofbeats pounding down the path at midnight.

This morning, David needed to think…specifically about Anna Leighton.

When his sister told him she was hiring someone to teach him Signing, he reacted with many fist-shakings. Aware of what that meant, she reprimanded him sharply, the words on the slate thick and wide, written with a heavy hand.

Stop. Now.

Eleanor was correct in her guess that David equated a teacher with a doctor. He expected Anna to be another stodgy spectacled gentleman who'd stick cold metal instruments into his ears, hold down his tongue with a flat piece of wood while peering into his mouth, and prod his chest and palpate his neck, then straighten with a sad shake of the head and say words to his sister that he knew by heart though he couldn't hear them: *I'm sorry, Your Ladyship, there's nothing I can do.*

David had had enough of that. He wouldn't stand for it again.

Instead, he'd been introduced to this beautiful…delightful…little creature…the girl he'd mistaken for someone applying to be a maid like Jane. Only she was much prettier than Jane. She was to be the one to help him communicate? Not with one or two words scribbled on a slate but with…what? How?

She was smart, too, he realized, for she'd already discovered he could sometimes tell what people were saying by watching their mouths. She didn't let herself be frightened easily, as when he dragged her into the dining room. He expected Ellie to protest his ill-manners about that but she hadn't, and the girl hadn't complained, either.

That was another mark in her favor.

Anna. He thought her name, mentally caressing it.

There was something else about Anna, however, and that was the thing David needed to think about…

The first time she touched him, standing in the driveway, she'd startled him. He hadn't been expecting it, hadn't felt movement behind him as she approached. The second time, however, when she pulled him to the desk in the library, he'd been surprised again, but in a different way. *Disturbed* was a better description. The warmth of her hand seemed to penetrate the cloth of his sleeve, spreading up his arm and through his body. The feel of her gloved fingers sent a bolt of fire directly into the very center of his being, and from there it trickled to somewhere a little lower and more basic. No one, especially no woman, had ever made such a sensation occur within him before, and he wondered why.

What was it about Anna that made those odd feelings within him? He didn't understand.

It wasn't that David was kept isolated from female company. There were many young women in Mayfield Village. He knew most by sight and a few by name because they'd more or less grown up together. He rarely had anything to do with them, however. He knew them, he recognized them, but that was all. Al, Jem, and the others were more his companions.

The only women at the manor were his sister, Jane, and the cook who had been with the family since David was ten. Jane had trod an uneasy line between servant and companion until he was around fifteen. Jane was pretty, but Anna…

She's beautiful, David's rudimentary thoughts declared. Like the fairy princess in the books his mother used to read him before Nanny put him to bed.

Nanny was the only other woman David had ever been close to, but she was gone now. He didn't remember if she had been young or old, pretty or plain. His only memory of her was that she had taught him his letters and praised him for being such a quick study. Then there was that fatal carriage ride and the driver, the footman, and Mama and Papa went away, and Nanny went with them. She'd been riding on the side of the carriage where David sat but he was thrown clear, hitting his head.

He awoke into eternal silence, with Elly crying by his bedside and the realization he hadn't been allowed to go with Mama, Papa, or the others to wherever it was they went after that.

Reaching into the hollow, David drew out the oilcloth-covered box, unwrapping it and taking out a single *cigarito* and one of the matches Al had also supplied. Lucifer matches cost extra because they were still a rare item, but Al explained with elaborate gestures that as long as David gave him a few more coins, he'd make sure he got some.

He replaced the box, dragged the match along the sole of his boot, and held it up as it flared. Touching it to the tip of the *cigarito*, he waited until the cornshuck cover blackened and the tobacco inside glowed. Then he inhaled and expertly blew away the smoke.

Snapping the matchstick in half, he dropped it to the dirt and ground it under his boot.

As he walked along the lake's shoreline, raising the *cigarito* to his lips and puffing methodically, he studied the ducks lazily paddling across its length. There was a mallard, green head gleaming iridescent in the sunlight flickering through the trees, the characteristic and very noticeable curl in his tail feathers marking his breed. Beside him floated his hen, a drab brown little creature looking insignificant beside his colorful plumage. Occasionally she floated closer, so their sides actually touched. Once the drake stretched his neck, rubbing his bill against the side of her head. She opened her own bill—David imagined she was making some noise—then returned the caress.

What would it be like to have someone ride beside me…let me hold her hand as we rode along…perhaps the leather of our boots would brush because our horses were so close together…

Would he feel the same heat through the thickness of a riding boot as from Anna's hand on his sleeve?

He blew smoke into the air, watching the other birds, several gray geese, a couple of other mallards. The birds realized they were safe on Mayfield land. One or two were recognizable as having returned from previous springs. They generally produced a small flock of ducklings and goslings, bringing them to near-adulthood before the weather changed and they flew south.

David wished they'd stay and not leave. He liked feeding the creatures, holding out a hand filled with grain and feeling the blunted little pecks against his palm as they scooped off the kernels. Once or twice, he'd actually coaxed one of the babies to come close enough to pet, though the mother bird hovered anxiously behind.

That had given him a bit of a tremor internally. Why

hadn't his own mother hovered and kept the carriage from overturning? Did she fly south and leave him like the birds did every year? Only…the birds came back.

As if realizing his reminiscences weren't getting him anywhere, and experiencing a rare occasion of frustration in which he actually wished he were able to express himself, David wandered back up the slope to where Run waited patiently.

Taking a final puff on the *cigarito*, he tossed it to the dirt where it was crushed under the toe of his boot.

The wind had died down and smoke floated about him in a very visible cloud. He swatted the air but it barely moved. Raising his arm, he sniffed at his sleeve. The scent clung. His fist struck the air. He didn't dare give his sister a chance to smell the least scent of tobacco about his person. That meant he'd have to bathe before returning to the manor and discovering what Anna had planned for that first lesson, a session he was actually looking forward to, though he pretended otherwise.

Shrugging, he pulled his shirt over his head, dropping it to the ground as he started down the slope. Boots followed, with an awkward struggle as he hopped on first one foot, then the other, pulling them off. Unbuttoning the drop panel of his riding breeches, he stripped them away. As he neared the lake edge, he shucked his drawers and pulled off the ribbon holding back his hair. Lastly, he removed the slate from around his neck.

David waded into the water. It was cold but felt good. He looked up. The sun was almost over the trees now. The water would be warmer when those golden rays struck it.

An inquisitive duck floated near. Cupping his hands,

he splashed at it and it scrambled away, wings flapping and spraying water, bill open, though as far as David was concerned no sound emerged.

David continued into the water. It was now at his shoulders, his hair floating around him like the fronds of dark lake weed. The duck stopped a few feet away, settled itself, and glided in a circle, regarding him with a round orange eye.

David grinned back at it and, lunging forward, began to swim.

****

Early on, Eleanor had developed a fear of his falling into the lake and drowning, so she'd had Shelton teach him how to swim. At the age of ten, David and the old man, both clad in their smallclothes, waded into the water while Eleanor stood higher up on the bank, hovering like that mother duck.

Paddling close to the bank, Shelton demonstrated what David was to imitate, while he cast many glances at Her Ladyship, obviously embarrassed by appearing before his employer in his underwear.

David thought that funny. Shelton was tall and thin and reminded him of a crane. Eleanor ignored everything except what he was trying to accomplish.

When they finally emerged from the lake, soaked fabric clinging to their bodies and the footman hastily draping a blanket around both of them, David had the rudiments of staying afloat well-learned, and his sister's fears were assuaged. He'd since refined his swimming technique and now was quite a strong and accomplished swimmer, as his many clandestine dips with Al, Jem, and the others attested, when they shucked their clothes and swam naked in the part of the creek after it left the lake, where it meandered behind the miller's and become a stream turning the mill wheel.

Eleanor didn't know of that any more than she did his smoking. If David had his way, she never would.

****

Diving, David surfaced near the ducks, sending them scattering. He spun in the water, moving with clean, strong strokes. As he returned to the shore, he rose to his feet in the shallow water, ducking his head and rubbing his hair to make certain no smoke still clung. Then, he scrubbed at his shoulders and arms.

There, that should take care of it.

The sun was directly overhead now. Reluctantly, David decided he'd better return to the manor. He waded toward the bank, looked up the slope...and froze.

Silhouetted against the sunlight was a small figure.

Chapter 13

Anna had been enjoying her walk, looking at the trees, trying to identify them. So far, she'd seen a couple of oaks much like those near the edge of the highroad. There were also one or two she recognized as silver birch by their distinctive white bark, and of course the many pines towering above everything. High in the branches, small, yellow blossoms dangled from vines. She thought that was yellow jasmine. Below, here and there, small purple-and-white-striped late-blooming crocus peeped through the grass.

The carrion crows were no longer about, and she was glad of that. They always seemed to place a pall over everything. She spotted a starling or two, and heard a couple of songbirds. Something that might be a chipmunk skittered through the trees, while a small squirrel scrambled up the trunk of an oak, a large acorn bulging its jaws. Along the way, she discovered a gooseberry patch and sampled a couple, but it was too early and they were incredibly sour. Grimacing, she spat out the berries, promising to repay them a visit at a later day to see if they might be ripened enough to pick.

If I'm around long enough.

If David proved too difficult, she might possibly find herself in Ogilvie's pony trap on her way back to the train station this very evening, no matter how Eleanor felt about her becoming a 'member of the family.'

The sun was getting higher overhead. Anna decided she'd better start back. She hadn't found the lake Eleanor spoke of, but by the time she arrived at the manor, luncheon would probably be ready. Afterward, the *ordeal*, as she was beginning to think of it, for both her and David would begin.

Before her on the path, sunlight struck something, making it gleam whitely. She paused, stooping to pick it up.

What's this?

She stared at the odd thing, turning it over in her hands. It was brittle and paperlike with minute wrinkles...*a corn-husk?*...wrapped around what appeared to be shredded bits of brown plant. It was charred and crushed as if it had been burned and then stamped on. Anna raised the thing, sniffing loudly.

Why, it's tobacco!

She was familiar with cigars. Her own father smoked them occasionally, but this was too small and narrow.

Is this what they call a cigarito? She'd heard Papa mention them. *Who would be smoking one of these out here?*

There was a sound...a horse's snort...

Anna looked up. Through the trees, she saw a tall chestnut, its reins tied to a branch, bit dangling under its chin. The animal raised its head, looked at her, and neighed as if in recognition.

That's David's horse. She looked again at the *cigarito*, remembering Eleanor's statement at dinner the evening before. *Oh, I see...putting one over on your sister, are you?* She glanced around. *Where are you, David?*

Her gaze traveled down the slope. Anna frowned as she saw the scattered clothing. Her attention was caught by the lake and the ducks paddling peacefully, barely breaking the water's smooth surface. Abruptly, there was a racket as the ducks fluttered into the air, quacking loudly, wings swooping.

A dark head broke the lake's surface.

Anna froze. *If David's in the water and his clothing is there…oh no…*

Slinging his hair out of his face, David rose from the water, wading toward the lake bank.

He doesn't see me. And calling to him would do no good.

Still clutching the *cigarito* stub, she backed away a few feet, then stopped as he turned his head and looked up the slope.

Though he didn't wave or acknowledge her presence, he definitely saw her.

He'll stop now. He won't come out of the water.

David didn't slow his progress. Splashing, he emerged from the lake and stepped onto the grassy bank.

Anna stared at him, startled eyes once again taking in that broad bare chest, gleaming wetly in the overhead sun. She could see little droplets of water falling from his fingertips where his hands hung at his sides. He took another step and that pulled her eyes toward his thigh, also covered with a sheen of lake water, also golden in the sun, and from there to…

Her hand went to her mouth to stifle her gasp. *Surely he'll turn his back…or I should…*

She didn't move.

David didn't turn his back. Instead, he raised a hand, waving to Anna before reached for his drawers, pulling

them on in a slow and leisurely fashion.
Anna whirled and ran.

Chapter 14

How could I do such a thing? How could I stand there and watch him like that?

Anna's thoughts were a frantic, horrified jumble as she rushed along the path. Though she was aware the young farmers around Little Riversreach often shed their shirts as they worked in the fields, and the smith generally wore only his breeches and a thick leather apron while he toiled at the forge, she'd never stared at any of them. She'd certainly never seen any man completely naked before.

Now, not only to see exactly what she'd always wondered about, that hidden mystery inside a man's trousers, so blatantly displayed without a single iota of shame by the man who was to be her pupil…

Which of us was worse?…he, for not covering himself more quickly after he realized she was there…*or I, for not looking away? Did he not know he should be modest? Perhaps he hasn't been taught one didn't bare one's body to the opposite sex.*

All she knew was that she couldn't face David Woods now. The next time they met, she was certain what would happen. Those sky-blue eyes would light with devilment, and though he couldn't speak the words, his smirk would say it all. He would know what she was thinking…that she wanted to see more of His Lordship, unclothed.

I have to find an excuse to leave.

She heard hoofbeats behind her. Not looking back, Anna continued walking, hurrying her pace. The sound came closer. She walked faster. Briefly, he trotted the hunter beside her. She didn't look around, staring determinedly ahead.

He rode the animal in front of her, pulling on the reins. Anna tried to go around them, but he moved the horse forward, making its body block the path. The only thing she could do was allow a confrontation then and there or turn and bolt into the forest.

Glancing desperately at the trees, Anna looked up, meeting David's eyes. His expression told her nothing.

For what seemed an eternity but was surely only mere seconds, his gaze held hers, dark brows scowling, lips in a steady, straight line. His hair had been hastily finger-combed and tied back with a sodden riband. It was plastered to his forehead and cheeks, water trickling down his temples onto his collar and from there to his shirt which was already damp from being pulled onto a wet body. Both shirt and riding breeches clung tightly.

He pulled the slate from his pocket, scribbled something and held it toward her.

Saw you. Why you not wait?

Anna didn't answer.

Shoving the slate back into his pocket, he slid his foot out of the stirrup and twisted in the saddle, holding out his hand.

Anna didn't move.

Impatiently, he gestured, the scowl deepening.

He doesn't act as if anything is wrong. Perhaps, to David, it wasn't.

With a feeling of surrender, Anna raised her skirts

and awkwardly put a foot into the stirrup. She placed her hand in his and was hauled upward, his other hand going around her waist.

In a moment, she was settled on the saddle in front of him. As he gathered the reins in his right hand, she clutched at his arm, fearing she might fall. The arm tightened around her, pulling her body against his chest. Through the shawl, warm, damp heat suffused her shoulder blades.

With a faint moan, Anna closed her eyes, then opened them quickly, looking down, as she realized she was still clutching the *cigarito* stub. His chin grazed her shoulder as she opened her hand. He plucked the stub from her fingers, flinging it away.

Then, he once more wrapped his arm around her, holding her securely as he touched heels to the chestnut's sides and turned its head toward the manor.

Chapter 15

David sat guzzling his soup. He didn't raise his head.

Why won't he look at me? Anna wondered. *What is he planning?*

****

Anxious to rid herself of the damp dress as well the disturbing sensation of heat lingering in it, Anna had hurried to her room as soon as she was inside the manor. Nodding to Shelton as he answered the door, she gave some vague and quick answer to his inquiry if she'd enjoyed her walk. In her room, she pulled out the first dress she found in the wardrobe, hastily divesting herself of one and replacing it with the other. She didn't ask for Jane to come help her, not wanting to draw more attention to herself. Then, she returned downstairs to the dining room.

David wasn't there. Anna expected some remark from Eleanor as to why she was late, but Her Ladyship didn't appear to notice. Perhaps because of her brother's haphazard attention to time? *Can he even tell time?*

When he entered the dining room after Anna was seated, Eleanor made no remark about the fact of his being even later, merely acknowledging his hasty bow with a nod.

Though she'd taken time while upstairs to tidy her hair and splash her face with water in an effort to relieve the warmth inundating her skin, David seemed to think his dip in the lake was refreshment enough. He'd removed the riband, and his hair, now dry but uncombed, lay in a dark mass of wild waves on his shoulders, curling in all directions.

His shirt was still damp and Anna waited for Eleanor to comment on that, but Her Ladyship also appeared accustomed to her brother coming to table clothed in wet garments for she didn't remark on it, either. Indeed, she didn't even blink.

All Anna could think was the fact there had been no inch of untanned skin on David's body, which meant he'd often cavorted naked in the sun, and how she wished she could've seen that. She squeezed her eyes tightly shut as if to dispel that image, then hastily opened them again as the meal was served.

Taking his place at the head of the table, David attacked the light beef broth with the enthusiasm of someone who hadn't eaten in a week, looking neither at his sister nor Anna.

His continued avoidance of glancing at her worried Anna.

Does he think I'll guess his next scheme if I look into those innocent blue eyes? Is it possible he was embarrassed by my presence at the lake?

"Did you enjoy your walk, Anna?" Pausing in dipping her spoon into her broth, Eleanor broke the silence.

"Most certainly." Anna brought her own spoon to her mouth. She sipped slowly. The broth was warm and a bit spicy.

"Tell me, did you see anything interesting?"

Anny choked on her soup, spraying broth.

"Oh, I'm so sorry…it…I swallowed wrong."

Immediately, David gestured frantically at the footman. Edward started forward with a pitcher of water. Anna waved him away.

"That's quite all right. I have water." She lifted her own goblet, drinking noisily. "Oh, dear…the tablecloth…"

In the meantime, David left his seat, holding out his napkin, dabbing at the greasy spot the broth left on the white lace.

While Eleanor made soothing noises assuring her the fine linen wasn't ruined, David pressed the napkin against a large stain on the bosom of her dress.

"That's quite unnecessary!" The ice in Anna's voice would've frozen a man with hearing. The way her body stiffened and cringed from his touch made him jerk his hand away.

He took a step backward, mouth dropping open.

"I-I mean… Thank you, David." She regained her composure and began dabbing at the spots with her own napkin.

David returned to his chair. He saw his sister staring at him and asked, *What*? with raised brows and shoulders.

"I merely asked Anna if she saw anything remarkable on her walk." She wrote an abbreviated version of that on her slate. She looked again at Anna, who was once more attempting to eat her soup. "Shelton said he saw you two ride up together on Horse." Eleanor glanced at her brother, rubbing away her previous words and writing new ones on the slate. "Did you show Anna around the lake, David?"

"As a matter of fact…" Anna began.

He spun in his chair to stare at her, abruptly shaking his head and managing to make it seem a movement as he turned. She was startled by the panic in his eyes.

What does he think I'm going to say? Oh certainly, Eleanor. I watched your brother swimming stark naked and feasted on his manly charms? Apparently so, if the desperation in those wide eyes was any indication. David definitely didn't want his sister aware they'd been in such a confrontation.

Brow wrinkling, he waited for her reply.

"I met David on the way back. He very courteously offered to give me a ride so I wouldn't be late."

"I'm glad you can show you're a gentleman on occasion." Eleanor gave her brother a left-handed compliment verbally and a single-word one on the slate. *Good.*

Nodding hesitantly because he wasn't certain exactly what Anna had said since she'd turned away from him as she spoke, David locked his gaze on Anna's lips.

"I also noticed a fine gooseberry patch. I'm hoping I might pick some when they're ripe and have Cook prepare some gooseberry tarts…if that will be permissible?" She spooned broth, blithely aware how closely he was watching.

The relaxed relief to David's body was very noticeable.

****

Anna excused herself from luncheon as quickly as she could without appearing rude. David didn't look at her again but slumped over his plate. Not daring to look up for fear of again meeting that blue gaze, she also keep her attention on the food before her, though later she was unable to remember anything else she'd eaten.

At last, with the excuse she had to prepare for the momentous first lesson, she left the dining room and hurried to the library.

She'd thought long and hard the night before of what she would do this first day, and now that the time was rapidly approaching, she was understandably nervous, undoubtedly aided by that morning's encounter.

She still was uncertain whether David was aware their meeting in such a way was an impropriety, though his obvious fear that she'd mention it to Eleanor seemed to confirm that. Nevertheless, she believed he would do something unexpected but embarrassing to her, though she hoped he'd also cooperate and try to learn. More likely he'd display some of that mulish temper and balk, while committing some act to remind her of what had happened between them at the lake.

What exactly did happen? Anna's conscience asked her. *You came upon him swimming. You were so startled you couldn't move. Then you came out of your shock and ran. Even if you saw something a young unmarried woman shouldn't, it won't happen again, and if David decides to keep reminding you…well, Anna, there is such a thing as lying…making it look as if His Lordship's simply being a disruption.*

Anna had to admit those thoughts made sense and offered an easy way out of a potentially embarrassing situation. After all, David already had a reputation for being difficult, so it would probably be very easy to convince his sister anything he said was untrue.

I don't want to do that, Anna protested. Teaching was difficult enough without the pupil being on the defensive or the teacher making him even more so. *I don't want to make an enemy of him.*

At last, she decided to simply not refer to the event. If David continued trying to, she'd ignore it.

****

In the dining room, David pulled his napkin from his shirtfront, dropped his spoon to his plate with a clatter, and stood. Pointing to the door, he scribbled on his slate…*Anna… teach…go?*

Eleanor nodded and waved him on. "Go ahead."

With a hasty bow, he was out the door before she spoke the second word.

The moment David came through the library door, Anna met him with a quick movement of fingers.

He stopped, frowned, and lifted the slate from around his neck.

What? Scowling so deeply, his dark brows nearly met, he wiggled his fingers at her to indicate what he meant. Anna noticed he managed to copy exactly one of the motions she made.

Her own slate lay on the desk. She picked it up, writing, *Good afternoon.* She moved her fingers again.

He appeared to consider that. There was more hand waving and another notation on the slate. *Good afternoon? Show me.*

Nodding, Anna made the signs again. He attempted to copy them. She held out her hands, making each curve and wave slow and slightly exaggerated so he could see the way her fingers moved. On the fourth try, face grimacing in concentration, he made them correctly. She congratulated him by seizing his hands and squeezing them and smiling while nodding.

Briefly, his expression went blank. Then he pulled his hands from hers so quickly she feared she'd angered him. Instead, he wrote something on the slate, thrusting it at her.

More.

Relief flood through her. He wanted to know more. He wasn't going to do anything to prevent her from teaching him. For the moment, they had a truce.

Quickly, she went through basic phrases and words...*My name is... Hello, how are you...Please, thank you...*

He was a remarkably quick study. By the third attempt he had the formation and movements correct on most of the words he tried. In spite of her worry, Anna felt pride at his accomplishments. She began to relax.

The finger-spelling alphabet was used for names and places. When she spelled out D-A-V-I-D...he touched her hands, fingers closing around them for the briefest moment, then placed a hand on his chest, brows arching in a question.

She nodded and wrote on the slate, *You. David. My name is David*, and Signed all of it again.

He copied the movements, then asked, *Elly?*

Though she'd never have thought of Lady Eleanor as an *Elly*, Anna quickly spelled out that also.

His next request shouldn't have been a surprise, but it was.

Anna.

She supplied him with the spelling of her own name.

Before she could learn what he planned to do with that knowledge, Eleanor appeared in the doorway.

"I'm sorry I'm late." Apparently, David had given her permission to be present. "I had to speak with Cook about dinner…"

David whirled. He couldn't have heard her. Anna

decided he'd felt the vibration of her footsteps. She noticed he didn't appear guilty as he had at luncheon, however. Advancing eagerly to his sister, he gesticulated, waving his hands in broad gestures.

She stopped.

"What…what's that?"

Immediately, up came the slate and chalk. *Good afternoon, Elly*. He performed the movement again.

Eleanor stared. David glanced at Anna, frowning slightly, his look seeming to ask if he'd done something wrong.

"He actually said that?" Eleanor looked past her brother to Anna who nodded. She turned to David, putting her hand over his as he'd done to Anna and enunciated slowly, "Show me. Again."

She didn't need to write it. He seemed to understand. Again, his fingers curved and twisted, forming the words. Awkwardly, she attempted to copy them. He smiled and glanced at Anna, motioning her over.

"It's like this." Anna showed her the signs.

Eleanor tried again. David made another sign.

"What was that?" Eleanor asked, as if afraid he'd said something impolite.

"He was thanking me for showing you."

"That…" she gestured. "That meant *Thank you*?"

"That's right."

"Oh, Anna…" She looked tearful. "I've been so foolish."

"What do you mean?"

"I stupidly thought if you taught David to Sign, he'd be able to communicate…"

"But he can…" Anna protested. "He will."

"Not unless he has someone to translate."

That was true.

"I'm sorry, Eleanor, I simply assumed...I mean...it's generally accepted family members will attend a few classes and learn how to Sign also. When I said the family didn't usually attend the first session, that's what I meant—the first session, but not the rest."

"I didn't think that far ahead, but I shall. I'll be here every day also, and..." Eleanor stopped as if abruptly having a moment of enlightenment. "So will Shelton and Jane and...the rest of the staff." She took a deep breath, continuing. "Perhaps some of the villagers would like to learn also. Yes, that'd be helpful when David goes there. I'll have Shelton post a notice..."

"B-but..." Anna hadn't counted on teaching an entire village. "I didn't..."

"Surely the more people who can communicate, the better off David will be?" Eleanor's question was a trifle sharp as if she thought Anna was attempting to deprive her brother of this gift.

"Of course, it's simply that..." Mentally, Anna sighed and accepted the task. "I'm sorry I didn't think of it." She rallied, putting enthusiasm into her voice. "By all means, invite the entire village to come learn. Do you think they'll all fit into the library?"

"If we have to, we'll open the ballroom and have Shelton bring in chairs, or adjourn to the garden." Eleanor became enthusiastic, missing the tinge of sarcasm in Anna's question. "I'll speak to him directly." Before Anna could move, she threw her arms around the girl, hugging her tightly. "If I felt hopeful before, Anna, now I feel exhilarated!"

With that, she whirled and hurried out.

David watched after her before looking at Anna.

Elly happy. His scribble made it a statement.

Yes. Anna nodded. *Happy for you.* She made the signs, pointing at him.

I happy too. His forefinger tapped his chest over his heart, then he leaned toward her.

She should've expected it, but there was no warning. He copied his sister's gesture, hugging her. It was a light embrace, no more than a tightening of his arms around her shoulders. Before she could stiffen in protest, he released her and stepped away, but the brief brush of his body against hers, and its warmth, jolted through her like a gentle rush of fire.

Turning to the desk, David didn't see her expression of bewilderment. The paper they'd used the night before still lay on the desk. He flipped open the inkwell, picked up a quill and, dipping it into the ink, wrote *More*. Following that was a list of words, laboriously printed out.

He held it out to Anna.

You…ride…horse…run…dinner…lake…apple…water… and so on.

Though that deviated from the lesson she'd prepared, she didn't want to dull his enthusiasm, so she obediently Signed the words he'd written. There were more phrases, such as *Good morning, It's a beautiful day,* and others, and much to her amazement, David parroted the signs back to her almost perfectly.

At last, she called a halt to the lesson, saying, "I think that's enough for today."

She put a hand on his, pushing them down and stopping their movement. He shook his head, raising his hands again.

No. Sullenly, his lips formed the word.

Yes. She pointed to the paper. *Study. Tomorrow show me you remember.* She wrote that on her slate. He appeared to think about that, then nodded, and smiling, made the sign for *yes.*

"In that case, class dismissed." Anna curtseyed and started to the door.

David's hand on her arm stopped her. She looked back. He began Signing again. Her eyes followed the movements.

*You see...*the facile fingers moved, spelling out words he'd ask her to show him, then gesturing down his body. *You like?...* He smiled but Anna saw it as a leer.

Her mouth dropped open as a rapid blush flooded her face.

"Oh!" Striking his hands away, Anna fled the library, leaving David standing there.

She didn't see his expression of shock or how his own mouth opened in surprise, though she did hear a plaintive, "Ah-na..." behind her as she sped down the hall.

Chapter 16

I mustn't let him keep embarrassing me, Anna scolded herself. *Eleanor may have taught him a few manners but she obviously didn't teach him anything about morality.*

Immediately, she knew that was incorrect. David had probably already been tutored in etiquette before his accident. Even at age five, the child of a baron would have to know certain rules of polite society. After that, his sister probably hadn't thought about anything except getting him well. The few manners she taught him later were probably so he wouldn't become a complete animal, living in squalor. She made certain he bathed regularly and combed his hair...Anna thought of the unruly damp curls touching his cheeks...and didn't feed himself with his bare hands.

What Anna termed *morality* probably didn't enter into it. She imagined David wouldn't beat an animal or kill someone or steal, and she'd never seen a curse written on his slate... He simply said what he thought, much as a child would. About *anything.* She forced herself to consider the situation at the lake and what he'd just said to her.

If I look at it from the prospective of a five-year-old, I might consider it amusing.

The problem was, David wasn't five, he was twenty, and if she were able to bring him to the point where he could enter Society, he was going to have to learn not to say such things. Otherwise he might find himself challenged to a duel by some protective father, brother, or sweetheart.

I suppose it's going to be up to me, she thought glumly, pausing at the foot of the staircase. *I'll have to teach him not only how to speak but also what* not *to say. Your Lordship, you are becoming a great challenge!*

"Is there anything wrong, miss?" Shelton appeared in the foyer.

"Not a thing, Shelton," she lied, while thinking, *Yes, Shelton, your young master is proving more of a handful than all my other pupils put together.*

To cover her own agitation and hoping to diminish it, she said, "I was wondering…"

"Yes, miss?"

The old man took a step nearer. He was very tall, as tall as David, and reminded her of a thin, scrawny water bird. That analogy brought a smile to Anna's lips.

"Last night, I thought I saw a room with a piano…"

"Yes, miss. The music room." Shelton smiled as at a pleasant memory. "The entire family was musical. Lord Harold played the violin, Lady Beatrice the flute, and Miss Eleanor is very accomplished on the pianoforte. They used to have family musicales in the evenings and often played during the house parties. Miss Eleanor even taught Master David to pick out a few little ditties before…" He shrugged slightly and looked away. "Afterward, I suppose she felt there was no place for music in this house."

"Do you suppose Lady Eleanor would mind if I played the piano?" Anna asked. "I'm certain I'm not as accomplished as she, but I do fairly well. If it wouldn't be too much of a presumption."

"I'm certain she wouldn't, miss." Shelton actually smiled. It dispelled some of his resemblance to a stork. "It might be good to hear some melodies around here again."

"Thank you, Shelton." Anna started down the corridor toward the music room.

"It may be a bit dusty, miss," he warned. "It's been closed off except when Jane goes in monthly to give it a bit of a sweep."

"If I have to fight my way through the dust bunnies, I'll let you know," Anna promised.

****

The music room wasn't as neglected as Shelton hinted. Throwing open the heavy draperies and letting in a little sunlight worked wonders. The room was a little chilly because no fire had been laid, and that perhaps contributed to the abandoned sensation seeming to hang in the air, but otherwise Anna found it a lovely room.

Though hidden under dust covers, divans and chairs were arranged in little groupings, with other chairs lining the walls. Anna imagined those were formed into rows for the audience during the musicales. Raising a cover on a table near one group, she discovered a violin and bow, a flute beside it, as if their owners had merely stepped out for a breather before proceeding with their concert. Several sheets of music were nearby.

Anna pulled the cover off the piano, folding it and dropping it to the floor.

It was a parlor grand, a piano in a harpsichord case constructed of maple. The name written across the front plate was Broadwood, along with the date the piano was constructed.

Anna was well aware Broadwood pianos built around that time had a range of six octaves, where earlier ones had only five and an interval. Her own instrument in the parlor at Little Riversreach had been a small pianoforte created in Vienna, containing only five octaves. Papa had received it from a patient who was about to have it carted away because he was purchasing his daughter one of the newer versions having a wider range. He'd told Papa Broadwoods were more robust in sound but Viennese pianos had more sensitivity of tone.

Papa said he thought that was a quote, because he knew for a fact his patient was tone-deaf.

A couple of the keys were out of tune and one side of the frame had been splintered slightly when the movers carried it from the house. It took Papa a month to have the money to pay the piano tuner. The movers' wound was still there, though it had been sanded and smoothed somewhat.

Anna didn't care. She now had a piano, and she and Maisie played many songs in the evenings while Papa smoked a cigar and listened.

The Broadwood was still open, the lid up, as if whoever last played it had been called away with the violinist and flutist. There was still a sheet of music upon the stand.

Strolling past the silent violin and flute, poignant evidence of lost lives, Anna peered at the title on the open sheet. She was surprised to find it was one with which she was familiar, a sonata for four hands…a duet she and Maisie had often played, she taking the bass section, Maisie the treble part.

Settling herself on the bench, she moved it to a closer, more comfortable position, studied the notes, then raised her hands and struck the first chord.

The sound was loud in the stillness and she stopped, fully expecting to have Jane or Edward, or perhaps even Eleanor herself come running in, demanding to know what she thought she was doing. When no one appeared to chastise and order her from the room, Anna struck the second notes and continued to play with increasing enthusiasm. As always, she played the lower section, humming Maisie's part as she went along.

She was in the middle of the second page when the back of her neck began to prickle, and she was certain she felt a breath upon her skin. She'd heard no footsteps, but she was sure someone had come into the room and was standing directly behind her, watching. *Who can it be?*

Surely it wasn't Eleanor. She'd say something. She feared she knew the answer. Not daring to turn around, she continued to play. She struck the next notes, reached out to turn the page, and…

A pair of hands, arms encased in linen sleeves with wide-banded cuffs, reached past her. Forefingers touching the treble keys, David began tapping them vigorously, forehead wrinkled in concentration.

Though the sounds produced were discordant against the melody she was playing, if one listened closely, it didn't sound like mere noise but…a different tune.

Anna stopped playing. She looked up at David. He continued touching the keys a few more seconds before realizing she had folded her hands in her lap. Stopping also, he looked down at her.

"What was that you were playing? Who…oh!"

She broke off as he caught her about the waist and

lifted her off the piano bench. Setting Anna on her feet, he released her and flipped up the bench's lid. Inside was a storage area, filled with several folders of sheet music. David picked up the top folder, holding it out to her, letting the lid fall back into place.

Simple Piano for Four Hands...a duet, written for two people to play.

Tapping the title with a forefinger, he then touched his own chest.

Oh no, he wanted to play this piece with her. "David, I don't…"

She got no further as he set the music on the stand atop the music shelf, then gently pushed her back onto the bench.

Again, he tapped the title on the top of the sheet, then touched her shoulder and his own chest. Raising his hands, he curved them slightly and made a downward motion as if striking something.

"Oh, David, I don't think…"

Sliding onto the bench beside Anna, he caught her hands, placing them on the keys, and again tapped the printed title.

It was a close fit. The bench was a short one, made for only one person. They were pressed closely together, thighs touching. David's legs were much longer than Anna's, and in that moment, his left one, shoved tightly against her right, felt like a smoldering log spreading its warmth the length of her person, burning through muslin, foundation, slip, pantelettes, and stockings, straight into her flesh and bones.

With a struggle, Anna forced herself to ignore that.

Deciding at this point, that, though it might seem cruel, it was best to humor David while driving home the fact that he couldn't hear the music, Anna studied the sheet a moment, then began to play.

Out of the corner of her eye, she watched His Lordship glance from the sheet to her hands and back, nodding his head in time to the movement of her fingers.

He's counting out the beats.

To her surprise, he also began to strike the keys with two fingers, not in another discordant set of chords, but with the opening notes of the second player's section, the same ones he'd played before. The entry was a fraction late, throwing off the timing. Anna paused a moment, counting the rhythm, letting her notes blend in with those David struck.

It was a simple melody, one a beginning player, or a child, might learn. Once or twice, he missed a beat and fell behind but caught up quickly. Now and then he hit a wrong note, making a discord, but all in all he kept pace fairly well and his performance was relatively musical.

As the piece came to an end and Anna finished with a flourish, he simply stopped and straightened, letting his hands fall to his sides.

"How did you do that?" she demanded, turning on the bench to stare up at him.

His expression was startling. He looked as if he expected her to upbraid him. When she merely gave him a mild but inquisitive look and repeated her question by Signing, he shook his head.

As she realized he didn't understand, she also remembered she'd left her slate in the library. Seizing the one around his neck, she scribbled the question on it and turned it so he could see. Then she dropped it and Signed again.

Elly, his fingers answered. He tapped the sheet of

music, showing he recognized its title, then repeated the finger-stabbing gesture at the keys. *Teach me.* He patted his temple. *I remember.*

He looked proud to have recollected how to say that, while Anna was surprised he hadn't forgotten everything from that first lesson. He pointed to the violin and the flute, then looked back to the piano and shook his head as if seeing other fingers touching the silent keys, playing music he'd never hear.

*Parties...*he wrote. *Pretty ladies...Elly dance with me...* Dropping the slate so it bounced against his chest, he got to his feet, arms raised as if holding someone, and spun around twice.

Anna nodded to show she understood. Papa had done the same thing with her and Maisie, letting them stand upon his insteps while he held their hands and waltzed around the room. They'd felt so grown up, dancing with their father in the parlor.

David waved a hand at the piano, tapped his ear, and shook his head. *No...*his fingers began. He stopped, again at a loss for words and wrote, *No music...no dance.* He paused, then scribbled hastily, *I wish dance with you, Anna.*

"Oh, David..." She was about to tell him there was no way they could dance if he couldn't hear the music, then...

Why not? If, after fifteen years, he could remember how to pick out that bit of music with two fingers though he couldn't hear it, why couldn't he also remember the steps to a dance his sister might've taught him around the same time?

"Very well." Anna got to her feet, stepping away from the piano and holding out her hand. "Come here."

When he hesitated, she gestured again, and he very carefully took his place by her side.

How am I going to do this? she wondered.

"Watch my feet." Patting his arm to get his attention, she gestured, lifting her skirts so they cleared her ankles.

His gaze slid downward and—she might've expected it—he glanced back at her, rolling his eyes and smirking, one hand to his mouth.

"Do you want to learn to dance or not?" She slapped his sleeve gently, then wrote the question on the slate.

He read it, nodded, and affected a very serious manner, the threat that it might be broken evidenced only by a quivering lower lip.

It would be too difficult to teach him one of the contredanses such as Strip the Willow, which was generally danced at any get-together whether it was a village social or a society ball. The steps were too intricate and depended too much on changes in tempo and sound of the music, as well as the movements in the dance being called out by someone. *Do I dare attempt a waltz?*

All waltzes had the same rhythm, so it would be much easier. The dance from Vienna had caused quite a scandal when first introduced. While gentlemen were eager to help it gain acceptance, it had taken several years before it was so well-received that young women could perform the so-called hold-close dance without their parents' permission and without being compromised.

Looking up at him, she said, "This is called the *waltz*."

He nodded, mouthed the word and watched.

She went through two sets of the steps, then looked

back at him. He was regarding her steadfastly as if not to miss anything. Gesturing, she pulled him beside her and waved a hand, then stepped forward, pulling him with her.

Stumbling slightly, he copied the action, *step forward…to the side, draw up, step back, draw up…step up again.* She counted with her hands, making certain he saw…*one, two, three…one, two, three…*

Once she was certain he had the movement firmly established, she swung him around, raised her hands, and waited.

He didn't move. She shook her right hand. Very gently, he took it in his left one, cradling it within his fingers as if it were too fragile to touch. Anna caught his right hand and placed it at her waist.

With the cautious movement one might make if easing past a hotly burning fire, he slid that arm around her, hand firmly resting against the small of her back. Immediately Anna felt the warmth of his fingers, that insistent, disturbing heat piercing the fabric of her dress. She started uncomfortably.

He moved his hand as if she'd slapped it. Reaching behind her, she caught and replaced it, looked up at him and nodded.

She began to count.

David stepped forward. Anna stepped back. He watched her lips, his own mouthing the words…*one, two, three…*as he completed the first box, then again. He slowed, ready to pause, relaxing his hold. She tightened her grip on his hands, pulling him into another set.

This time, he bit his lip in concentration. Anna pushed him into a turn. He stumbled, stepped on her toes, immediately jerked backward. His glance was apologetic. She nodded to show him she wasn't injured.

They moved smoothly into another set. Anna hummed softly to herself but even with no music to guide him, David managed to established a rhythm. He smiled in delight. His embrace was so secure, his arms so warm. Anna shut her eyes…

"What are you two doing?"

Anna jumped and opened her eyes.

Eleanor stood in the music room doorway.

Startled, David tripped, nearly treading on her foot. He immediately jumped back, releasing her, hands fluttering. *Sorry.*

He glanced at his sister with more guilt than Anna had ever seen him display in his expression.

That lasted a moment. Abruptly, the stubborn look was back. He straightened, wrote something on his slate, and held it to Anna.

Say Anna teach me.

Stunned, she supplied the gestures and he repeated them to Eleanor.

"You know I can't understand," she cried as she looked at Anna. "What did he say?"

"Merely that I was teaching him to dance." Anna wondered why they were acting so guilty. *Is it because David shouldn't be able to do such a thing…like he shouldn't be able to play the piano?*

"I suppose it was a foolish question," Eleanor replied. "When I could see very well you and he were dancing. What I should've said was, 'Anna, how did you manage that? It's a miracle!'"

"Not really." Anna didn't want to be given credit for something she hadn't done. "You used to dance with David, and…"

"I did," Eleanor affirmed. "Whenever Mama and Papa had a party, I'd go to his room to tell him goodnight before retiring. I'd let him stand on my feet and I'd hold his hands and dance him around the floor. His little feet looked so tiny and pink on top of my slippers…"

She stopped, hand going to her mouth as she looked at the young man standing before her. Anna wondered if she was remembering again that little boy in his nightshirt waiting for his big sister at the top of the stairs.

"Did…did I also hear you playing the piano?" She sniffled slightly, clearing her throat.

"You heard *us* playing the piano," Anna corrected. "It was a duet."

"That's absolutely impossible," Eleanor declared, shaking her head.

"I'm afraid not," Anna corrected her. "Shelton told me you were teaching David to play the piano when…" She hurried on. "He followed me in here, saw me playing, and remembered."

"Let me see." Plainly, Eleanor believed she was being guyed.

"David?" Gesturing, Anna seated herself on the bench.

After a moment's hesitation, David allowed himself to be pulled down beside her.

Turning the sheet of music back to the beginning, she raised her hands and began to play. David sat a moment longer, not moving. At the proper moment, when she nudged him, rather ungently and boldly with her knee, he jumped, raised his own hands, and began to again strike the keys with his forefingers.

Their duet was interrupted when Eleanor began to sob, quite audibly. Looking up and seeing the tears streaming down her face, David jumped from the bench, putting his arms around her. Once again, he turned a scowl on Anna, as he had the last time Eleanor reacted so emotionally to something she'd helped him do.

Releasing his sister, David Signed, *Elly unhappy?* He patted Eleanor's shoulder, and put his hand under her chin, forcing her to look up at him. *Elly unhappy?* He repeated the words on his slate.

Wiping at her eyes, Eleanor shook her head.

Why cry?

"Because I'm so happy," she told him, and wrote it on her slate.

The scowl changed to a smile as he shook his head. *Silly to cry.*

"I know," she agreed, leaning against him, forgetting he couldn't see her lips from that angle. "That's how women are."

David looked at Anna, who quietly translated what she'd said.

No. He startled her by mouthing the words while looking directly at her. *Not you. Not Anna. Never silly.*

Before she could react to that or ask what he meant, he turned Eleanor and escorted her from the music room, arm across her shoulders.

Chapter 17

David was absent from dinner that night. Once again he felt a need to think, and sitting across from Anna at the dinner table was not the place he was going to easily do that.

Conveying a terse message through Shelton that he was tired and wanted to get an early rest, he retreated to his rooms, locking the door.

Unlike his sister and Anna, who had rooms on the second floor of the manor, David occupied the third story and had the entire floor to himself. The only other rooms there were the nursery, the nanny's room, and some empty guest rooms, none of which were going to be filled any time soon, if ever.

At the time he was injured, David had been an occupant of the nursery. He stayed there through his recovery and until he was twelve, at which time he moved into the largest of the nearby bedrooms. He made it plain to his sister he wanted isolation and, as usual, he got his way.

Satisfied he wouldn't be disturbed, David went to his bookcase, pressing a small lever on the bottom of a shelf. There was a click and he pulled the shelf and the books on it outward.

Behind them was a recess in the wall. Within it were the rest of David's *cigaritos,* matches, a book from his father's library, and a bottle of his father's very best

French brandy, remnant of several cases bought before the war with France cut off all vintner supplies except those smuggled in. The filched crystal goblet, for which the servants had been docked pay, nestled beside the bottle.

Taking out his contraband treasures, David pushed back the drapes and opened the windows to the evening air. He lit a *cigarito*, breathing smoke in the windows' direction. He always made certain there was no smoke scent for Elly to discover.

Half-filling the goblet, he returned the brandy to the recess and leaned against one of the windowsills, looking up at the sky rapidly darkening behind a sunset glory of flaming crimsons and brilliant golds. *I may not be able to hear, but at least I can* see *pretty things…like sunsets…and Anna.*

It was Anna he had to think about. More seriously this time.

After the way she made him feel while they danced…and earlier at the pond, he knew he had to do some in-depth self-searching.

Carnality was something new in David's life and he still hadn't come to terms with it.

He hadn't been aware of it at all until the year he turned fourteen when he abruptly shot from being four feet high to a towering five-eleven, looking down at his sister whom he had always considered so tall.

That was the year he also sprouted black bristles on his jaw and chin, and his forehead became decorated with a mass of pimples. Frequent ministrations of witch hazel poultices banished the pimples, and the gift of Papa's straight razors and several lessons from Shelton on how to wield them without exsanguinating himself rid him of the whiskers, though he had to shave every morning, which was a bother.

David hated shaving. If he had his way, he'd have a beard growing past his knees. He'd once hidden his razors, attempting to grow a beard, but Eleanor nixed that quickly enough, saying it made him look like a bear. He'd laughed and growled, and she scowled and searched his room until she found the razors hidden in his shirt cupboard. Slapping one into his hand, she ordered him to get rid of what was already, after three days, more than a very heavy shadow.

David came to understand his rapid height, beard, and those pesky pimples meant he was becoming an adult. Whether through embarrassment or the belief he'd never need to know, Eleanor didn't bother explaining any of the other conditions accompanying adulthood.

David had to discover those for himself...

He'd learned the first of those also when he was fourteen.

Absalom Brown owned the stud farm across the highroad from Mayfield Manor. Before Eleanor sold all except the carriage horses, many of the animals gracing the Mayfield stables had been purchased from Mr. Brown.

When David received Run, who was also one of Mr. Brown's horses, he immediately remembered watching his father put his hunter through its paces, jumping hurdles and hedges. He wanted to learn how to jump also, and Eleanor gave permission for Mr. Brown to teach him. Accordingly, David rode Run up the carriage road and across to the farmyard where Brown awaited him.

He found that gentleman at one of the areas he called

the breeding paddocks. David tied Run's reins to a hitching post and was waved over to Brown's side. As with everyone else in that area, the man had known David since he was a child, seeing him with his father when Lord Harold came to ask Brown's opinion on a hunter he was thinking of purchasing, or such.

The breeding paddock was a small place, with another smaller pen built into the back of it. Inside stood two grooms, holding the bridles of two very nervous-looking mares, a sorrel and a dapple-gray. David climbed onto the planks of the fence, perching on the top board next to Brown.

"Breeding those two today." Brown shouted, gesturing at the mares. "Then we'll get to your lesson."

David didn't understand because Brown didn't bother to write it. He rarely did, being of the opinion if he spoke loudly enough, David would be able to understand. At that time, David was still teaching himself the rudiments of lip-reading and had to guess most of their conversations.

He glanced at the animals and, because he knew Mr. Brown expected it, nodded, then looked around, wondering where Charger, Brown's best stallion, was. He liked to watch Charger run, and Brown was always proud to let the animal out for a good gallop.

Before he could ask Brown about the horse's absence, Charger was there, brought from his stall by two grooms, each clasping the cheekpiece of his halter.

The stallion was a magnificent wild bay, coat a glistening dark red with a purplish tinge, his mane and tail dead-black as were the points of his slender but strong legs. Charger was a giant of a horse, almost seventeen hands high, though Brown claimed he had

Barb blood.

Lord Harold had often argued the horse was too tall to come from Barbary stock. Whatever his long-ago antecedents, the stallion was pedigreed appropriately, and he was strong, beautiful, and fast, as were all his get.

While David watched, one of the mares gave a high-pitched nicker and began dancing on her lead.

Charger stopped stock-still.

The grooms tugged on the halter. He refused to move, nostrils quivering, ears pricked forward. Without warning, a low neigh rumbled deep in his chest, and he reared so quickly one of the grooms was jerked off his feet.

The stallion aimed himself at the paddock gate at a fast trot, the grooms running alongside to keep from being dragged.

"Get that gate open!" Brown shouted.

On the other side of the paddock, the sorrel mare was maneuvered into the little pen.

As Charger headed for her and the grooms released their holds on the bridle, Brown murmured, "The old lad'll get his fun now."

David frowned, waiting for an explanation of that sentence, but the breeder was too busy watching what was happening on the other side of the paddock. Charger galloped into the pen with the mare and the grooms slammed the gate shut.

What happened next was confusing to David.

Briefly, the two horses milled around in the small space. He'd thought they were going to fight, as the mare gave little squeals and Charger answered with deeper neighs. Not that he could hear them, but the open mouths and bared teeth indicated something violent was about to happen.

When Charger rose into the air, forehooves flailing, David was certain the mare was going to be killed. Gripping the fence board tightly, he wondered why Brown didn't have the horse pulled from the paddock.

He was about to shake Brown's arm and gesture to the two horses when Charger settled, forelegs seizing the mare about the ribs as if pulling her rump against his belly, and then…

David nearly fell off the fence.

He'd seen the thick thing protruding from the nether part of Charger's belly, how it seemed to come alive on its own. The mare's tail came up, and that thing thrust itself under. She screamed, snuffled slightly, then as if overpowered by the other horse's weight and grip upon her, subsided.

David couldn't see what happened next, though he imagined there were more sounds from the horses. Brown slid from his seat beside David, and he and the grooms crowded around the paddock, speaking loudly. When they opened the gate, the two horses were still, Charger resting his chin on the mare's poll while she leaned against him. They led the trembling stallion from the pen, the two grooms seeming to support the horse as he stood with head down and shaking limbs.

In a remarkably short time, he was once again put back into the paddock, this time with the dapple gray. The same thing happened, and he and the dapple went through whatever had gone on with the sorrel. This time, however, when Charger was led away, Brown slapped the horse's neck happily.

"We'll have two good colts in a bit, lad, thanks to you."

Out of that sentence, David managed to understand only one word...*colts*. From that he puzzled out whatever had happened would result in two baby horses. He'd seen the heavy-bellied mares in the field and later the same horses with foals, and often wondered where the little ones came from, and now he had an answer...of sorts. All that bumping around and struggling, and screaming...all that violence somehow produced a beautiful baby horse that might look like Charger.

David came away from the stud farm that day with a wealth of information he had to sort out for himself because he felt it wasn't something he dared ask anyone. Indeed, if he had, there probably would've been no way anyone could explain it to him.

Unfortunately, there were no animals at Mayfield Manor except the carriage horses and Run, all geldings...no cats or dogs who could have kittens or puppies by which he might see the cycle of life on a lesser scale. The only real fact he'd culled from what he'd seen was that he also had an organ similar to Charger's, if somewhat smaller, but it had never done anything such as he'd seen that day. *It*, as he termed the member nestling against his thighs, had never been any trouble at all until recently, when the little pouches resting beneath began increasing in size. Now, however, occasionally *It* jerked and twitched of its own accord.

David's other brush with the carnal part of life came from his father's library. He'd always been aware his papa had books only he was allowed to read. They were kept on one of the top shelves in the bookcases.

Once, when David was around four, he'd tried to climb the shelves and reach them. Papa pulled him off the shelf and lectured him on the danger of attempting such a thing, then informed him, "Those are Papa's books, Davy, and not for youngsters. When you're much older, you can see them…if Mama doesn't find out."

When Papa went away, the books were forgotten until one day when David was fifteen and bored, and tired of looking at the pictures in his own books. He remembered those volumes. Eleanor wasn't around and neither was Shelton, so he stood on a chair and pulled down the thickest. He couldn't read the title. It was in some language other than English.

Pornografia Mundus.

He'd taken it to his room and leafed through it, discovering it had many words in that foreign tongue but also a multitude of woodcuts…pictures much more interesting than those in his own books but at the same time confusing…of men and women totally naked…doing very odd things to each other, but they all had one feature in common. The men had very large organs, almost the size of Charger's member, and they all put them inside the women while lying or standing in various positions. If the expressions on the women's faces were any indication, they enjoyed whatever was done to them, however. David wondered if that meant all the women had babies afterward. He wished he could read the strange words so his questions would be answered.

He didn't return the book to the library but hid it in the bookshelf recess where later it would be joined by his *cigaritos* and brandy. Occasionally, when *It* acted up and twitched and stiffened and made riding difficult, he'd get out the book and look at the pictures and surprisingly, *It* would behave. Then one night, *It* did a very frightening thing…

David awoke from a disturbing dream that he couldn't remember, only to find a thick sticky splotch on his nightshirt. Frightened, certain his insides were somehow liquefying and oozing out, he went in search of help. He didn't dare tell Elly. Both she and Jane had stopped helping him bathe when he was nine, so he didn't think he should reveal *It* to her in its current condition, now he was so much older.

Instead, he sought out Shelton who was already going about his rounds of opening the manor for the day.

"Master David? What are you doing up so early?" The old man was surprised to see him standing at the foot of the staircase to the main floor. "And in your nightshirt? What's the matter, lad?"

Not understanding anything the butler asked but believing from his expression he was concerned, David pointed to the stain, while clutching *It* tightly lest it begin leaking again. Miraculously, Shelton understood, ushering the boy back up the stairs and into his room.

Getting a clean nightshirt from the clothes chest, he poured water into a basin and motioned for David to cleanse *It*, then put on the shirt. David did as instructed, and watched as Shelton shoved the soiled nightshirt into the clothes hamper. When the old man straightened, he asked with a frantic word on his slate and many shrugs and waving of hands, *Why? What?*

"You're becoming a man, lad. Nothing to worry about. It happens to all of us."

That was all Shelton said. While that calmed David slightly, assuring him he wasn't dying, the butler's reply gave him no answers, except that in some way, anything male suffered this same affliction and it was simply to be accepted. The boy couldn't know that as Shelton left

David's room, he'd muttered to himself, "No need for you to know anything more, poor lad. You'll never get a chance to use it."

At the age of twenty, David had barely enough knowledge to be dangerous while being utterly ignorant at the same time.

Then Anna Leighton strolled out of the woods and into his life, and she touched his arm and a lightning bolt of *something* shot through him, and here he was… With *It* wanting to assert itself, and his body threatening to become as raging as Charger with the mare, while David was afraid to touch Anna's hand.

What am I to do? What am I supposed to do?

David had never felt so ignorant, so cut off from his fellow humans than in that moment. He wished there were someone who'd sit him down and scribble on his slate or use that wonderful new sign language and say, *Here's how it goes, lad…laid out plainly…all the mysteries revealed…*

Nothing was revealed and David was certain it never would be. All he knew was that when he was with Anna, he wanted to whirl her around the room as he'd seen the men in their evening clothes do the ladies in their beautiful gowns…he wanted to hug her as he remembered Papa doing Mama, he wanted to kiss her…he wanted to be naked with her, swimming in the cool waters of the lake…to do the things he saw in the woodcuts in his father's book…he wanted…

He didn't know what he wanted, except whatever it was, he wanted it to be with Anna Leighton.

At that moment, he had a great desire to see her again.

While he'd paced, puffing on the *cigarito* and

gulping huge swallows of Papa's brandy, *It* was asserting itself, most painfully this time. A few instances before, *It* had acted that way, persistently stiffening and thickening until David feared the organ were going to burst. His attempts to soothe *It* by stroking and petting, resulted in a burst of that sticky stuff onto the lining of the panels of his riding trousers. Though it brought instant relief and startling satisfaction, David didn't particularly like doing that. He feared if it happened enough, the sticky stuff would be depleted and he might die from its lack. He still had no idea what it was used for. With that thought, he successfully managed to distract *It* from further misbehavior with icy dips in the lake, grateful to his sister for having Shelton teach him to swim.

Tonight, however, *It* wasn't to be pacified. *It* wanted to be in Anna's presence. That was the only thing that would appease *It*.

David knew what he had to do.

Anna's room was directly below his. Next to his window, huddled as close to the manor wall as it could get, the ancient oak rose as if steadying that section of the house. Often David climbed into the tree and looked at the stars from the shelter of its branches. Tonight, he planned to do something else.

Flicking his *cigarito* into the fireplace, he watched it flare and be consumed to ash, falling through the grate. He downed the last of the brandy in the goblet and returned the glass to the depression in the wall, then rushed to the rightmost of the three open windows. Kicking off his boots, David climbed barefoot onto the windowsill. He was about to do something he considered both desperate and daring and wondered what would happen if he were caught.

What would Elly say if she knew her brother were about to become a Peeping Tom?

He didn't care.

Seizing a branch, David hoisted himself out the window and into the tree.

Chapter 18

Jane helped Anna into her nightgown and brushed her hair. Then she took away the stained dress, promising she knew a miracle cure for removing grease spots that wouldn't leave a mark.

"It'll be good as new and ready to wear by morning, miss."

Alone, Anna sat at the vanity, staring at her reflection. Though she didn't want to, scenes from the music room kept returning to her mind, interspersed with images of David rising from the lake, water dripping from his tanned skin...sunlight sparkling off drops of moisture beading on his chest...like a water god emerging to lure some hapless mortal maid into the depths for forbidden aquatic pleasures...

Stop it. Stop being so fanciful. This is serious. She hadn't realized how serious until that moment.

In Little Riversreach, Anna had indulged in mild and harmless flirtations. She'd been to dances and picnics and proms where her card was always filled, and she'd walked with handsome youngsters her own age, young men from the village as well as a few more prominent and well-to-do families, all under her father's watchful eye. There had been one or two stolen kisses but nothing serious, and indeed she'd never felt about anyone the way David Woods made her feel.

From the moment he rode into Mayfield Manor's

yard and she mistook him for a groom to this very night as he held her in his arms and whirled her about the music room in that awkward, silent waltz, she'd felt such a devastating exhilaration…an overwhelming elation…if she'd been of a less strong constitution, she might've given in to a fit of the vapors and fainted dead away.

Indeed, she was still slightly lightheaded. There was a ringing in her ears, in fact. She remembered how riding before him on Run had felt…his embrace, his closeness, even that faint horsey scent to his clothing, combined with the lakewater-clean smell of his skin…

She wanted him to kiss her, while wondering if he had any idea how.

I'd gladly teach you that, David…

Getting up, she walked to the window, pushing open the center shutter and staring out at the gathering darkness.

I'm falling in love with David Woods, twenty-seventh Baron Mayfield. A man I've known such a ridiculously short time. How absurd is that? I want him to hold me in his arms, crush me in that burning embrace. I want to be naked with him in his bed…to know all those things forbidden to someone in my current state, those things only married couples, hot-blooded society bucks, and wanton hussies know…

Anna's conscience was having none of that nonsense. *This is ridiculous. Face it, Anna. This isn't some fairy tale. This is real life. Even if David Woods were a normal young man who could hear and speak, all you'd get from him is a momentary dalliance. Barons don't marry the daughters of country doctors. There is no such thing as love at first sight. You're merely infatuated, so stop it. Now.*

"It's no use," she said aloud. "I'll drive myself insane thinking about it. I simply have to accept the inevitable and do what I was hired to do."

And that was to ensure David Woods was declared competent, able to enter Society and find someone from his own class and marry her.

Sighing, Anna closed the window and hurried to the bed, throwing herself into it. She turned down the lamp to its lowest level, and lay back, settling herself for sleep.

****

Outside, David leaned against the trunk of the tree. The oak had grown branches at conveniently-spaced intervals as if preparing itself for a confused young man to climb.

He'd watched Anna as she sat with Jane brushing her hair, envying the maid, wishing it were he gathering that wheat-colored mass into his hands. He wouldn't comb it, however. He'd press his face into those curls, open his mouth and let his tongue taste the golden strands, while the smell of lavender on her skin permeated his senses. He'd noticed that scent about her the moment he met her. It smelled so good, so clean. He wished he could place his nose against her neck and sniff up and down her throat and determine the source of that enticing fragrance.

When Jane left and Anna wandered over to the window, she was so close he could've touched the hand she rested on the sill. Instead, he hid behind the oak's thick leaves.

He thought she looked unhappy. Was she thinking of the things he'd done, how badly he acted upon her arrival…or perhaps the scene at the lake? Had she really been as shocked as she appeared? Did *she* know of the things he'd seen in the book? Was she aware of *It* and the things *It* wanted to do?

How can I ask her? How do I find out if she feels as I do? How do *I feel?*

When Anna spoke, it was getting too dark for him to see the movement of her lips. In fact, he wasn't even aware she said anything. All he knew was that she left the window, closing it. When she got into bed, turning down the lamp, he wished he were lying beside her, both of them curled together, warm and safe.

He'd hold Anna in his arms, resting his cheek against that wheat-colored hair. She'd snuggle her body close to his so he could feel her warmth through her nightgown…and *It* would sleep silent and happy because she was near…while the scent of lavender floated over them like a sweet cloud.

With a sigh echoing Anna's own, though he was unaware of that, David climbed up the oak and from it through his own window back into his room. He undressed, put on his nightshirt, and climbed into his own bed. Sleep didn't come right away, however, because *It* protested, keeping him awake for another hour before surrendering and allowing slumber to come.

Chapter 19

"The gooseberries may not be ripe, but David says there are some early raspberries on the other side of the lake if you're interested."

The next morning at breakfast, David was again absent, leaving Eleanor to deliver his message.

"By the lake?" Mentally, Anna went on the defensive. She'd seen no raspberry bushes. Of course, she'd been focused on something much more attention-holding than a mere raspberry.

Is this another of David's schemes?

She was certain he knew exactly how far to push and would never try the same ploy twice, especially since she'd now be wary. Perhaps there *was* a raspberry patch and he was attempting to make amends, though she seriously doubted it. David's *amends* might pave the way for something worse.

Nevertheless, having no genuine excuse not to accept his offer other than to lie and say she despised the richly tart fruit, Anna found herself answering, "That's very thoughtful of him. Why don't I walk there after breakfast and see what the bushes hold? Perhaps there may be enough for us to have tarts with dinner tonight."

She hoped berries were all the bushes held.

"That'd be lovely," Eleanor enthused. She looked thoughtful. "When David was small, he and I used to walk to the lake and pick berries for Cook." There was a sigh. "You're bringing back memories, Anna."

"Good ones, I hope."

"Good? Yes," Eleanor admitted. "Also sad, in a way, because I remember how David used to chatter as he skipped along in front of me. He was too small to carry the *wazbewwy bucket*, as he called it. He couldn't pronounce his R's back then. He'd only become able to differentiate between R and W when…" She stabbed her fork into her cutlet, sliced off a bit, and ate it before continuing with a decided tremor in her voice. "He always ate more berries than he picked, and his little lips would be fairly purple when we returned, as would his pinafore-front. Nanny always had to re-dress him."

There was a soft sigh while Eleanor ate another mouthful of veal.

"He was such a precious little boy then. I wish you could've seen him, Anna."

"I wish I could've, also," Anna replied dutifully.

She *did* wish she'd known David as a child. She imagined he'd been as mischievous as he was now but without the spoiled stubbornness, a pinafore-garbed moppet whose big blue eyes and curly locks won over everyone crossing his path.

"We still have the same bucket," Eleanor said. "It's old but serviceable. Some things seem to last longer than others." She reached for the little silver bell by her plate. "I'll have Shelton fetch it."

****

Approximately half an hour later, Anna found herself trudging down the path to the lake, swinging the berry bucket in her right hand.

It was definitely a beautiful day, even more than the previous one. The sun was struggling to shine through

145

the trees as if determined to light up the entire forest.

Anna felt her spirits lifting. Briefly, she wanted to act like a child, sprinting down the path with her skirts above her ankles, the bucket bouncing. In fact, the only reason she didn't do so was because she feared David was lurking somewhere, like the Big Bad Wolf in Red Riding Hood's story, spying and ready to pounce as soon as she was out of sight of the manor. Remembering his reaction to seeing her ankles as she showed him the steps to the waltz, she decided she didn't need to be displaying them any more than necessary.

She found the lake and the berry patch, with no David in sight. The berries were luscious, ripe, and juicy. They'd make delicious tarts, Anna decided as she sampled first one, then another, and finally, a third.

I'd better stop, she chided herself. *Otherwise I'm going to be like little David, eating more than I pick.* She set to picking with enthusiasm and soon the pail was half-full.

That was when she heard the hoofbeats.

Looking up, she saw David and Horse coming down the trail at a leisurely saunter. It was so leisurely that Horse looked as if he were sleepwalking. David pulled the animal to a halt. He touched his chest, then gestured at the berries.

"Of course you may." Anna hoped he was asking permission to dismount. Deciding to be cautious but not hostile, she waved him over. "Come help me."

Sliding from Horse's back, he looped the reins over a limb and walked over, looked down at her a moment, then dropped to one knee and began to pull the berries from their stems.

They worked in silence for several minutes, Anna

seeing no need to speak and David lost in his own thoughts as he concentrated on his task. He'd become better at berry picking in the intervening years. Unlike Anna, whose fingers were now stained a deep purplish-red, his own were completely untouched by any foreign color.

The bucket was nearly full when Anna straightened.

"I think we should stop." She waved a hand to get his attention, and when he looked at her, repeated what she'd said, also Signing.

He agreed, dropping the raspberry he held into the bucket and seizing his slate. *Yes. Leave rest for birds.*

"Sign it," she told him, enunciating carefully.

Frowning, he thought a moment, then cautiously gestured. When she nodded to show he made the Signing correctly, he smiled. He got to his feet, dusting the knees of his riding trousers, then held out his hand to assist Anna in standing. That little courtesy surprised her.

Today, David was in a gentlemanly mood. He even offered to carry the bucket.

Smoothing her skirts, she decided to give in to the temptation to eat a few more of the berries she'd managed thus far to ignore. They certainly had enough for a raspberry fool plus at least a dozen tarts. She reached into the bucket, scooping up several so ripe the slight pressure of her fingers immediately reduced them to pulp.

Anna shoved them into her mouth, chewing enjoyably. David watched her. Waiting for her appraisal of the taste? Or appalled at the dark stain now smeared over her lips and palm?

"Delicious," she announced and reached for another. She held it out to him. "Would you like one?"

It was more the gesture than her words, she told herself. After a moment's hesitation, he took it from her, held delicately between thumb and forefinger, and bit into it. Briefly, he closed his eyes as if savoring the dark, tart taste. When he looked at her again, he thrust the bucket at her. Anna took it and he gestured.

More?

She was surprised he'd ask her permission. "I believe we can spare a few."

It was difficult Signing while holding the bucket. She looped the handle over her arm, awkwardly using both hands to reply, knowing she was utilizing symbols he might not be familiar with this soon.

He didn't move, except to nod at the bucket on her arm and point to his mouth.

Does he want me to feed him? What cheek!

She had a momentary vision… David lounging like the sultan in the *Thousand and One Nights* while a slave girl—herself—dropped berries into his mouth. That made her smile.

Very well. I'll humor His Lordship.

She studied the mass of berries, selected one nearly the size of her thumb, and held it out. "Say 'Ahhh.'"

That stopped him a moment. He didn't understand at all. When she repeated it, he obeyed literally, making a similar sound, "Uhhh," flat and nasal. Anna placed the berry on his tongue, jerking her hand back quickly as if she thought he'd bite her finger. He made short work of the berry, then gestured again.

Anna fed him another. It became a game…again and again berries disappeared into David's mouth, like a chick accepting food from a mother bird. Anna laughed and he did also, though without a sound.

A pink stain appeared on his lower lip, her fingers even more darkened with juice. A purple drop trickled down her wrist. She held out another berry. He chewed, swallowed, and…

…caught her wrist, holding her hand immobile. Before Anna realized what he intended, his tongue slid up her wrist, stopping the errant drop and following the little stain it made on her skin. He finished by licking the juice from her fingers.

Anna shivered at that warm, damp sensation gliding over her skin.

"Don't!" She jerked her hand from his, nearly dropping the bucket, catching it as it slid from her arm. She clenched her now-clean fingertips against her palm. "Why did you do that?"

Setting down the bucket, she asked again with a flurry of fingers.

He shrugged, hands waving helplessly as if he didn't know how to tell her. Lifting the slate, he wrote something, studied it as if trying to decide whether or not to show her, then turned it around.

Wanted taste you.

"Don't ever do that again," she flared, not bothering to Sign it.

He understood her expression if not the words.

I do this? his fingers asked. Seizing her by the shoulders, he pulled her toward him, bent, and stroked his tongue across her lower lip.

Body shuddering visibly, Anna jerked out of his grasp. Her hand shot out, striking his cheek.

It wasn't painful. To someone of David's size and build it was probably no more than a glancing blow. He didn't even wince.

Anna rushed past him, the bucket swaying in her grasp, berries flying out of it, striking her dress and leaving small purplish stains. She gathered her skirts so she could move quickly, forgetting her previous caution about revealing her ankles.

How dare he? How could he? Her mind was in a turmoil, shocked…filled with a startling longing…how warm and sensuous it had felt…how…utterly disgusting…

She heard the jingle of bits, the evenly-spaced thud of Horse's hooves. Anna didn't look around but stared determinedly ahead. Out of the corner of her eye, she saw David, leading Horse. He reached her, falling into step beside her. When he pulled the bucket from her hand, she didn't react.

He stepped in front of her. She had to stop or run directly against him. He set down the bucket.

I'm sorry… you so sweet …his fingers said.

Anna frowned. *How do I interpret that? He's sorry and I'm sweet or he's sorry that I'm sweet?* Either way, it was highly improper to say, as well as what he'd done. *What does he mean by* sweet, *anyway?* She didn't reply.

You… He continued as if attempting to clarify. *Taste so good…like sunshine and honey…*

Anna still didn't respond. She didn't move except to turn her head.

He picked up the bucket, spun on his heel, and pulled on Horse's reins. The animal walked past Anna, and Horse and David continued up the path to the manor. He didn't looked back.

****

By the time Anna reached the manor, David was nowhere in sight.

Good. I don't want to see him at the moment.

She'd deliberately walked slowly so they wouldn't arrive at the same time, though the determined stalk of those long legs quickly left her behind. Opening the front door, she went inside, not bothering to ring for Shelton, thinking by now she could dispense with that formality.

It was nearly eleven.

And now, after that embarrassing episode, I have to become the teacher again, instead of...what?

She wondered exactly what David considered her. His plaything? His playmate? Someone to tease and plague like the playground bully did the classmate weaker and more helpless than he? She didn't believe David was a true bully. This was simply more of his undisciplined life revealing itself.

He'll stop such behavior once I explain it isn't acceptable, she told herself, adding, *I'd best do that soon.* She wondered why she hadn't already.

In the library, she found Shelton and Edward rearranging the furniture. They'd pushed back the chairs and the tables, leaving a large space between the hearth and the desk. Into that area they were placing chairs she recognized as having lined the walls in the music room, three rows, four chairs in the back two, three chairs in front.

"What's this?"

"They're for the villagers and us, miss." Shelton straightened from setting down the chair he held. "Edward rode to the village this morning and checked the notice I posted on Monday. Five people signed up for your class."

"Oh, yes." Anna had forgotten about that. *Today, I'm to have a full dozen students...* Eleanor, the villagers, the staff…and her star pupil and chief worry. David.

"They should be here soon," Shelton continued. "Miss Eleanor put eleven o'clock as the meeting time." At Anna's look of consternation, he explained, "You're to teach through lunch so no one will be traveling back to town in the dark. Going to really throw our schedules out of kilter." He shook his head, then said quickly, "But it'll be worth it to be able to understand Master David."

There was a raucous jangling of the doorbell.

"I imagine that'll be the first of them. From the sound, it's probably one of Master David's acquaintances."

Chapter 20

It was *two* of Master David's acquaintances, Jem and Albert, in fact, though Anna wasn't certain if 'acquaintances' was the correct description for the two young men. 'Cohorts' was a more apt term, she decided, for the two greeted David as if he were an equal. *Perhaps partners in mischief?*

Ushered into the library by Shelton, whose expression held severe disapproval of their dusty breeches and rough boots tracking mud and who-knew-what-else down the polished hardwood hall and across the carpeting, they raised their hands in a salute, then began pounding His Lordship on the shoulders. He returned the favor, and a large cloud was raised from all that battering of clothing exposed to the dust of both the forest path and the highroad.

When the dust cleared, David saw Anna staring at them and immediately remembered his manners. Signing, he said, *This Anna. My teacher.*

"'ere now!" One of the two looked from David to Anna. "Is it some of that sign-speaking stuff? Wot'd he say?"

"That's right," Anna replied, aware of David's gaze fastened on her lips.

That made her remember the way he'd licked his tongue across her lower lip. The young man stared at her. *Does it show? Did his touch mark my lips somehow?*

She told herself that was a ridiculous thought and forced herself to answer his question. "He said, 'This is Anna, my teacher.'"

Nodding, David pointed at Anna, fingers repeating what she'd said.

"So you're his teacher?" The young man gave her a look one degree below a leer. "Lucky sod." He turned back to David, saying, "Lucky you," and tapped David on the chest.

There was absolutely no reverence for David's station or title in his tone. He acted as if he and the twenty-seventh Baron were cut from the same social cloth.

David agreed, with a nod and a smirk of his own. Anna felt her hands, hidden by her skirt, clench into fists.

"David…" She waved a hand to catch his attention. He glanced at her. "Introduce me?" She Signed the word, then wrote it on her slate because it was a new one for his Signing vocabulary.

He caught her hand and pulled her to his side, making her stumble slightly. Both of the visitors' eyebrows went up at that.

A-N-N-A L-E-I-G-H-T-O-N, David surprised Anna by including her surname, spelled correctly. He said, "Ah-na." He nodded to Anna, then gestured at the other two, spelling A-L-B-E-R-T, then J-A-M-E-S. "Ah-ber'…Zames…"

He mangled the second name terribly.

"Albert, James." Anna acknowledged them. "So very glad to meet two of David's friends."

She decided she'd be cordial if it killed her because their learning to communicate with David was important and also she could see he thought a great deal of the two.

She wondered where Eleanor was and her opinion of her brother consorting with such rough characters as these two seemed to be. They were fairly pleasant to look at, both a little shorter than David, with heavily muscled arms revealed by the rolled-up sleeves of their homespun shirts. Their thick blond hair was short-cropped but not in that hideous *à la Titus* style, but more as if someone had simply grabbed a handful and hacked at it with a scissors.

"It's just Al and Jem," the older one corrected. He appeared a few years older than David and was the stockier of the two. "I'm Al, this is me li'l brother." He jerked a thumb at the shorter one, who'd been silent after greeting David. "Our da owns the smithy."

That explained the muscles and the shorn hair. It got very hot inside a smithy, and longer hair would be uncomfortable.

"When will your father get here?" Anna asked, wondering if the smith would be an older version of his sons.

"Oh, 'e ain't comin'," Jem spoke up. "Got too much work. Seems of a sudden ever'one's 'orses needs to be shod." He glanced at his brother. "Almos' didn't let us come, then said we could learn and teach 'im what 'e needed to know." He winked and aimed a mock blow at David's chin. "Got a soft spot for Davy, 'e has."

David laughed and dodged, sending an equally false strike back at Jem.

"I'm sorry he can't make it," Anna said. She waved a hand at the chairs. "Why don't you be seated? As soon as everyone else gets here, we'll begin."

They bobbed jerky bows, with sideways grins at David as they did so, and dropped into the first two chairs, slouching and each propping a booted ankle against the opposite knee.

Eventually the others trickled in and were summarily introduced—Mr. Greeley, owner of the mercantile, and Roger and Alfred, whom David greeted with the same enthusiasm as he had Al and Jem, but with no explanation of who they were other than their names.

Anna immediately marked them as two more members of the *gang*, as she unconsciously called the four young men, though the new arrivals were a bit more subdued than the blacksmith's offspring. Then came Edward, Jane, the cook, Shelton, and a man she hadn't seen before, whom Shelton introduced as the groom. His equally dusty boots and clothing as well as the strong horsey smell would've revealed his identity if Shelton hadn't.

Lastly, Eleanor appeared. She nodded to everyone, spoke briefly to Jem and Al, asking about their mother, and took the remaining seat on the front row. She sat next to Al with no hesitation, only a brief nod that the youngster returned with a tug on the hair hanging over his forehead.

Everyone waited, quiet and expectant, for Anna to speak.

With a deep breath, feeling as if she were about to jump into very deep water, she took her place behind the desk, gesturing for David to join her.

"Thank you all for coming." She cleared her throat, hoping she didn't sound like someone about to deliver a sermon. "David has already had several lessons, so I think what I'll do is simply go back and review what he's learned for your benefit…"

Things went better than she expected. Everyone

appeared eager to learn and surprised by the things they managed to say using only their fingers. Al and Jem couldn't stay serious, of course, joking and grimacing throughout, but they also retained a great deal.

When it was over, all promised to return the next day at the same time, Mr. Greeley stating he was looking forward to the next lesson. "Now when my wife starts some of her chatter, I can talk right through it and still not interrupt."

Jem suggested they bring a picnic lunch. "So's Al's belly-growls don't interrupt."

At one point, near the end of the lesson, his brother's hungry stomach made a rather loud background to Anna's explanations.

"'ey, yours weren't so quiet, neither," Al said. He glanced at David. "'Sides, Davy can't 'ear me tum, so what does it matter?"

David walked with them to the door, the brothers being the last ones to leave. They lingered a moment on the stoop, trying out their new skill, also using the gestures and grimaces they'd always employed with David. Anna waited at the foot of the stairs, watching.

Something happened.

She wasn't certain what, except that Al turned to go, then looked back with a smirk and a wink, saying something too low to hear and nudged David in the ribs. Until that moment, David had been responding quite jocularly to whatever they were saying. Abruptly, he stiffened, glared at Al and shook his head, rapidly. Both brothers looked surprised. Al looked apologetic, said something more, then waved, and the two walked away.

David came inside, pushing the door shut a little too violently. One fist pressed against the door frame, he stood there a moment, forehead resting against his hand.

"David?" Anna hurried over. He didn't react until she touched his shoulder.

Looking at her, he seemed visibly attempting to shake off anger.

"What is it?"

He glanced from her lips to her hands and shook his head.

"There's something wrong. What did Al say?" she persisted.

Had he ridiculed David somehow, perhaps mocking her, or been scornful of David's attempts? Protection of her pupil blossomed. She felt herself becoming angry at the smith's son.

David looked away. Anna caught his arm, shaking it.

"I want to know what he said." She enunciated the words tightly, fingers slashing the air.

He lifted the slate. Anna made a mental note to have him stop wearing it. He was still relying on writing to get his messages across. He wrote, *He want to know,* and stopped.

"What? What did he want to know?"

There was a long pause before he wrote, *if I*…and again stopped.

"If you what?" Exasperated. Anna gave his arm another shake. "If you did *what*, David?

He bit his lip, tapping the chalk against the slate, not looking at her. At last, he scribbled something on the board and held it up.

He want to know if we grind corn.

For several seconds Anna's expression was blank. *Grind corn? What? The manor doesn't have fields to harvest.* She had no idea what that meant.

Another look at David's expression, however, at the pressure with which his teeth were sinking into his lip, the whiteness around his mouth, and she believed she understood.

Al thought she and David were… *Oh!*

Color flooded her cheeks.

I tell him no. David's hand hacked downward as if to chop something. *We not do that.*

She was grateful he was angry, knew he was aware he shouldn't be saying such a thing to her though she had insisted. She was even more grateful he'd defended her.

"Thank you, David."

He shook his head, fingers spelling out the shocking words. *No thank me. I want to.*

Before she could react, he pushed past her and ran down the hall.

Chapter 21

This has to stop. Now. Anna didn't hesitate but rushed after him.

David's long legs took him out of sight quickly. Anna followed, but he'd gone into a section of the house she'd never been before, another smaller parlor at the back of the manor, a room also unused for some time. The furniture was shrouded in dust-covers. On the far side of the room, floor-length doors were closed to the outside…except for one, partially open.

Barely noticing the surroundings, Anna went through that door, finding herself in a very large and well-kept garden. Surrounded by a high hedge beginning beside the door, it was filled with roses and tea olive bushes, blending to fill the air with a scent so heady and overpowering Anna momentarily paused to catch her breath.

Before her lay a stepping stone path bordered by tulips and marguerites, and she sped down this, looking around frantically.

As she passed a marble birdbath, disturbing a pair of sparrows fluttering in the water, she saw David ahead. He was seated on a stone bench, half-hidden in the shadow of a wisteria-entwined trellis, head down, arms resting against his knees.

"David!" Worry made her forget he couldn't hear.

Sensing her footsteps, he leaped to his feet, hurrying

around the trellis.

"Stop." She caught his arm, pulling him to a halt.

He jerked from her grasp but didn't turn around. She walked around him so he was forced to look at her.

You must never say that to me again. Her fingers fluttered sternly.

Why not? His shrug and raised brows asked.

A gentleman does not say such things.

Al said it, he replied, scowling.

Al is no gentleman, she declared.

Neither am I. His answer was quite stolid, halfway a defense of his friend as well as a declaration of his feelings.

Yes, you are. Her fingers made a determined beat.

How? How am I gentleman?

You are twenty-seventh Baron Mayfield. Remembering he hadn't been taught some of those words, she wrote out part of that statement, pulling at his slate and forcing him to lean forward. He peered at the words she'd scribbled. *That makes you a gentleman.*

Then I…

He stopped, anger making him forget everything she'd taught him. Snatching the chalk from her hand, he pulled the chain over his head, then scrawled the words so frantically the pencil cracked, white flakes falling to the flagstones.

I love you, Anna.

"David, don't say that." In shock, she spoke aloud.

Why? That one word stabbed at her like the blade of a knife.

Again, she had to resort to the slate, writing the words her conscience told her the night before. *Barons don't love country doctors' daughters.*

161

Why not? He refused to accept that. His brows slanted, a furious scowl darkening his face.

She didn't answer, shaking her head.

Not be barron, he stumbled over his title, misspelling it, and that brought an even worse frown. *Not be gentleman. Want to do those things with you. I love you.*

"David…" She shook her head and attempted an answer. Her hands were shaking so badly she could barely Sign.

He put his hands over hers, halting the words, holding them until she stopped trembling.

I want grind corn with you, Anna… His own fingers hurried on. *Knock boots…make you wear green gown…those ungentlemanly words…* His fist struck the air in his version of a curse. *I love you, Anna. Nothing change that.*

"Oh, David." In the face of that declaration, her resolve gave way. She looked up at him, feeling the frustration, anger, and longing emanating from him in almost palpable waves, and her own body reflecting it back. "You can't love me. We barely know each other."

Seizing Anna's shoulders, he pulled her toward him so quickly she stumbled, catching at his arms to keep from falling. Immediately, she was swept into such a violent embrace she cried out. David's mouth coming down on hers muffled any other sound she might've made. It was an inexpert kiss, awkward and at the same time so ardent it shook her.

Pushing her away, he stared at her, breath coming in loud exhalations clearly audible throughout the garden, then caught her arm and pulled her back to the trellis and the bench. Pushing her upon it, he dropped beside her, wrapped her in another embrace and kissed her again...more expertly this time.

Gently, Anna pushed David away. She was careful not to do it as roughly as she could have, but she was struggling to control her own emotions, trying to see what had happened from his point of view. Getting angry or reacting violently was no help. She waited until he straightened, then moved slightly, turning out of his embrace.

It was so quiet...too quiet. A misleading sense of peace had fallen over everything, while the sun moved across the sky and the shadows deepened. More birds splashed in the water and flew away. Wind wafted the fragrance of roses, tea olive, and wisteria over them.

"You mustn't do that again," she told him. Catching his face in her hands, she forced him to watch her lips as she spoke.

Why? he questioned. *Liked it.*

"That's beside the point," Anna answered. "Teachers don't kiss their pupils. Not adult ones."

Am I adult?

"I think you know the answer to that."

I love you, Anna.

Anna didn't answer.

They had gotten into territory that was very dangerous. She had heard of students developing serious feelings for their teachers, the relationship between teacher and pupil becoming strained because the pupil was generally a child and saw the teacher, the one suddenly opening the world, in the role of a benevolent parent. Sometimes a child would make an idol of his teacher, to the detriment of his bond with his family. When that happened, the association had to be broken, sometimes gently, often cruelly. Occasionally, the teacher was replaced so the tie between parents and child could be re-strengthened.

She didn't want that. Not for David. Even in their short acquaintance, she was certain it would be detrimental to his case. They didn't have time for him to start over and become accustomed to another instructor.

Anna had to say something, and she spoke the first thought popping into her head, inappropriate as it was.

"Who cares for the garden?" She looked away. "I haven't seen a gardener."

He turned her to face him, mouthing, *What?*

She repeated what she'd said. He laughed, that silent huffing. She was slightly relieved. It distracted him.

Elly, he explained.

"You're joking." She was disbelieving.

He shook his head. *You think barron's daughter not dig in dirt?* He stumbled over the words, fingerspelling some of them because he didn't know the signs.

"I really can't envision your sister pulling weeds," Anna answered, truthfully.

Mama's garden. He waved a hand at the trellis and the rosebushes. *Elly feels close to her here. Wish Mama could meet you, Anna.*

"I'm certain she wouldn't approve of me," Anna said. "Not at all."

No. He raised her head with a finger under her chin. *She like you. Papa, too. Because I do.*

"I'm afraid, my dear David, you're too trusting," Anna muttered.

Getting up, he reached above his head and broke off a width of wisteria vine, offering it to her. *Smells good...like you.*

Anna took it, sniffing the heavy, sensual scent. She studied the wisteria florets dangling from a single stem, like a bunch of flowery grapes. He'd been sufficiently sidetracked, she thought.

"Let's pick some flowers." Rising, she walked to one of the flowerbeds and knelt, snapping off a large red-striped tulip.

David followed. He surprised her by pulling a small sling-blade knife from his hip pocket. She pointed to several blossoms and he deftly sliced through their stems. By the time Anna heard footsteps on the flagstones, she had accumulated an armful of tulips and marguerites.

"There you two are." Eleanor appeared on the path, looking a bit harried. "Luncheon has come and gone. Shelton couldn't tell me where either of you went after the others left, and I was beginning to worry. I didn't think to look in the garden until now. Whatever made you come out here?"

"We were picking flowers," Anna replied, raising her arms to indicate those she held. "I thought we could put them in the foyer." She looked at David. "If someone promises not to smash the vase."

David scowled, looking from Anna to his sister. With her hands full, Anna couldn't Sign. She shifted the bouquet, raising her hands.

"Wait," Eleanor said. "Let me." She Signed to David what Anna had said.

He laughed and made a single gesture. *I promise*.

"In that case," Eleanor went on, "come inside, and I'll have Jane find a vase. Then we'll have tea to keep us from succumbing to hunger before dinnertime."

They dutifully followed Eleanor down the path,

Anna acknowledging the current problem was unresolved and merely postponed for the present.

Inside, seated together with David on the loveseat, while Eleanor stood at the door speaking to Jane about bringing tea, Anna placed a finger to her lips. "Don't say anything to your sister. Of what happened in the garden."

Why? He looked puzzled. *Want to tell everyone.* He dared lift her hand and kiss her fingers. *I love Anna.* His free hand spelled the words with movements that were caresses in themselves.

No. Anna Signed, glancing at Eleanor. Luckily, she still had her back to the room. *Not until we've thought this out a bit more.*

Especially she. She had a great deal of thinking to do.

Very well. He glanced in a dramatically furtive manner at his sister's back, gave Anna a peck on the cheek, and got to his feet.

When Eleanor came into the room, taking her place in the chair by the fire, they were both sitting placidly across from each other, Anna on the loveseat, David in the chair she'd occupied that first day.

Chapter 22

The next morning, Anna found a stalk of lavender lying by her place at the table. Silently, she picked it up, glancing at Shelton and the footman. Like good servants, neither remarked on the flower. She had no doubt who'd put it there, for she'd seen the little purple blossoms in one of the garden beds. Would either Shelton or Edward aid and abet David by pretending they had no idea where it had come from?

She studied the blossoms. The stalk had been cut at a slant, by a knife, probably David's sling-blade. She remembered how deftly he'd used it on the tulips and daisies.

As usual, David was absent, so she couldn't tell him it was improper for him to leave her a flower, even if it was only a sprig of an herb. As Eleanor came through the door, she slid the little spray into her pocket.

"Good morning, Anna," Eleanor greeted her.

"Good morning," Anna answered. "Has David already breakfasted?"

"Of course." His sister shrugged. "He and Horse rode out some time ago. I think we should try to convince him to join us at table, though it may be a struggle. Old habits die hard, especially where David is concerned. He doesn't like change, as you're well aware."

She moved to the buffet. Edward immediately followed, selecting a plate and waiting for her to indicate her choices for breakfast.

Anna smiled at Shelton when the old man gently took the plate from her hands. "Then I suppose it's up to me to change his mind."

She had a feeling she had more chance of making David sit down to breakfast with her and his sister than she did of ridding him of the way he felt about her. It would be much easier, at any rate.

David returned in time for his classes, appearing shortly before the others. Surprisingly, everyone who'd been present the day before was back again. Anna had hoped David would arrive early so she might talk to him. She'd worried whether to acknowledge the gift of the lavender, then decided not to mention it. Doing so would only encourage him. With the others present, she was forced to go on with the lesson as usual. To her relief, David didn't say anything about the flower, or his feelings for her, either. She hoped that meant he would take the hint and, by doing so, let his emotions cool somewhat.

It probably simply means he remembers what Albert said and is practicing a little restraint. I hope.

The rest of the day went as usual, nothing different or deviating from their usual routine. It was only at dinner that evening that Anna realized how wrong in her assumption she had been.

She was grateful Eleanor was accustomed to meals with very little conversation. Otherwise she might've commented on how quiet both were…quiet as far as any verbal language was concerned, that is.

At his end of the table, David was Signing non-stop, chattering like a magpie. She was startled by his boldness, flattered by what he was saying while being totally dismayed. His silence during his lessons had only meant he was storing up mischief for the evening.

He might not be saying anything to Eleanor, but he was telling Anna a great deal. Though he devoured his meal in his usual starveling manner, his left hand hovered below the table's edge, fingers deftly saying things Anna was grateful his sister couldn't see from where she sat.

I love you, Anna...want to tell world...David loves Anna...love, love, love you...

Even after she shook her head and Signed quickly, *Do not say that,* he ignored her entreaty, continuing with even more flowery compliments.

Love Anna's blue eyes...like sky...Love her lips...sweet as strawberries...cheeks so pretty...angel's hair... the fingers of his left hand waxed rhapsodies of compliments while the right speared a slice of beef loin and brought it to his mouth. He chewed, licked a drop of gravy off his lower lip and winked.

Anna put her napkin to her mouth to hide an involuntary smile. In a moment, if she wasn't careful, she'd might blush. Heavily. She couldn't help it.

Forgetting her earlier admonitions, she alternated between wanting to slap his hand as if he were a disobedient child, and laughing at his antics because the disobedient child was also a favorite one. Truly, if they'd been alone in the dining room, she might have burst into laughter, then hugged him while remonstrating sharply that he should *behave immediately*. She was thankful for Eleanor's presence as well as that of the servants, preventing that.

How can I be angry with him? He was as guileless as a child. *But he's not a child.* The warning David had given through that fable's moral was true. *He definitely isn't what he seems. But is he the cat or the mouse?*

As for *decorum*... If David took it into his head to kiss her in front of everyone, she had no doubt he'd do so. That was her greatest fear, his lack of the niceties of societal manners. Discretion? She was certain that word wasn't in his vocabulary.

I must make sure he learns it. Soon.

Telling herself her reactions weren't helping, she Signed, *Stop. Others than Elly can read now, you know*, and jerked her head in a nod toward Shelton, standing near the door. The moving fingers immediately stilled. David seized his knife with his left hand, sawed at the slice of beef and applied himself to his meal.

After that, Anna refused to look at him, though she was uncomfortably aware of that hand and its twitching fingers, as if, at any moment, he'd again burst into movement with more embarrassing compliments. Finally, she could stand it no longer.

Getting to her feet, she dropped her napkin beside her plate. "I'm sorry, Eleanor. Would you excuse me? I feel I should retire early."

"My dear, don't you feel well?" Eleanor looked disappointed. "I was so hoping we could have a nice chat in the drawing room after dinner."

"Ordinarily, I'd like that," Anna replied. "However, I think I've a megrim coming on. Too much excitement, I imagine…what with teaching everyone, and giving so many explanations, and missing luncheon."

"It has been a bit of a whirl today, hasn't it?" Eleanor agreed. "Though I declare you're managing everyone so valiantly. You're a good teacher, Anna."

Anna nodded her thanks. To forestall any more talk,

she put her hand to her forehead, rubbing her temple.

"You do look pale," Eleanor decided. She waved a hand. "Go, go, dear. I'll send Jane up to help you prepare for bed."

Without another word, Anna hurried out.

David watched her go. He ate stolidly for a few moments more, then dropped his knife and fork to his plate. There was a loud clatter.

"David…" Eleanor looked up, scowling. Her fingers scolded. *I have told you…careful with silverware…. could chip plate.*

He ducked his head, then touched his temple, an exact copy of Anna's gesture. *Sorry. Head hurt. Too much riding in wind today. Excuse?*

Of course. Eleanor gestured but as he hurried out, she said aloud, "Both of them not feeling well? I hope there's nothing going around. Shelton?"

"Yes, ma'am?" The butler took a step forward.

"There's been no mention in the village of a miasma or any kind of epidemic, has there?"

"Not that I've heard, ma'am. Everyone appears hale and healthy."

"Good. I suppose I won't worry, in that case. Would you pour me some more water, please?" Eleanor returned to eating her braised carrots. "Then, summon Jane."

"Certainly, ma'am." Shelton gestured to Edward, who retrieved the water carafe from the sideboard.

****

"Don't you worry, miss," Jane assured her, as she trotted behind Anna to her room. "I know just the thing to help with those pesky megrimes."

Sent by Eleanor to assist Anna, the maid rushed

ahead to open the door to the bedchamber. By the time Anna reached the room, she'd opened one of the windows and was waiting by the door.

"Some good fresh evening air will do wonders," she informed Anna. "A nice hot bath, also. Edward's bringing up the tub, and Cook's heating some water."

By now, Anna's imaginary megrim was rapidly turning into a real one, so she merely nodded listlessly.

When Jane continued, "You sit here by the fire and compose yourself, miss," she was only too glad to do so.

Edward soon arrived, lugging the tub, a tin and copper contraption looking to Anna like nothing more than an over-large coal scuttle. It appeared heavy and awkward, but the footman had hefted it to his shoulder. Anna thought he must be much stronger than he looked, for he carried it with no apparent distress.

Placing it in front of the fire where Jane gestured, he bowed to Anna and walked out. Jane followed.

"I'll be bringing up the hot water now, miss."

Anna nodded and closed her eyes, shading them with her hand. Her headache was disappearing. Because she wasn't in David's presence, she imagined. Worry that Eleanor would see his messages made her head hurt. She'd never had a megrim in her life, but the reality of what happened in the garden and not knowing what David would do next made the dull ache in her temples seem magnified.

Far in the back of her mind where she could keep it out of sight was the vague idea that she wished she wasn't David's teacher and he wasn't a baron, so they could kiss with no repercussions. The ache intensified.

At the moment, all I want is to sleep. In the morning, perhaps an answer will present itself. An answer we can both accept.

In a surprisingly short time, sounds on the stairs told her Jane had returned, lugging two heavy cast-iron kettles from whose spouts steam poured. She emptied both into the tub, then hurried out again, returning the next time with the kettles filled with cold water. That also went into the tub.

Jane tested the water with her fingertips, declared it "Just right," and went to help Anna to her feet. "Come now, miss. We'll have you right as rain in no time."

She helped Anna undress, steadying her while she stepped into the tub. After soaking a washcloth, wringing it, and folding it across Anna's forehead, she turned back the sheets and got Anna's nightgown from the wardrobe. Laying it across the foot of the bed, she turned down the lamps.

"You lie there and relax, miss." With that, Jane hurried out, shutting the door behind her. In a moment, however, she popped back in. "Don't worry about the tub. Edward can take it down tomorrow morning. You just get into bed when you feel like it and have a good sleep."

"Thank you, Jane. Good night." With a sigh, Anna leaned her head against the tub's unyielding back. It was cold, in startling contrast to the water's heat, which felt very soothing. Anna settled into the wet warmth and tried not to think.

That was an exercise in futility. All she could see was David's face as he pulled her under the trellis. Instead of warm water surrounding her, she felt the heat of his arms as they held her close. The weight of the washcloth against her forehead became the press of his lips to her temple.

"It's no use." Anna realized she wasn't going to get any rest. In that case, she may as well go to bed and lie sleepless upon a feather mattress instead of in rapidly cooling bath water.

A breeze floated in through the open window.

"…or catch cold allowing a night wind to blow over my damp body." Dropping the washcloth into the water, Anna grasped the sides of the tub and pulled herself to her feet.

A bath towel conveniently lay on the chair in which she'd sat, placed there by Jane. Stepping from the tub, she dripped water the few feet to the chair, then stood on the hearth, wrapping the towel around herself. The low fire felt good as she blotted away the moisture from arms and legs, counteracting the wind making the flames flutter.

Sliding the nightgown over her head, she reached for the sheet, then stopped. Something lay on the pillow.

A flower?

Peering closer, Anna recognized it as a sweetshrub bud. No wondering how it had got there. None of the bedchambers were locked. Sometime after they'd had tea, David came into her room and tucked it between pillow and sheet.

She picked up the dark red flower. Clasping it between her hands, she inhaled the sweet fragrance before placing it in the dresser drawer where she had hidden the lavender sprig before changing for dinner.

Both lavender and sweetshrub are used in potpourri sachets, she thought. *These two can add their fragrance to this drawer…while I forget them.*

When she climbed into bed, however, she found it wasn't so easy. The flower's scent had transferred itself to the pillowslip and the fragrance floated around her all night.

Chapter 23

Each day after that, a new flower lay by Anna's place at the table...a spray of wild aster, a buttercup's petal-encased trumpet, a sky-blue bachelor's button, a minty sprig of catnip, those funny little white flowers called Dutchman's breeches... At night, her pillow held some other treasure. One evening, it was a small river pebble, worn smooth by the water, and of such a wondrous shading of blues and greens, it would've made a ring's beautiful setting. Another time, it was a small twig with two perfect golden acorns attached. The flowers went in with the lavender and the sweetshrub, the other items into a small empty drawer meant for trinkets.

By the end of the week, Anna was no closer to a solution on how to end David's courtship, for that was plainly what he was doing, she admitted—courting her, in his own childlike way.

Childlike in that he seemed to see his behavior as a kind of game with which to bedevil her, the way a schoolboy might a girl he likes but for whom he has no idea how to express his feelings, yet with enough adult understanding that no one else must know what he was doing.

Otherwise, the classes were going well. It was surprising how quickly everyone was learning. If others could see their progress, Anna thought, no one should ever belittle the intelligence of the common people again.

That day, she'd decided to speak to David, to "put her foot down," as her father would say. Whose toes were going to be trodden on when that happened, however, she wasn't certain.

"David, wait a moment." She caught at his arm as he prepared to follow the others from the room.

He looked around, coming back to stand before her as she straightened the items on the desk.

What is it?

I think you know. Now that the time had come, she wasn't certain how to begin.

He shrugged, a look of complete innocence on his handsome face. *How? Not read minds. Can not even talk.*

In answer, she took the things from her pocket…the lavender, the sweetshrub, aster, and the other herbs and flowers. Without saying a word, she placed them on the desktop. They were drying now, but their scents were still strong, swirling around them.

You like? A hand gestured.

Very nice, but you must stop doing that.

You not like? He scowled.

It is not that I do not like it, it is that you must not do it.

Why? You say I not kiss. I do not. Not say I love you. I do not. Can not give you pretty things, either?

David…

That silly. I do as you say, not say I love you. Let flowers speak for me. All those—again, he gestured to the desk—*all those mean I love you, Anna.*

With a remembrance of reading in one of her father's books, she knew there was a secret meaning of flowers and herbs. Buttercups, asters, bachelor's buttons, catnip, even the Dutchman's breeches…all meant *I love you*. She wondered where David had learned the fact, then decided it didn't matter.

Nevertheless, you must stop this…flowers, gifts, saying you love me…all of it.

You not like me, Anna?

The hurt in his expression, mingling with what she thought was disbelief, that something he'd thought could be so incorrect, shook her.

Of course I like you, she hurried to assure him.

More than like, the truth be known. She wouldn't admit it, but he was slowly wearing her down. Those little bits of flowers and acorns, pebbles, and herbs were worming their way into her heart.

I am fond of you.

Fond? He brightened.

I suppose I would say I have a great affection for you.

In her heart, a little voice spoke, *Keep going, Anna. Draw the noose around your neck. Admit you're falling in love with this young man in spite of yourself. That, in some perfectly ridiculous way, in the short time you've known him, and in spite of his handicap, he's found his way into your heart in a way no other man ever has.*

He seized her hands, kissing her fingers.

She pulled her hands from his, making a sharp gesture to the door. *No more of that. Ever. I am your teacher. You are my pupil. That is all.*

She turned her back, becoming very busy with the books and papers on the desk. David stood there a moment longer, then stalked out. Anna waited until the sound of his footsteps died away. Then, she put her hands to her face.

****

Dinner was as silent as a funerary meal. All it needed was crêpe covering the mirrors and cypress and yew draped over the thresholds. Tonight, there were so secret messages from David's facile fingers. He ignored her, sulkily keeping his attention on his meal. Though he ate with his usual appetite, he didn't appear to enjoy the food and, soon after dessert was served, tossed down his napkin and got to his feet.

With a curt bow and an even briefer, *Excuse me?* he was gone, not waiting for Eleanor's permission. He hadn't looked at Anna once during the entire time.

"Is anything the matter?" Eleanor asked.

"What do you mean?" Anna was determinedly eating her way through the dessert, though as far as she was concerned, it, like the rest of the meal, was completely tasteless.

"David was so…quiet…tonight." She laughed softly. "I know that may seem an odd thing to say, but he's generally availing himself of Signing, and tonight…he looked, I don't know, sad." She thought a moment. "No…angry. He seemed angry."

"I've no idea." Anna shrugged. She didn't dare look directly at Eleanor, fearing she might read something in her expression. "He learned some difficult words today. Perhaps he's thinking about those."

Difficult words, indeed. Words he hadn't heard very often before now. *No* and *Do not*.

She laid down her spoon. It made a gentle tapping against the dessert dish. "I believe those same words have given me another headache. Would you mind if I retire early, also?"

"No, of course not." Eleanor looked concerned. "I hope the lessons will go easier tomorrow."

"I'm certain they will," Anna spoke with no enthusiasm.

It wasn't going to get easier, she was certain. *Somehow, I have to keep going, and keep David at bay, until the day of the trial. Once he's declared a competent, contributing adult, then I can leave.*

At that moment, all she wanted was the solace of her room. She hoped David had left no token on her pillow.

Chapter 24

In his room, David immediately kicked off his boots and divested himself of his stockings. Tossing them aside, he padded barefoot to the bookcase and got his *cigaritos* from their hiding place.

Need to think. Serious think.

He lit one, opened the window, and pushed the shutter wide, pouring himself a full goblet from the bottle he'd filched from the cellar before coming upstairs.

Instead of the brandy in his decanter, David's choice that night was a red Bordeaux, his father's favorite. It was a dark *rosé* Lord Harold always called *clairet*, instead of *claret* as everyone else did. David had a particular taste for that wine because once, when he was four, Lord Harold sneaked him a sip of the fruity-tasting vintage and was severely chastised by Lady Beatrice when she discovered that.

Taking a rather large swallow from the goblet, he paced before the hearth, puffing frantically while his thoughts were even more so.

What must I do? Why not tell anyone I love Anna?

Anna had said barons don't love country doctors' daughters. She also said teachers don't kiss pupils.

If I not a baron, would everyone know? If Anna not teacher, could she kiss me? Why do I have to be baron? That was the main question worrying David. Anna said he was born a baron so he *had* to be one, but he wondered about that. The answer appeared simple enough. He'd stop being a baron and then he could love Anna.

A new problem arose with his next question. *If I not a baron, what will I be?*

In his brief thoughts past the desire to kiss Anna and attempt some of those things he'd seen in his father's book, David had a vague image in his mind of being in a cottage with Anna, where children came to be taught Signing while he…did what?

Taking a deep draw on the *cigarito* and letting the smoke trickle out his nostrils, David was brought up short by the realization he'd been trained to do exactly nothing. His only accomplishment was riding, and caring for Run. His one venture into manual labor was the day the blacksmith fed his curiosity about making horseshoes. He'd motioned David into the smithy, showed him how to hold the tongs and the hammer, then allowed him to pull the hot metal from the forge and pound it against the anvil. David's arm had ached with the impact of the hammer against the malleable iron, but under the smith's guidance, he created a fairly serviceable shoe.

At least he supposed that was what the smith's pats to his shoulder and his many nods meant.

Tossing the cigarette stub into the fireplace, David lit another. He finished the wine in his glass and refilled it and continued his pacing.

Could I be a smith…like Al and Jem's da? He was certain with a little practice he could be as good as those two in shoeing horses, and in tending them, also. Al had been hinting at moving away and opening his own smithy in another town. *Take Al's place, let his da train me. Then…Anna teach children to speak with their hands while I shoe their fathers' horses, or…*

Another idea occurred.

…I could be a groom, work for Master Brown. After all, he knew how to care for tack, to saddle and bridle a horse, as well as how to curry and cool it down after a ride. He could use a pick to clean hooves and a file for smoothing roughened ones.

Nodding with satisfaction, he decided he'd solved the greatest obstacle to his problem.

The second *cigarito* was smoked to ash. It followed the first into the fire. David raised the goblet, gulping the claret, startled his glass was once again empty.

When that happen? Surely I not drink so fast.

As he stared at the cut-glass goblet, it blurred. He blinked and the image cleared, but the room spun slightly. Closing his eyes, he leaned against the mantel, arm on the carved shelf, forehead resting against his forearm.

The whirling stopped, and he opened his eyes again.

What I thinking? Oh yes…groom or perhaps a coachman. He reached for the *cigarito* box once more. *Something to do with horses.* He resumed his pacing.

He began to think of Anna, of what had happened in the garden. It felt so good to hold her, kiss her, though he'd sensed her uneasiness. Or maybe it was simply surprise. His entire body was suffused with fire, but a glowing gentle one. Thinking of the woodcuts in the book, he'd wanted to do more, of course, but had enough sense to realize in his sister's garden in the middle of the day was definitely not the place to strip naked and make love to his woman.

My woman…Anna…mine…

She was his, just as he was hers. He hoped she

wanted to be with him as much as he wished it. He thought back to the way she'd blushed and hidden her expression with her napkin to her mouth. Surely that was to keep his sister from seeing how she enjoyed what he was saying. She only looked angry to keep Ellie from guessing what she was feeling.

Wish I knew more words so I could tell her how I feel.

David wondered if there were actually words to describe the violent turmoil within him, the deep, hot welling as if his body were filling to overflowing and the only way to keep from stifling was to tell her, *I love you, Anna.* What if Signing wouldn't work? What if his love smothered him and he expired instead of sharing that love with her, simply because he couldn't speak them?

By now, the third *cigarito* was half-smoked and the level in the wine bottle had gone down drastically. David coughed, fighting his way out of the thick cloud slowly wafting toward the open window. Waving his hands, he continued coughing as he fanned the smoke away.

The things Anna had said today after class… She didn't mean them, he was certain. She was merely saying them because she had to.

There was movement outside the window. A faint breeze ruffled through the tree. He peered through the haze at the oak's branches, its leaves fluttering.

Must tell Anna…make her happy I solve problem…

He had to see her.

David took a step toward the window, stubbed his bare toe against one of his boots, and nearly fell. As he regained his balance, sloshing wine, he took a last drag on the *cigarito* and sent the stub joining its predecessors in fiery immolation in the hearth. After he drained it, the goblet found its way to a nearby table, though he nearly missed the table and dropped it to the floor. The delicate crystal wavered, rolled, and toppled onto its side, a single drop of wine trickling onto the lace doily on the tabletop.

Awkwardly, David righted it, made certain it wouldn't again fall, and staggered to the window.

Odd. There appeared to be *two* center windows instead of one. How…?

Blinking made them merge into a single casement. Taking a deep, alcohol-filled breath, David scrambled onto the window seat, leaning out and reaching for the branch directly overhead.

The wind blew again, heavier this time, pushing it out of reach. The branch wavered, swaying back and forth. David placed one knee on the sill, stretched with an effort, and caught the branch, hauling himself up and out of the window. Briefly, he clung to the limb, thinking how odd he felt—as he had that very first time after drinking the wine stolen from Jonathan's father—his head so light, as if it might float off his body and away into the evening clouds. His arms were abruptly numb and too weak to pull himself against the tree's trunk.

Never have trouble before…

He attempted to touch the lower branch with his feet. That was his usual routine…stand on the branch, balance, and walk to the trunk, then lower himself to the next one. His body didn't want to cooperate, legs limp and uncoordinated as a new colt's. He felt confusingly dizzy, leaves and branches seeming to swirl amid the wind's disruption.

What happening?

Carefully lowering himself, David positioned his bare foot over the branch. His toes touched it. He reached for a limb between the other two…his hand slipped…he fell forward…

****

Once again, Jane had opened one of the windows, the breeze wafting through them making the fire's low flames flutter.

I should shut that window, Anna thought as she climbed from the tub. Thankfully, there had been no gift from David on her pillow tonight. She'd dismissed Jane, telling her she'd turn down the covers herself, just in case, then checked to make sure before she stepped into the water.

She didn't want to think, forcing her mind to become a blank as she simply lay in the water, letting its warmth ease away some of the tension in her body. Now, the water was cooling and it was time to get out and go to bed and hope sleep would pick up where the bath's soothing heat left off.

A sudden disturbance outside, a violent rustling of leaves made her look in that direction. One thick branch hung low, nearly touching the window. It shook violently.

I hope a bird isn't about to fly inside. That would be a fitting ending to this day, calling Edward or Shelton to chase a frightened bird out of her bedchamber.

The branch shook again, bouncing up and down this time as if someone were jumping on it. Picking up the towel, Anna wrapped it around herself as she hurried to the window. She stopped short as a pair of bare feet appeared below the upper edge of the casement.

As she stared, they dangled, swinging up and out of sight. Something fell below the window frame…

David's face, hanging upside down.

Anna's hand went to her mouth.

David righted himself, swung back and forth, then, lifting his legs, arched his body and vaulted through the window. He landed inside, wavered and regained his balance. Looking around, he saw Anna and smiled.

She didn't move. Neither did he.

"What are you doing here?" she whispered. She couldn't have raised her voice if she had to.

David didn't answer. Instead, he simply held out his hand.

She took a step backward. Again, she asked, *Have you come to dishonor me?*

How could I do that? He revealed his ignorance of what she meant. *Love you, Anna.*

Anna's eyes met his. In that moment, she knew everything she'd been thinking, anything she'd intended was useless. No matter what she said, she was more than fond of David, had more for him than a teacher's affection for a pupil.

It was absurd. People don't fall in love that quickly, no matter what the novels say, but she felt it was true nevertheless. In spite of her own intentions, David had won…he was an unskilled rake, the ultimate novice in seduction, but his persistence plus the force of his innocence had broken her defenses…and now came the moment of truth.

If she rejected him, she was certain he'd accept she meant it and go. His coming here would never be spoken of, and she could finish her assignment and escape to safety with a heart *mostly* unbroken, but…

Do I want to? If she succumbed, if it were discovered how she betrayed her trust, she would lose her position and never be allowed to teach again, and…

There could be other more obvious repercussions. Her reputation would be destroyed.

Papa would take me back, she told herself. *No matter what, he'd allow me to return home.*

The last thing she wanted to do was send David away. She knew what would happen if she didn't. When she and Maisie were old enough, hadn't her mother spoken to them of such things

Do it! Before you weaken and begin thinking clearly.

Taking a deep breath, Anna took a step toward David…and her own condemnation. He caught the edge of the towel, pulling it from her grasp. Her nerveless fingers let it go. It fell to the floor.

If Anna could've known his thoughts in that moment…

****

She looks like goddess.

Lord Harold had several histories of Greece and Rome, both containing etchings of statuary, pottery, and mosaics depicting those ancient cultures' gods and goddesses. David had taken one to his room, stripped, and compared his body to those in the drawings. He decided he looked as good as Apollo or perhaps Mercury. He saw Anna the same way. She was as beautiful as Diana or Venus…or any of the beautiful women in the many portraits adorning the manor's walls…

Falling to his knees, he put his arms around her, pressing his cheek against her breast. *So warm, so soft*…he kissed the hollow between them, nuzzling against her skin. Anna's hands clasped his shoulders, holding him tight against her body. His hands slid down her back, clasping her buttocks, pulling her tighter against him.

Abruptly, he pushed her away, hands coming up with fingers fluttering.

You my goddess. I your lover. Goddess, not destroy poor mortal. That was followed by a shy, tentative smile.

Rising to his feet, he scooped her into his arms and turned to the bed. Anna didn't try to stop him. Indeed, she didn't want to.

Whatever comes, let it…I love you, David.

Placing her gently upon the bed, David pulled his shirt over his head, tossing it to the floor. He slid out of his riding breeches and rid himself of his drawers. Then he simply stood there, waiting.

Goddess accept me?

Shadowed by the bed's draperies, lit only by the lamp's flickering flame, he was highlighted into a godling.

She remembered how he'd looked as he walked out of the water.

David was more beautiful than he had been that day at the lake…he was transmuted… the river god come onto dry land, his long dark hair untouched by water, curling about his shoulders, skin gleaming in firelight instead of water drops…prepared to carry her into forbidden magic…his body a treasure for her to discover. That mystery no longer lay quiet against his thighs. Now it rose from its nestling of dark curls, offering itself to her.

Take me, Anna, I am yours…

She looked at him with a lover's freedom.

I have that right. In a moment, we'll be lovers in fact.

She knew that, accepted it…it was inevitable no

matter what she thought, and she didn't care.

Anna raised her hand.

David took it in his and climbed onto the bed.

Chapter 25

David kissed her forehead, her eyelids, her cheeks, and chin.

Then he pressed his mouth to hers, tongue thrusting. It was cool but burning, a spear of ice.

How can it be so hot and cold at the same time?

He leaned away from her, fingers declaring, *You are my goddess, Anna,* then kissed her again. His fingers were busy now, too busy to speak…exploring her body. One palm cupped a breast, thumb stroking across the nipple.

Anna trembled as it tautened, peaking into a sharp tight bud. He transferred his mouth to it, using his tongue to lave and caress while the other hand trailed down her ribs. He rubbed his cheek against her belly, bristles of his whiskers maker her shiver with the most delicious *frisson* she'd ever experienced.

Kisses trailed down her body—one pressed into the bend of her thigh, another sought the golden nest of curls, and then…

Anna stiffened. She nearly cried out as his tongue thrust inward, grazing across her most intimate part, a place she herself never touched except in bathing.

"David…" she began in protest, then let it trail away as the caressing touch came again.

Her mother had said, *On your wedding night, you'll learn of your man's mysteries, and how every inch of his body will please yours as much as yours pleases his.*

Was this what she meant? Had she and Papa ever done this? Oh, David, where did you learn this? She lay still under his touch, body trembling, aware she was moaning softly, knowing the sounds she made fell on ears that didn't hear, that only she knew what caused the whispers within her or the sounds escaping. She hoped somehow he could sense the pleasure she felt in his touch.

Abruptly, she wanted to touch him…to let him know how she felt. Hadn't Mama said their bodies would please each other? That mean she had to respond with caresses also. She touched his shoulders, grasping tightly and tugging. At first, he didn't respond, then stopped his attention to look up at her as she pulled more sharply.

Grasping his arms, she pulled him up beside her, then kissed him again, marveling at the odd flavor upon his lips.

She remembered he'd said he wanted to taste her. *Is this what he meant? Is that how I taste?*

She stroked fingers down his chest, trailing gently over his ribs, felt his body quiver under her touch, as hers had done. David lay motionless, body visibly quaking. She could see his shoulders tremble in the lamp's dim light.

Anna's fingers slid to his groin, brushing through the dark curls, seeking that greatest mystery she'd already glimpsed in both its quiet and aggressive states. It rose to meet her hand. She didn't have to seek it further. There was a moment's awkwardness as she looked down at what she held…shadowed and rampart, wrapped in its leaflike sheath of flesh.

He made a sound as near to a grunt of pain as she'd

ever heard from someone not injured, the mystery jerked out of her hands. David caught her by the shoulders, rolling her onto her back. Grasping his member, he pushed her thighs apart with his knee, lay between, and fitted that stiffened rod of flesh against her.

He looked up, eyes meeting hers.

It's going to hurt. It'll be worth it to be David's. She seized his face in her hands and pressed her mouth to his.

David caught her about the hips, thrusting his body forward, pulling her against him.

Anna's cry was captured between them. She couldn't stop the tears, but she muffled her sobs against his shoulder as he began to move. She put her arms around him, running her hands over the smoothness of muscles in his shoulders, feeling them flex and relax with each thrust and retreat, slowly at first, then faster and faster.

David stiffened. Briefly, his body convulsed, shaking so violently the bed itself shook. Anna tightened her grip around his shoulders, but he pushed away, head thrown back, eyes shut, mouth open in a startling grimace of a wordless cry.

Abruptly, he collapsed, face nestling against the little space between her neck and shoulder. She felt his lips moving against her neck and knew without seeing that he was whispering her name over and over while his body continued quaking.

…Anna…Anna…Anna…

She stroked his back, fingers moving over his hips, down his thighs, crooning, "Shh…shh…" until the trembling stopped and he lay still against her.

I'm lost. Now she knew who was the cat and who the mouse.

193

David raised his head, eyes managing to find hers in the dimness. They caught the light from the lamp, seeming to reflect onto her face. He touched her cheek, kissed her lips again, then pushed away, raising both hands.

You're not a goddess...no, no...I was wrong...

No? Then what am I? She feared his answer.

You're an angel...taking me to heaven...

With that, he rolled onto his back, sought and found a pillow and, resting against it, pulled Anna into his arms. Cuddling her against his chest, he threw one leg across her thighs, capturing her in a possessive embrace. He raised himself to say one last thing.

Beautiful naked...with you like I want...Sleep now with my angel...

Chapter 26

Anna awoke to the sensation of a very warm male body cuddled against her back. Briefly, she started in shock at the intrusion of a stranger into her bed, then memories of the night before flooded in.

Closing her eyes, she snuggled into David's warmth. Still sleeping, he reacted by tightening his embrace, pulling her closer against him. He lay with his face burrowed against the back of her neck, his breath a warm whisper against her ear. It tickled against her skin, stirring her hair over her shoulder.

Below stairs, there was the faint sound of movement. Shelton went about opening the house for the morning, Cook fed the fires in the iron stove to prepare breakfast while Edward and Jane began their chores. Distant noise from the yards floated through the open window.

They were no longer alone in their love. With those hints of life, reality set in.

He called me his angel, but would anyone else? Will Eleanor? Not likely…fallen woman, wanton… harlot… She could almost hear the accusations. *Seducing your charge, an innocent because of his disability… They'll say I abused my responsibility, took advantage of David. Once it's learned, I'll never be able to teach again.*

The cat had devoured her in one gulp.

Oh, Papa. I hope you'll be understanding.

Completely excluding David from any wrong-doing, Anna blamed only herself for what had happened. *That'll be enough scandal in itself, but what if...* She wasn't so naïve she was unaware of the possible outcome of what they'd done.

If there's any result from this, David must never know. I'll finish what I came here to do, make certain he's accepted in his world, and leave...to bear my shame alone... He'll forget me once all those debutantes discover him...

She pressed her hands against the ones lying against her breasts.

But I'll *never forget* you. *Oh, David, if only...*

"Miss?" There was a tap upon the door. "Good morning. Are you awake?"

Rolling over, Anna seized David's shoulders and shook him. His eyes opened, glancing around in confusion before settling on her. Recognition set in and he smiled, pulling her toward him for a good morning kiss. Instead of allowing herself to revel in his caress, she pushed him away.

He scowled.

Jane knocked again.

You must go. Anna glanced over her shoulder toward the door.

"Miss?" Jane called again.

Not understanding and not hearing Jane's knock, David shook his head, again reaching for Anna and pulling her close. She wriggled out of his embrace, Signing, *Jane...here...go,* and pointing to the door.

He sat up, eyes going wide, then looked back at her.

Go! Anna struck his shoulders so violently he tumbled backward off the bed.

Landing on the carpet with a solid *thud*, he sat up and looked around. Crawling on hands and knees, he found his shirt.

"Miss? Are you still feeling ill?" Jane's voice rose in concern.

Ann glanced at the door, then peered over the edge of the bed at David.

He'd pulled on his shirt, thrusting his arms into the sleeves. Tossing his breeches over his shoulder, he climbed onto the windowseat and turned to look back at Anna, crouching in the center of the bed. Blowing her a kiss, he clambered through the window and reached for the branch. The morning breeze lifted the tail of his shirt, giving Anna a brief glimpse of a tight, naked bum as he pulled himself up and out of sight.

Anna touched her own fingers to her lips, and looked down as David had.

There was a red smear on the sheet. *Oh no…*she couldn't let Jane see that, nor the fact that she was naked.

"Miss?" There was another knock on the door.

If I don't answer soon, she'll come charging in, thinking I'm ill, or have Shelton do so…or tell Eleanor. There was a flare of anger. Anna didn't particularly want to see anyone at that moment. She'd wanted to bask in the aftermath of David's love, and now that idyllic moment was ruined.

"I've still a bit of a headache, Jane," she called hastily, "Let me rest perhaps a half hour longer, and then could you bring me up a tray with some tea?"

"Of course, miss. You just take your time. I'll come back later."

Later would come soon enough…and in the meantime…

197

Jumping from the bed, Anna plunged her hands into the now-cold water in the tub, found the washcloth, and wrung it. Hurrying back to the bed, she frantically scrubbed at the stain, relieved to see it fade and disappear under her ministrations. Now, however, the bed was damp.

How to explain that?

Desperately, she looked around as if something in the room would provide an answer. She saw the nightgown, wadded at the foot of the bed where it had been pushed by their movements.

Jane'll expect me to be wearing that. An idea presented itself.

Slipping the nightgown over her head, she ran to the tub, again dipping her hands into the water and wiping them down the front and back of the muslin gown, not enough to soak it but merely dampening the fabric. Anna shivered as the wet cloth clung to her thighs and ribs. She returned to the bed, climbing into it and settling herself somewhat uncomfortably onto her pillow.

A damp bed isn't restful. She hoped her ploy worked.

When Jane returned with another discreet knock, opening the door to Anna's call, she carried a tray holding a china cup and saucer and a teapot wrapped in a knitted cozy.

"Here we are, miss." She set the tray on the table near the hearth and seized one of the pokers. Remarkably, the fire hadn't died during the night. "Let me get this fire stirred so it'll be warm for you."

As she was speaking, Jane hurried to the wardrobe, retrieving Maisie's shawl. Anna sat up and Jane wrapped it around her shoulders.

"There, now. Sit yourself and I'll pour you a nice cup of morning tea."

She set about doing so as Anna obeyed. The fire felt good, warmth seeping through the damp nightgown. Anna decided she'd speak before Jane noticed how the cloth clung to her legs.

Handing Anna the teacup, Jane was already turning to the bed, however, still talking. "I'll put the bed to rights…Goodness, the bedclothes are so disarranged. Did you have a restless night, miss?"

Oh, Jane, you couldn't possible guess how restless it was. Anna hid her reddening cheeks behind her teacup. *How can I possibly blush* now*?*

Before she could answer, Jane seized the top sheet and comforter, throwing them back as a prelude to smoothing the bottom sheet. "Miss! There's a damp spot…"

"I'm afraid I was feeling so wretched last night I didn't bother to dry properly after my bath." Anna made her voice a touch embarrassed. It wasn't difficult. She took another sip of tea. "I felt so sleepy from the warm water that I got directly into bed, wet as I was. I'm sorry, Jane." She injected a bit of apology. "I know the sheet'll have to be changed…"

"Don't you worry about it, miss. It's Thursday. Today's the day I change the linens anyway." Seizing the offending sheet, Jane practically ripped it from the bed, tossing it upon a chair. She spun to look at Anna. "Do you feel well enough to get dressed now?"

Anna finished her tea. "That warm cup seems to have fortified me. All trace of my headache has been vanquished." She smiled. "I'm ready to face the day, Jane…thanks to your tea."

But am I ready to face David? The Lord only knows how he's going to act, now that we've...

She let the rest of the thought die away as Jane opened the wardrobe and asked her which of her remaining dresses she'd like to wear.

****

Breakfast was pleasant, partly because of the way Anna felt, as well as the fact that David behaved...to a certain degree.

She'd barely entered the dining room and spoken her good mornings to Eleanor who had decided not to wait to be served, when David bounced in. That was the only way to describe the way he moved, springing along like one of the baby goats she'd seen when she once accompanied her father on a visit to a patient at a farm outside Little Riversreach.

He was also dressed semi-formally, in knee breeches, stockings and hose, shirt, and a completely buttoned weskit. Not aware of the fact that a gentleman never appeared without his coat even at home, David had ignorantly foregone that item of apparel.

Good morning, Sister. His nimble fingers seemed to sing. *Good morning, Shelton...Edward.* He turned to include the butler and footman in his salutation. Shelton answered in kind, bowing slightly. Hands full of a serving tray, Edward merely bowed.

Good morning, dear. Choosing to answer David also by Signing, Eleanor set down the spoon with which she'd scooped an aromatic mixture of creamed eggs and spring onions onto her plate.

You look happy.

Why shouldn't I be? When I'm dining with my...

He bestowed a brilliant smile upon Anna whose

heart sank even as she smiled back at him. She braced herself for the rest of that sentence.

...favorite teacher and my beloved sister?

Breathing a quiet sigh, she relaxed. *Thank you, David.*

He nodded, seizing her hand and bowing over it. Glancing quickly at Eleanor and making certain she was involved with the toasted muffins and jam, he winked at Anna and turned her hand, pressing a kiss onto her palm. A moment later, his tongue traced the pattern of the kiss against her skin.

Anna started, barely preventing herself from jerking her hand from his. He held it a moment longer, then released it, still smiling. *I love you, my angel*. His fingers told her. *Moreso than last night.*

Shhh. She tapped her forefinger to her lips, glancing at Eleanor, who chose that moment to look up.

I hope you're feeling better? David's question was as solicitous as his expression. *Your megrime...* he had to spell that word...*is gone?*

Quite, thank you. Anna answered.

"I'm glad your headache is gone, Anna. It's so good to see David carrying on a normal conversation," she remarked. Abruptly, she burst into a quick laugh. "Oh, dear, I just thought of the most amusing thing."

"What's that?" Anna asked.

Eleanor has thought of something funny, she told David, who hadn't been looking at his sister, his gaze fastened to Anna's.

Brows raised, he gave his sister his attention.

I've only just realized people who Sign can't have secrets.

"What do you mean?" Anna asked hastily. She

grimaced at the startled note in her voice.

"Well…" Eleanor paused to eat a spoonful of egg followed by a large bite of muffin and jam. She chewed and swallowed before answering. "Hearing people can whisper or write notes if they don't want someone to know something, but the deaf…"

As if the answer should've been obvious, she gestured with her muffin, sprinkling crumbs onto the tablecloth. Shelton was immediately there with a crumbcatcher, brushing them into the pan and backing away from the table.

"…whenever they Sign, everyone in the room knows they're speaking whether they can read what they say or not."

David stiffened.

Anna turned away slightly, dropping her hands to waist-level. *Surely you realized that.*

He shook his head.

Forgot. Looking back at Eleanor, he nodded. *You right, Elly. Have to be discreet, do they?* Again, he had to spell out the words he hadn't yet learned to Sign.

He took a step closer to Anna.

Too close, she thought, trying to inch away, but Eleanor was again concentrating on breakfast, inquiring of the footman about the fried ham slices. Shelton was busily returning the crumbcatcher to its place at the end of the sideboard. A moment later, she felt David's left hand brush against her ribs, then trail down her back. He cupped the curve of one buttock in his hand, squeezing lightly.

Anna swallowed her gasp, shooting him a glare.

He smiled innocently.

Well? Why are you two standing? Eleanor looked up

again. *Sit down.*

Bowing, David offered Anna his arm and led her to her chair. He waited until Edward seated her, then returned to his own place.

The rest of breakfast went boringly without further incident, either seen or unseen by Eleanor, for which Anna was eternally grateful.

Chapter 27

The day went through its boring routine.

The townsfolks appeared.

Anna went over that day's lesson.

David asked to be taught words seemingly innocent in themselves but to Anna's suspicious eyes held double meanings. Al and Jem were their usual irreverent selves.

After the lesson, Eleanor asked Shelton to serve everyone tea. To assist Al's digestion, she said. It was a bit of fun watching Al, Jem, and the other two young men handle the delicate cups and saucers in their big calloused hands. Even David thought it amusing and said so.

It a tea cup, Al. Not hen egg.

Good thing there is ladies present, Davy. Else I would give you an answer to that as would singe that curly pate o' yours.

"Isn't it wonderful to see David chatting with his friends?" Eleanor whispered. "It's so…natural."

Anna agreed it was.

Afterward, while Shelton shut the door after they'd bade everyone goodbye, David turned to her.

By your leave, Anna. Must see Run.

Who is Run? Anna asked.

My horse.

While Anna digested the fact that the horse actually had a name, David straightened and she saw that mischievous gleam in his eyes.

Been neglecting him for a filly interesting me. He smiled as if thinking himself very clever for saying that.

Filly? Eleanor came into the hall. *Have you been to Master Brown's?*

He nodded. *Thinking of buying her.*

Anna frowned. His smile grew wider.

Tell me about her. Eleanor looked interested.

Nice little mare. His eyes twinkled.

Against her better judgment, Anna reflected his smile back at him, though she still tensed.

Golden sorrel. Dainty but sturdy. Maybe good breeding stock.

Her smile faded. *No, David, oh, no, no. Do not think that way.* It was all she could do not to let her fingers say that to him.

That is nice, dear. Eleanor frowned. *Except we have no stallion.*

No? David looked directly into Anna's eyes. Her own gaze skittered away.

"All our horses are geldings, dear." Eleanor spoke aloud, blushing slightly. "You may not understand but geldings can't sire colts."

But, Elly... David reflected back her frown. *Why not?*

"I don't believe this is quite the time or place to discuss that." Eleanor whirled and got very busy walking in the direction of the kitchen. "I really must speak to Cook." She fluttered her fingers. *Anyway, we have no need for another horse.*

David shrugged, though he still looked confused.

Aiming himself after his sister, he headed for the kitchen and the quickest way to the stables, leaving Anna with more than a slight sense of foreboding.

Oh, David, we must have a very long and serious talk.

Though it might be embarrassing, she had to discover exactly how much he was aware of male-female physical relations as well as the seriousness of what they'd done. It came to her his actions the night before might have been mostly instinct or simply a response to physical sensation.

I should've asked this before I...we...were so foolish. A little late is better than never, I suppose. All she had to do was get David alone so they could talk without Eleanor reading what they were saying.

The only chance came that night. As soon as the house was silent and everyone presumably asleep, he appeared through her bedroom window. Anna wondered what he'd have done if the shutters had been closed.

What would happen if I refused to let him enter? Not that she'd ever do that. *It may be weak-willed of me, but I can't refuse him.* She wanted David's love for however long she might have it.

If the window was shut, she imagined he'd simply break it somehow. After all, what was mere glass to a lover's steel will...or he'd do the unthinkable and stamp down the hall and pound on her door until she opened it while the sound awakened everyone in the household and informed them of what was going on between the master and his tutor.

In the dim light from the lamp, he regarded her with the adoring gaze of an acolyte, reminding her of his comparison of her to a goddess...but he was an acolyte impatient for the goddess's favor.

David, we need to talk...

She never got to finish.

He kissed her, picked her up, and carried her to the bed. Once they were lying in it, side by side, he Signed, *Talk later. I have much to say*. Then he proceeded to make love to her.

****

Anna was sleepy and sated, imprisoned within the heat of David's embrace. He'd been still for so long she thought him asleep, and though she knew they should talk, to discuss their situation before the night grew older, she was loath to disturb the contentment she felt.

It was David himself who did that.

Now then… Releasing Anna, he seized the pillows, fluffing and piling each behind them. Leaning back, he turned Anna so they were face to face. *You said we must talk*.

And you said you had much to say, she reminded him.

I do. Shall I begin? Or… A hand graciously gestured. *Ladies first?*

Anna hesitated. Wondering what he was going to say, she decided it might be best to let him speak first. She shook her head.

Very well. Settling himself, he held Anna's hands, kissing her fingers, then released them, and drew in a deep breath. *Anna…*

His fingers paused. He looked away, inhaled a second time, and raised his gaze to hers again.

She tensed, fearing whatever was coming.

Why can a gelding not sire colts?

She nearly laughed. It was such an inappropriate question. Thinking back to the other things he'd said to Eleanor, she realized it was much more.

207

Because… Her fingers fluttered helplessly, wondering what to say and how to say it. She wasn't certain of the exact procedure, simply the result. *They are…disabled.*

Disabled? He frowned.

They lack the… Oh, why must I be the one to do this? *…the proper equipment.*

The frown deepened. *But Charger does?*

Charger?

Master Brown's horse. He makes colts.

Oh. I see. Charger must be a stallion. Yes. They can make colts.

But not a disabled horse? Is Run disabled?

I…yes. Eleanor said all the horses at the manor were geldings.

Abruptly, he seized her hands so tightly she bit her lip to keep from crying out, then released them, asking in a rapid gesturing, *Anna, am I disabled? Am I a gelding?*

"Oh, David, no!" She spoke the words aloud, then glanced around fearfully as if afraid someone might've heard. The rest of her answer was silent. *Not in that way.*

But I unable to hear…can barely speak… That is disabled.

It is not the same thing.

Then you and I could make a baby…like Charger does with the mares?

We could—she wouldn't lie to him, though she hated to answer truthfully—*but we must not.*

Why?

We're not married.

Oh, I see…and a baron not marry a country doctor's daughter. Nimble fingers parroted her words back at her once again. *So I must not make baby with you though I like to.*

She nodded.

How do I not do it?

Anna had no answer for that. Her mother had never mentioned any way of preventing birth. Though she imagined her father might know, he was too far away to ask, and she couldn't have brought herself to bring up the subject with him anyway.

There is only one way I know.

That is…?

Do not make love to me.

Not… No kissing? No… He nodded at the bed. *No grinding corn?*

She nodded.

Will not do that. Love you, Anna. Make baby and marry you. He put his arms around her, hugging her so tightly she couldn't move, couldn't raise her hands to argue. A moment later, he released her so violently she fell against the pillows. *I have another question.*

What else can he possibly ask? Anna braced herself.

What is it?

This morning…I saw…blood on the sheet. His hand brushed against the percale beneath them. *Why?*

By now, Anna was ready to weep. These were questions she never thought she would be asked, much less have to answer. She'd always believed her first lover would also be her husband and he'd know all the answers and be answering *her* questions, if she had any.

I was a virgin, David…

His fingers came up with the expected question. *What is…*

That means I never had a lover. Virgins always

209

bleed the first time.

He thought about that. Then he asked the one question she'd never expected.

Did I bleed, too? I virgin also.

She shook her head.

Why not? He looked chagrined, as if cheated somehow.

Men never do. At least she didn't suppose they did.

Not fair. His lip protruded in a brief pout, and then he shrugged it away. *No matter. Will it happen again?*

She shook her head. *Only once.*

Glad. Now I love you again, Anna.

She was swept into that overpowering embrace, letting David's kiss wipe away any thought of right or wrong or the impropriety of what they were doing.

It would end soon enough. She may as well enjoy her crime as it happened.

Chapter 28

Things went quietly but swiftly after that. To Anna, it felt as if she were living a masquerade of some kind.

By day, David was her pupil, being instructed in words and phrases necessary to carry on daily living in Mayfield Manor and at the village. At night, he became her lover, a passionate but silent incubus coming to her through that open window, sweeping her away to what he termed *Paradise* and Anna silently agreed, though with pangs of conscience as she allowed herself to be enfolded into the false safety of his embrace for a brief peace before he left her again, traveling *via* oak branch back to his own rooms.

She was startled but thankful no one suspected anything.

Thus far.

During the next week's lessons, Al told her he and his brother wouldn't be back. "This is the last day for Jem and me. Da says we knows all we needs to and he and us'n can talk good enough to Master Davy now. We's to thank you, miss, for the teaching." He bobbed his head.

"Same here," Mr. Greeley spoke up. "I need to get back to the store. My wife doesn't like waitin' on customers. She's eager to be tending the hearth again."

The others gave similar excuses.

"Well," Anna remarked aloud, watching them

trudge up the path. "It appears I've lost all my pupils."

Still have me. David reminded her. *Forever.*

She put a hand over his. He caught her fingers and squeezed them, then lifted her hand and bowed over it.

You have conquered Signing, she told him. *I think it's time you started speaking along with Signing. That is part of the curriculum for the Academy...Sign-supported Speech.*

He nodded, looking eager.

We'll start tomorrow, she told him.

In the meantime... His smile held a wicked tilt.

What? She was almost afraid to ask.

Gooseberries are ripe. Like to pick some?

She glanced toward the library where Eleanor had told her she would be going over the household accounts, writing out bank drafts for various creditors.

Already told Eleanor. She looking forward to gooseberry tarts for dessert tonight. David looked past Anna to the butler walking toward them. *Here is Shelton with bucket.*

He seemed to have thought of everything.

They decided to walk to the patch instead of riding Run.

Once away from the manor, David was remarkably silent. Now that they were alone, Anna had supposed he'd chatter away, saying risqué and blush-inducing things. Instead, he simply walked beside her, swinging the bucket and scuffing up dust with the toes of his boots. They found the gooseberry patch. As he'd said, the berries were indeed ripe.

So it wasn't simply a ploy to get me alone. Anna felt a slight disappointment, then told herself that was a good sign. David was learning to exercise discretion, and she wasn't his sole subject of thought.

It didn't take long to pick the berries. As Anna got to her feet with David's assistance, he released her hand, fingers rippling out, *Warm. Walk by lake? Cooler there.*

All right. Anna nodded. *I think it is time you began Signing in complete sentences. You know enough words now, and I am certain it will help your case.*

Very well. He switched the bucket to his left hand. *Whatever you say.*

Taking her hand in his right one, he gave her a smile, so obliging Anna wondered if she should be suspicious.

Once again, they walked along in silence.

As soon as the lake came into view, David stopped. Setting the bucket at the foot of one of the pines, he looked at her.

That day… Why did you run?

Young women are not supposed to see young gentlemen without their clothes.

Why not? Do they not like it?

They are not supposed to like it.

That does not answer my question. Did you?

Perhaps a little, she hedged, looking away.

Silly…and stupid. His fingers under her chin turned her back to face him. *I love looking at your body, Anna. Should I not admit it?*

It's one of the rules of Society, David.

Foolish rule.

I agree, but there it is.

Are there other rules?

She nodded.

Are they all so stupid?

Once more she nodded, suppressing a smile.

And I have to follow them because I am a baron?

I'm afraid so.

Why has Elly not told me about them?

Because she never thought you would need to know.

And now I do. Why now? Wait. He held up a hand. *I know. When we marry, I will have to know these things.* He shrugged as if that answered his question.

David...

He looked away, deliberately not seeing what she had planned to say, turning his attention to the lake.

So peaceful here. Do you think Eden was like this, Anna?

That startled her. She hadn't thought David would have any idea of the Bible or its teachings.

Perhaps.

We're alone here.

Not even the ducks or geese were present, having abandoned the lake for other locales.

Let's be Adam and Eve. David swung around, catching her hands. *Let's shed our clothing and swim. I want to see you in the water, Anna.*

Oh, no! She pulled her hands from his. *We can't.*

Why not?

I can't swim. Besides, someone might come along and see...

...and be the Serpent, spoiling our fun? Eve can't swim? Very well. He dropped to one knee, catching her foot and placing it against his thigh. *Will you wade with me, then?*

I suppose...

His hand crept up her ankle past the pantalette ruffle to her thigh, found her garter, and worked it loose. Anna's stocking was gently rolled down. David removed her slipper, dropping it to the grass. The stocking followed, as did the other slipper and the stocking's mate. Releasing her, he slid to the ground, sitting and removing his own boots and stockings while Anna wiggled her toes in the grass's coolness.

He got to his feet, caught her hand, and pulled her to the lake bank. Releasing her, he waded into the water ankle-deep, turned, and waited.

Lifting her skirts, Anna gingerly dipped one toe into the water. It wasn't cold at all but sun-warmed. She lowered her foot into the water, then the other. Draping her skirts over her arm, she caught David's hand and they splashed happily down the shoreline and back.

As they neared the spot where shoes, boots, and stockings lay in an intimate jumble, Anna glanced up.

We must get back.

The sun had passed overhead and was now edging behind the trees again. She sank to the grass, picking up one of her stockings.

If we're to have gooseberry tarts for dessert tonight…

…I want my dessert now.

David fell to the grass beside her. Putting his arms around her, he pushed her onto her back. Kissing her stopped any refusal Anna might make as he trailed a row of kisses from her mouth to her bosom, raising his head long enough to mouth, *Don't argue, my Eve. The Serpent hasn't arrived yet.*

He quickly maneuvered her skirts above her knees, then flicked open the drop panel of his riding breeches and fumbled with the buttons of her pantalettes.

Wait. Anna put her hands against his chest. *Adam didn't know Eve until after the Serpent arrived.*

You're wrong. He shook his head. *It was merely bad*

timing. God was about to reveal everything to them... He kissed her, tongue caressing hers before he continued. *...when the Devil showed up and spoiled His plans and got blamed.*

****

Afterward, David insisted on helping her put on her stockings, pushing her skirts high and kissing every spot as he rolled up the cotton tubes...ankle, knee, thigh. He tied the garters with little bows, tucked the ruffles of the pantalettes around them, and slid her slippers onto her feet. Then he pulled on his own stockings, smoothed them inside the cuffs of his breeches, and stamped into his boots.

As he got to his feet, the sun burst through a gap in the trees. Briefly, David was enveloped in golden light. He spread his arms, spinning, caught Anna, and whirled her about in the sunny glow. Then the sun moved on and they were in the trees' cool shadows again.

Holding the bucket between them, they returned to the manor.

I'm terrible, Anna thought. *I'm more wanton than the worst harlot. I've not only known this man without marriage but I like seeing his body and I admit it. Now, I've made love in the open where anyone might come upon us and I enjoyed it. Oh, David, are we both mad or is it simply I who've gone insane?*

Rebelliously, in that moment, she didn't care.

Chapter 29

Back at the manor, while David took the bucket of gooseberries to the kitchen, Anna strolled into the music room. It had become her custom to go there after their sessions and play as a way to relax, while David generally took Run for his daily ride and Eleanor tended to household duties.

Seating herself at the pianoforte, she leafed through the sheets resting on the music stand, selected one, and began to play.

Briefly, she lost herself in the melody, fingers brushing the keys. There was a step behind her, a pair of arms slid beneath hers, hands caressing her breasts. David pressed his lips against the nape of her neck. Her hands left the keys. She twisted on the piano bench, touching his cheeks as he raised his head to kiss her on the lips.

From the hallway came a loud shout.

"Get out of here. Get out! Shelton, if he isn't out of here in two minutes, throw him out."

Anna pushed David away. He frowned, then glanced over his shoulder in the direction she was looking.

What? his fingers asked.

Eleanor…shouting, she explained.

At Desmond. He replied as if this were nothing new.

"Desmond?" She spoke the name aloud. *The cousin?* "He's here?"

Arrived while I was in kitchen. I stay away. I don't like Desmond. They always fight when he visits. He shrugged that fact away, bending to kiss her again.

Someone stamped into the foyer. Evading David's embrace, Anna slid off the bench, seizing his arm and pulling him to the music room door. They came through it as Desmond, pursued by a red-faced Eleanor, arrived in the foyer.

He was around David's height and she could see the family resemblance. Desmond was also dark-haired and blue-eyed, a startlingly handsome man around Eleanor's age. He was dressed—to the point of dandyism—in buff knee breeches and white stockings, with silver-buckled shoes. His tailed cutaway was such a dark green it was almost black, complemented with gold braid on its turned-up collar and cuffs, and his neckpiece was a folded masterpiece.

At the moment, however, there was nothing gentlemanly about his expression, for his face was dark and twisted with rage.

Clutching a stiff-brimmed hat and walking stick, Shelton stood at the open door. He glanced with dismay at David and apologetically at Anna.

"If there's anyone going to be thrown out of here, it's you, dear cousin," Desmond declared. "You and that idiot brother of yours. As soon as the judge speaks his verdict, I want you gone…and it won't be to the gameskeeper's cottage. I'm throwing all of you onto the highroad where you can beg or starve."

Anna gasped, and he swung around, angry gaze lighting on her. It immediately turned curious. "And who might you be?"

"I-I'm Anna Leighton, Lord Mayfield's hearing

teacher." Anna's hand unconsciously crept to David's. His fingers tightened around hers.

"Oh, yes, I'd heard Elly brought in someone from one of those schools. So you think you can teach this dummy to talk, do you?" He glanced down, spying their clasped hands. "So that's how it is, eh?"

"Is there a problem, ma'am?" Hearing raised voices, Edward appeared behind Eleanor. She turned to look at him.

Beside Anna, David shifted his weight, his own gaze fastened on his cousin's mouth.

"Well, David, didn't think you had it in you." Briefly, Desmond's eyes held brief admiration. "Don't worry, my dear, you won't lose your status when I'm Lord Mayfield. I'll keep you on. You must be a saucy bit between the sheets if you can liven the simpleton here. Mayhap you can teach me a thing or two."

David lunged for him. Anna reached to stop him, only to be hurled aside.

Dropping hat and cane, Shelton leaped forward, catching David's shoulders. In spite of his age, he managed to haul his young master backward.

As servant and master struggled, Desmond took two steps out of reach. Clawing the air, David broke from Shelton's grasp and Edward moved past Eleanor as the old man again reached for David.

Between the two of them, butler and footman kept him from knocking Desmond down.

"Better watch that," Desmond threatened. He retrieved his hat from the foyer floor, brushing a bit of dust from the brim, then stooped to get his cane. "You might find yourself up on assault charges, Cousin, and on your way to Australia."

He placed the hat on his head and turned, throwing over his shoulder, "I imagine they'd make short work of a halfwit like you."

"How dare you speak to my brother that way!" Eleanor flew at him. The sharp *slap* of her hand colliding with his cheek echoed through the foyer.

Desmond staggered, surprise on his handsome features.

"Will you have me arrested, too?"

"You're going to regret that," he shot back. Before any of them could recover, he was through the door and gone, walking hurriedly to the coach waiting on the far side of the courtyard, facing the carriage road.

Shelton released David.

You...that... David's hands flailed the air as his fingers tried to find a word expressing his anger.

Anna stepped in front of him, seizing his chin and forcing his head around.

Bleeding sod, her own fingers supplied.

She'd heard those words used only once. They'd been taking an evening stroll when a drunkard lurched out of a tavern, nearly knocking down Maisie, who was much smaller at that time.

"You bleeding sod!" Papa had seized the man by the shoulders and hurled him away. "How dare you knock down a child?"

With a muttered apology, the man clambered to his feet and staggered down the street into an alley. Both his words and her father's expression stuck in Anna's memory. She hadn't believed her peace-loving parent could look so deadly. That phrase was exactly the one to describe Desmond Walters.

David's facile fingers seized the movements,

repeating the words over and over...*bleeding sod...bleeding sod...* The look on his face frightened Anna. It was exactly as her father's had been.

Remembering what Desmond said, she began to cry. David put his arm around her, drawing her against his chest, then reached for Eleanor who stood with tears trickling down her own cheeks. He embraced both women. Their sobs drowned out the sound of the coach driving away.

Awkwardly, David guided Anna and his sister to the parlor. He looked back at Shelton, raising one hand to sign, *Bring tea.*

The old man nodded and hurried to the kitchen.

In the parlor, David seated Eleanor in her chair, then led Anna to the other. With the aid of the tea Shelton hurriedly served, he managed to calm both women in a remarkably short time, during which Anna thought of Desmond's insulting words to her.

Did Eleanor hear? Or Edward? Surely Shelton had, but... Everything was so sudden and violent, and noisy, perhaps no one really knew what had been said. She hoped. This definitely wasn't the time for Eleanor to learn of her brother's involvement with his tutor. While David paced back and forth between them, she stifled her own tears, forcing herself to sip the tea and let its warmth calm her.

"Thank you, David." Eleanor looked a little more composed. The flush had left her face and she was once more her collected self. "I feel much better now."

And you? He glanced at Anna, fingers moving so quickly she barely got a glimpse of what he asked.

"I, also," she assured him.

We must talk of this, David signed.

221

I agree. Eleanor set down her cup, fingers moving rapidly.

Even in her distress, Anna could only marvel at the speed with which they were conversing. Perhaps their heightened emotions was a good thing, since it forced them to utilize their knowledge.

David's hands fell to his sides, as if waiting for Eleanor to open the discussion. When she didn't move but simply clasped her hands in her lap, he raised his own again.

Why was Desmond here? What did he want?

I told you, Davy…remember?

David shrugged. *When he came before? Some nonsense about wanting my title?* It was obvious he'd simply brushed whatever Eleanor told him aside. *Desmond always spouting some twaddle.* He spelled that last word.

Not nonsense. Eleanor's fingers took on a desperate motion. *Desmond gambles. He has debts. He wants your title and everything going with it.*

David thought about that before again raising his hands.

He can have it.

What are you saying?

His reply shocked both his sister and Anna, but for different reasons. Eleanor stared at him as if he'd lost his mind, Anna with fear he was about to say the wrong thing.

He did.

I don't want to be barron. He still misspelled the word. *I want to marry Anna.*

Marry Anna? Eleanor glanced at her, the confusion on her face reflected in Anna's horrified gaze.

Apparently, she hadn't understood Desmond's remarks. *What are you talking about?*

A barron can't marry a country doctor's daughter. Therefore I want to not be a barron. I love Anna.

Oh. I see. Eleanor's fingers fell to her lap. She studied them.

Carefully, Anna set down her teacup, her hands clenched in her lap. She waited for the outburst, the denunciation.

Instead, Eleanor asked, *Is this…serious?*

Anna didn't move. David took a step toward her, body tensing. She put up a hand. It struck his thigh, stopping his approach. He stood still.

I go to her room every night…

She gave him an imploring look. *David. No.*

He ignored it. *Stay until dawn.*

Anna buried her face in her hands.

You…and Anna… Eleanor's hands shook. She looked at Anna whose eyes met hers over her fingertips before glancing away, face brilliant crimson.

Anna's hands slid to her mouth, stopping its trembling. Eleanor looked up at David.

I hadn't realized you were aware of… How long have you been doing…this?

Since the day everyone came for class, David supplied before Anna could answer.

He caught her hand, bringing it to his lips. Too frightened to react, Anna didn't pull away but let it lie listlessly in his grasp.

Are you angry, Elly? David's fingers slashed the words as if they were a challenge. *I may as well confess. I smoke and drink, too.*

Eleanor took a deep breath. *I'm sorry. It's taking me*

a moment to accept the fact my brother's a rake.

Do all these things plus my loving Anna make me a libertine? That last word was meticulously spelled.

I'm afraid it does, dear, she answered. One corner of her mouth twitched. She bit her lower lip to stop it.

Anna had the startling notion she was about to laugh. *Is she going into hysteria?*

"Please, Eleanor…" She spoke aloud. "David's not…"

"*You* didn't seduce *him*, did you?" Eleanor shot her a sharp gaze.

"Well, no…but…"

"Then he was the one…" The look she turned on David held a confusion of emotions…wonder…horror…*happiness*?

Could it be?

My little brother… Her hands came up in a flurry of words. *…unable to hear or speak, yet he's a womanizer…*

Not a womanizer. David corrected. *I love Anna and no one else.*

At the moment, that isn't important. With a stern set to her mouth, Eleanor waved David's amorous activities aside. *We'll speak of that later. I daresay this is something serious that must be dealt with, but not just now.* Fixing him with a gimlet eye, she continued, *This problem with Desmond is…* She fumbled a moment, then spelled the word, *…paramount.*

I'm sorry I didn't pay attention before, David truly looked apologetic.

Desmond has managed to have the competency hearing moved up. It's to be next week instead of six months from now.

"Oh, no." Anna breathed. "How could he manage that?"

"By convincing His Honor that David's condition isn't going to change and waiting six months wouldn't make a difference." Eleanor's laugh was a harsh, ironic bark. "My opinion is that our cousin's creditors refused to be held at bay any longer." She looked at David, signing, *Do you now understand how important it is that you learn to communicate as well as possible?*

Not all of it. He made a gesture indicating his uncertainty.

If the judge decides you aren't capable of being Baron Mayfield and awards the title to Desmond, we'll be turned out…penniless.

Good.

Don't say that. If you care for Anna, you'll need money to keep her.

Keep me? Anna started at that but forced herself to stay silent.

Already thought of that. I'll go to Mr. Brown, ask to work as a groom. I know horses.

True, you do, she agreed. *You seem to have thought that part out, and it's very well and good for you, but what about me? I've no training for anything except being a lady…and there's Shelton and the others to think about.*

Won't they stay here?

Didn't you see what he said? Desmond intends to dismiss everyone. I'm certain he won't give them characters. They won't be able to find new positions. Shelton's too old.

David's expression said plainly he hadn't thought how his losing the title might affect others.

You have to be baron, David. You have to keep your title, and your fortune, for all our sakes. Too many people count on you.

But I don't want... He turned away, leaning against the table, fingers silently drumming a tattoo against its polished top.

Neither Eleanor nor Anna moved except to glance at each other. Anna was shaken to see there was no hatred in Eleanor's eyes.

Anna thought back to what she'd said...*If you care for Anna...* Did that mean Eleanor accepted their relationship? Or was she merely sweeping it aside for the present, concentrating on the more important thing first, as she said? Then she remembered the rest of that sentence...*you'll need money to keep her...* and realized David's sister was relegating her to the position of her brother's mistress. She sighed.

What else could I expect?

What are we waiting for? There was a change, not only in David's expression, but also in his manner. *I have to learn to speak, that's all there is to it.* He looked determined, yet also eager to accept the challenge. He dropped onto the couch. *We'll start directly after dinner. For now, I want you two to go to your rooms and rest.*

It was evidence how shaken they were that neither Anna nor Eleanor protested his ordering them about, but mutely nodded, stood, and went out together.

They'd no sooner left the parlor than David caught the bell-pull, giving it a vicious jerk.

Shelton appeared in the doorway. He saw David was alone, noted his expression, then signed hesitantly, *Sir...you rang?*

Bring me a bottle of Papa's brandy, Shelton, David

ordered. *I need a drink.*

Sir? Shelton didn't move.

You heard me.

But Master David, Lady Eleanor doesn't allow…

I'm the master here, not my sister. The movement of David's fingers was so forceful, Shelton visibly started. *Bring me some* grape marc. *Now.*

Yes, sir. Shaking his head in wonder and foreboding, Shelton exited the parlor, hurrying to the wine cellars.

****

Anna didn't speak until they reached the stairs.

"Eleanor…I'd like to explain…"

"Later," Eleanor interrupted. "We'll discuss what your relationship with my brother means—and where it may lead—later. Right now, Desmond is the problem."

With that, she hurried up the stairs, leaving Anna standing there.

Chapter 30

David's determination was evident the moment he arrived in the dining room. Barely giving either woman time to be seated, he raised his hands.

I've decided I won't wait until after dinner. Lessons begin now. He looked from Eleanor to Anna as if expecting argument.

That may be a trifle difficult. Anna immediately gave him the opposition he anticipated. She had been sitting in excruciating silence, avoiding glancing at Eleanor for fear of what she might see in her expression.

Oh? How? He looked on guard as well as a little surprised. He hadn't believed an argument would come from *her*.

It's going to be awkward to sign and eat at the same time. We can do one or the other but not both. Your first lesson will also involve other things, she added, then wished she hadn't said that.

Very well then. To Anna's relief, David didn't pounce on the chance to say something suggestive but accepted her statement, hurrying on, *There's something I must do first.*

What's that, dear? Eleanor asked. With forced calm, she'd picked up her soup spoon but immediately put it down again to wave the question at him.

Do you have your slates?

Of course. Eleanor's lay by her place. She held it up.

Anna took hers from her pocket, doing the same.

Good. Moving from his place, David walked first to Anna and then to his sister, taking the slates from their hands. He returned to his chair, set both objects in it, and pulled his own from around his neck. *We won't need these any more.*

What are you going to do? Anna asked.

David didn't answer. Instead, he took all three slates, raised them above his head, and hurled them against the hearth. There was a sharp, brittle crash as the thin plates struck the marble tiles and shattered.

Using the toe of his boot, David nudged them together.

Remove those, Edward. From now on, there will be no more writing. Only Signing…or speaking. David dropped into his chair and picked up his spoon. He glanced at the bowl of soup Edward had placed before him. *Now let's eat…but hurry.*

He began to spoon the soup into his mouth, swallowing loudly.

Not too quickly, Eleanor warned. *No sense getting dyspepsia. Being uncomfortable while you're being taught won't help.*

David didn't reply. He simply dipped his spoon into the soup again, though his next swallow was a bit quieter.

****

After possibly the fastest meal ever consumed, Anna found herself with David in the library.

I'm going upstairs to rest, Eleanor told them. During the meal, she had kept her attention centered on David, avoiding looking at Anna at all. For Anna, that was a very disturbing sensation, especially when compared to Eleanor's warm treatment before David's announcement.

As she left, Eleanor told them, *I believe I'm getting a headache. Nervous exhaustion, no doubt. Besides, I imagine David will do better without an audience.* With that she was up the stairs, calling for Jane to bring her some tea.

David didn't wait for her to be out of sight. He whirled, gesturing, *Where do we begin?*

I was going to start your advanced lessons, Anna answered, *which include lip-reading. You can already do that to a certain extent, can't you?*

She noticed how intently he kept his gaze on her fingers.

He nodded and looked up. *I enjoy reading your lovely lips, Anna.* He leaned toward her.

She backed away, leaving him kissing air. *You can't do that and learn at the same time.*

Can't I? He caught her about the waist, delivering a very firm kiss to her lips. *There. Kissed Anna. Now, learn.* He made a permissive gesture.

Very well, then. Anna became very businesslike. *From now on, whenever you Sign, you'll also speak. I'm also going to speak without Signing.* She dropped her hands, saying aloud, "Do you understand?"

David's gaze went from her hands to her mouth, then back again. Plainly he expected her to sign and when she didn't, he frowned.

"Do you understand me?" Anna said. "If so, repeat what I just said."

There was a very long silence. As Anna decided he wasn't going to say anything, David spoke, hesitantly, "D-do…yuh…unnerstaand…meh." He smiled, fingers asking, *Was that correct?*

"Yes." Anna returned the smile, unconsciously raising her hands. His voice was as flat as ever, completely without inflection, so the words weren't a question though they were fairly intelligible. She forced herself not to Sign, saying instead, "Very good. Now, let's go over some daily phrases."

Once again, she went through the common words a person used in everyday speech, *Good morning, How are you, My name is…* Once or twice, she spoke a word David didn't know. As his hands came up, spelling out *I don't know that* into a pause in the sentence, before speaking the rest, she would repeat it, then spell it for him.

They worked for three hours before Anna called a halt.

"Nuh…" David protested. "Nuh stop…keep goin'."

"We need to take a rest," Anna replied. "There's no need to exhaust ourselves."

"Nuh, Ah-na." David shook his head, fingers waving angrily.

"Very well." Anna sighed. She reached for the bell pull. "We'll have some tea. I don't know about you, but I need some fortification." For David's benefit, she spelled out *fortification.*

He agreed with a nod, waiting impatiently, tapping a forefinger against the desk until Shelton arrived.

The old man came through the door, saying, "Was there something, Miss Anna?"

Before Anna could reply. David put a hand on her arm, touching his chest. *I'll answer*, his fingers told her. Nodding, Anna remained silent.

David turned to Shelton.

"We wan' tea, Zelton." Realizing he mispronounced

the butler's name, David grimaced.

Mentally, Anna made a note to coach him on the *"sh"* sound.

"Pliss…bring it…an'…" He stopped, scowled fiercely, then looked at Anna, fingers moving rapidly. *I don't know bizcats.*

Bizcats? What? Anna thought quickly, then spelled the word she thought he meant. *Biscuits?*

"Biz…coo…its," David looked from her to Shelton, speaking the word phonetically.

Fortunately, the butler understood. He nodded.

"Speak out loud, Shelton," Anna whispered, though David was looking away from her at that moment.

Nodding, the old man said, "Very good, sir. Right away."

He hurried out.

"'ow…that?" David looked at her.

"He understood. So it was good," Anna told him, thinking to herself, *I must pay attention to "h,"also. He doesn't pronounce that letter at all.*

She remembered her father taking her and Maisie on a trip to London one time. The man who'd driven the coach had spoken that way. "Drops his *aitches*," Papa had said, adding the man was a Cockney, born within the sound of Bow Bells, the bells of the church of St. Mary-le-Bow.

"Now we wait." David flung himself into one of the chairs by the fire, slouching with long legs thrust in front of him. That blocked the way to the other chair.

Very carefully, Anna stepped over his ankles and seated herself. She slapped one ankle with her hand. "Sit up. Gentlemen don't slouch."

That wasn't true. She'd seen many of the young men

in Little Riversreach, both farm boys and gentlemen alike, lolling in sprawls when they thought no one saw, but David didn't have to know that.

Reluctantly, he straightened. "Westin'…not slouch."

R…Anna noted. *He has problems with "r."*

He gave her a belligerent look, prepared to argue the semantics of the words. Fortunately, Jane's entry with the tea tray prevented that.

"Zhane…pour pliss…" David didn't give Anna time to speak.

As Jane stared at him, amazed by his speaking with no signing, he gestured, and that broke the spell. Jane reached for the teapot, filling each cup, asking their preferences for sugar or cream, which David answered with a nod at the proper moments. Once they had their cups and Jane was sent on her way with a "D'ank yuh," Anna made another mental note.

Also needs help with "th."

David gulped his tea and had his cup and saucer back on the tray before Anna had taken the first sip.

"Be quick, Ah-na." He waited impatiently while Anna sipped slowly and deliberately.

At last, the tea was consumed, her cup returned to the tray. Seizing her hands, David jerked Anna to her feet. Before she could protest that rough treatment, he kissed an apology. "Now d'en…back tuh lesson…"

"Truly, David, you're doing very well. Progressing faster than one might expect. Perhaps we should stop for today…"

He gave her a frustrated frown. She'd been speaking too fast. He'd lost comprehension after "progressing." She repeated what she'd said, speaking more slowly and adding Signing to it.

Immediately he shook his head. "Nuh, nuh…keep goin'."

They did, for another hour more, until Eleanor appeared in the doorway, showing surprise they were still at it and announcing it was time for dinner.

David wasn't ready to stop. Once at his place in the dining room, he studied the platters and servers upon the table, reciting the name of each while Signing them, then looking to Anna for approval.

"It's amazing," Eleanor said. "If only I'd thought to do this directly after the accident, Desmond would have no room for his claim."

"…but Ah would not 'aff met Ah-na…" David interjected.

Eleanor didn't answer.

"Why don't we simply make small talk during the meal?" Anna suggested. She was startled to hear the timid tone in which she spoke, as if fearing Eleanor might order her from the table if she raised her voice.

David looked a bit rebellious at her suggestion, but she quickly quelled that with, "It's acceptable and customary." She spelled *customary*.

With a loud sigh, David sat, snapping, "Serve, Zelton." He waited until all plates were filled, then, as if uncertain it was a proper subject, said, "Askin' Wobert tuh wide Wun. No time fuh me do it."

His problem with 'r' was quite evident.

Oh, there's so much to teach him…and we've only a week. It generally took a full year for a student to confidently grasp the elementary skills of Signing and speaking. Anna wondered if she could possibly succeed.

Somehow, she managed to convince David to cut

the after-dinner session short. He protested, but she feigned exhaustion. Looking contrite, he acquiesced.

There was a preliminary and very basic covering of the letters he either couldn't pronounce or spoke incorrectly.

She began by letting him become accustomed to sounds, even if he couldn't hear them, taking one of his hands and placing it on her throat, thumb on one side of her larynx, fore and middle fingers on the other. She put the two fingers of his left hand on her lips. He immediately looked delighted, trailing his fingers across her lower lip while stroking her throat.

She slapped his fingers, catching his hands. "Lesson. Be serious."

His expression changed. Nodding, he raised his brows, letting his hands relax in her grip.

Anna began making the sounds of the alphabet. "A-A-A...Ah-Ah-Ah..." repeating them to accustom David to the *feel* of the sounds against his fingers. She had him speak them also, while touching his own throat.

She made it a game: She'd make a sound. He'd copy it.

At first, David's voice was very harsh, almost rasping. His lack of inflection made it seem even more so. Even as they progressed, his tone didn't change, making Anna wonder if perhaps his actual speaking voice would be rough and hoarse.

Definitely not smooth and cultured, but that's the least of our worries.

Not being able to hear, he spoke everything very low and soft. It wasn't an unpleasant sound. In fact, Anna forced herself to ignore the tremor that very quiet, husky near-whisper sent down her spine.

Once he's mastered speaking, I must teach him to raise his voice a bit.

"R," Anna said.

Taking one of David's hands, she placed it on her throat, then touched his other hand to her lips.

"R," Anna repeated. "R-r-r-r…" She pulled David's hand from her throat and placed it in the same position on his own and said again, "R-r-r-r," and nodded.

There was another of those blank stares. She could imagine him thinking, *Why are you growling? What do you want me to do?*

Moving his hand from her lips to her throat, she repeated the sound, exaggerating it so there was a deep vibration from her larynx. She tightened her own hand around his.

He gave her a startled glance, then began to simply make sounds. Somehow, the R-sound got into the mix. As soon as she heard it, Anna jerked her hand away. He stopped. She replaced it and again said, "R-r-r."

David repeated it.

"Robert," she said, moving her hand away to spell the name.

He nodded, dropping his hand. "Wobert."

She shook her head, again seizing his hand and replacing it, lifting the other to her throat. "R-R-Robert."

"Wo…" he began again, then stopped as Anna shook her head and made the "r" sound. "R-R-Robert."

"That's right."

"Robert…Robert…" David repeated the groom's' name, then stopped. His brows went down in a scowl. "Not Wobert. R-R-Robert."

"Yes."

"Robert." This time he said the name with a finality

making her know he understood. He smiled. "R-R-Robert r-r-ride R-R-Run."

"Fine, now let's see about 'h,'" she told him.

That one was more difficult. There was no sound involved, no vibration in the throat.

"Repeat this," Anna signed. "She held my heart in her hands."

Head cocked to one side, David stared at her as if she were making a joke. She was reminded of the way a friend's little terrier responded to something puzzling him. If he'd whimpered as Bosco always did, she wouldn't have been surprised.

Abruptly, he said, "She…'eld muh…'eart in 'er 'ands," and waited.

Anna's, "No, that isn't correct" wasn't the answer he was expecting. His frown went into a deep, dark scowl.

"Nuh? 'ow?"

Pressing his fingers to her lips, Anna exaggerated pronouncing the words, letting him feel the puff of air making up the "h" sound. "She HUH-eld my HUH-eart in HUH-er HUH-ands."

The scowl stayed in place as she pressed David's other hand to his own lips.

"You say it."

"She 'eld…" he began, only to break off as Anna shook her head.

"Huh…HUH-eld," she repeated.

"Huh…" He puffed against his fingers. "Huh…huh…"

"Say it." Anna went on, "HUH-eart."

"HUH-eart."

She smiled. "Good. Now say the sentence."

Taking a deep breath, David said, "She HUH-eld muh HUH-eart in 'er 'and."

"Almost," Anna told him. "Huh-er, huh-and."

Dutifully, he repeated the words correctly.

"Oh, David!" She pulled away, squeezing his hands. "You're doing so well. I'm proud of you."

Briefly, she forget where they were, wrapping her arms around his waist in a tight hug. The moment his own arms closed about her, she realized her mistake. She pushed out of his embrace.

He didn't let her get away, loosening his hold only enough for her to step back slightly. Seizing her hand, he pressed her fingers against his lips, breath huffing gently against them in a heated wave.

"You HUH-old muh HUH-eart in your HUH-and, a'r-r-ready, Ah-na."

Anna had no answer for that.

"Rest. Now." He pushed her away, dipping his head in a short bow, then left her standing there, hand raised as if it still touched his lips.

Chapter 31

In his room, David paced, thinking over all that had happened that day. Anna might say he was doing well, but he was very aware of the passage of time, the short number of days before he'd stand in front of the circuit magistrate who would decide not only his fate but also that of his entire household, perhaps even Mayfield Village itself .

I need to learn faster. Common sense told him that was impossible, unless Anna taught him nonstop, day and night. That couldn't happen because neither of them would last very long without sleeping or eating.

A *cigarito* and a glass of Papa's brandy, not the *grape marc* Shelton had supplied him but the last of that David had taken from the cellar, didn't help.

No solution came to mind. David decided he'd simply have to cram as many lessons as possible into a day, beginning before breakfast and continuing several hours after dinner. He had to make every minute a learning experience. For now, however…

He was going to see Anna. No matter how desperate the situation or what they had to accomplish as teacher and pupil, the night was for lovers…theirs alone, for private moments. David liked making love to Anna. He savored their closeness, the warmth of her body and the indescribable sensations it gave him. He wasn't going to let anything distract him from being with her every night.

He also decided he was no longer going to hide their association because, as far as he was concerned, it was nothing to be ashamed of or to keep secret. Tonight, therefore, he wasn't going to climb a tree or crawl through a window to be with the woman he loved.

Undressing and making a hasty *toilette* at the ironstone basin on his dressing table, he put on his nightshirt, and took his dressing gown from the wardrobe.

Buttoning the double-breasted front, he smoothed the wide lapels, studying himself briefly in the cheval glass. One hand came up, finger-combing his tousled hair and smoothing the damp curls into waves.

With a pleased nod, he picked up the single candlestick holder on the table, opened the door, and walked into the hall. His bare feet made no sound on the thick carpeting as he went down the stairs to the second story and Anna's room.

****

Helped into her nightclothes by Jane, Anna dozed in the chair by the fire. She was bone-weary, as if she'd done manual labor. She was certain the feeling was merely nervous exhaustion, like that Eleanor claimed. The tension of knowing what she had to do and the time limit in which to do it had already begun to wear.

David accomplished so much today. Surely if I tell the judge that, he'll admit there's no doubt of David's intelligence or mental capability.

Immediately, she knew that wouldn't work. His Honor would probably think she was merely fabricating to save David. She doubted if he'd believe Eleanor or any of the servants either, since all had a stake in David being declared competent. Any testimony in that direction would have to come from someone outside the household, someone uninvolved.

She decided not to think of that for a while, if that were possible, and was debating as to getting out of the chair and going to bed when there was a quiet knocking at the door.

"Who is it?"

There was no answer. The sound came again, a very soft, evenly spaced rapping this time.

"Who… Oh, no!" Anna ran to the door, jerking it open.

Lit by the candle in his hand, David stood there. He was wearing a dark blue brocaded dressing gown, its wide collar trimmed in gold braid matching the four large gold buttons at the waist. Through the open front, she could see the elaborate smocking on the yoke of his nightshirt, and his bare legs and feet where the shirt stopped a few inches below his knees.

"Ah cooom in?" he whispered and walked past her.

She pushed the door shut, waiting until he set down the candle and turned to face her before she said, "You shouldn't have come by the hallway."

She was glad she could speak aloud to him now, even if Signing did accompany it.

"Not coomin' t'rough duh window ever again," he informed her, glancing at the closed shutters and shaking his head. He held out his arms. "Glad tuh see me? Coom HUH-ere."

She went into his arms eagerly, desperately, meeting his kiss with one of her own. His hair was damp, his skin cool. He'd bathed, or at least taken a basin-bath…and shaved. She brushed fingers across a smooth cheek. A wisp of sandalwood wafted toward her.

She inhaled. He smiled.

"You laak? Sanda'wood…ap'rodisiac." He didn't bother trying to spell that word.

His mispronunciation made her smile.

"Ah say it wrong?"

"How do you know of aphrodisiacs?" She sidestepped his question.

"R-r-read in Papa's book…*Pornografia Mundus*…makes women want men."

"You don't need it," she informed him.

"Nuh?"

"I already want you."

He pushed her away, stalked to the commode where Anna's own ironstone pitcher and basin sat. Pouring water into the basin, he cupped his hands, splashing his face and neck, scrubbing industriously with his fingers while Anna hid her laugh behind her hands as it soaked into the neck of his nightshirt and the collar of the dressing gown. Lifting the towel from its little ring at the side of the chest, he dried his face, then came back to her.

"Dere…only me…all bare."

"Not quite," Anna whispered.

"Nuh?" He thought a moment, then held up a finger as if he had an idea. It was amazing how quickly his fingers opened the dressing gown, letting it fall to the floor. Stooping, he caught the tail of the nightshirt, pulled it over his head and tossed it to the floor.

"Dere." David spread his arms. "Now only me."

"You still need to work on 'th.'" Anna kissed him.

"Nuh lesson t'night," David told her in that husky whisper. He slid an arm behind her knees, the other going to her shoulders. She was lifted off the floor as he turned to the bed. "Knuh HUH-ow tuh do dis just fine."

Chapter 32

"You've changed," Anna said.

They'd made love in the brightness of lamplight. By mutual but unspoken consent, neither she nor David dimmed either the lamp by the bed or the one next to Anna's chair near the fire. Anna wanted to see David's responses as much as he wanted to say them to her.

"Not changed," he corrected, positioning himself so he could see her lips. "Same me."

"You're *not* the same," she argued, turning so they lay facing each other on the pillows. "You're different somehow. I don't know what it is, David, but you aren't as you were this morning…before Desmond came."

"Desmond…" He fell silent, face in a grimace of dislike. "Can I kill HUH-im?"

"Ki—David, no!" Shocked, she caught his shoulders, grasping tightly. "Don't even think that."

"Solve our problems."

"And make worse ones." His answer made Anna remember her thoughts on David's morality…remember and revise. Apparently, he had none.

"How?" He looked as if he really wanted to know. "Desmond be gone."

"And so would you." Her grip became even tighter. She saw him wince slightly, his own hand going over the one on his arm. "Don't you know what they do to murderers?"

"Not murder," he corrected. "Jus' kill HUH-im."

"That *is* murder."

He looked surprised. "Tuh kill pest?"

She hurried on, "David, they'd arrest you, and…if they didn't hang you, they'd put you away somewhere and you…all of us…would be even worse off than if Desmond is given your title." She bit back a sob. "Please…please, stop that kind of thinking right now!"

"Sorry, Ah-na," He wiped away a tear with his thumb. "Don' cry. Ah won' HUH-urt Desmond. Lahk tuh, but…won'."

"Thank you." She breathed out those two words and hugged him tightly.

"Ah-na? Tell you secret?" His question was muffled against her hair.

"Of course." She raised her head.

"Ah'm afraid." His voice sank so low she barely heard it.

"We're all afraid of something, David."

"Not yuh," he answered. "Not Elly. Bot' strong…"

"Yes, both of us are afraid," Anna replied. She touched his cheek, fingers rubbing gently across his jawline. "We're worried about you, and the trial, and…"

"Yuh don' show it." He pulled away, raising his hands.

As if he didn't want her to hear his words, he began to Sign. *I'm afraid of what's going to happen. I ask myself what would Papa do and I don't have an answer. I barely remember my father and I don't ever remember his facing anything like this. My Uncle William never wanted his title. My Aunt Estella would be shocked. I don't know what to do and you say I can't kill Desmond…Anna, all I want is to be with you and stay as we are now. What must I do?*

"Stop this kind of talk." Anna caught his face in her hands. "You *are* brave. To have lived for as long as you have, not hearing a sound, not speaking…now you can speak, and communicate, and…you've loved, David, and you *are* loved…by me, your sister, the servants, the people in the village. I admire your courage in learning all you have so quickly, of retaining the few memories you have. The judge will, too. He'll see how smart you are, and he'll make the right decision."

What if he doesn't? David refused to be lifted from his pessimistic mood.

"Then…I guess I'll find myself married to one of Mr. Brown's grooms." She kissed him.

He pulled away to laugh and flick his fingers against his heart and his forehead. *Love you, Anna.*

"If you really love me, say it," Anna answered. "I want to hear you tell me."

"Ah…luff…yuh…Ah-na." He punctuated each word with a kiss, to her eyelids, the tip of her nose, her mouth. Cuddling her close, he pulled up the sheet, tucking it around them. "Ah've nothin' tuh worry abou'."

Oh, God, please let me be telling the truth, Anna prayed silently as she snuggled into David's arms.

"Ah wish muh parents could've met yuh, Ah-na," he whispered, the same words he'd said before.

"Do you remember much about them? At all?" she asked, turning slightly so he could see as she spoke.

"Ah barely 'member Mama." His answer was apologetic. "Ah'm 'shamed."

"You were so young," she said.

"Bad son not 'member mother. Ah 'member Papa

better." That admission was even sadder. "Ah member he HUH-ad black HUH-air…like mine…an' he was tall. 'Least Ah t'ought so. Tuh me, he looked lahk a gian'. He lahked cigars an' brandy." David smiled. "He used tuh tiptoe to Mama, put his arms 'round HUH-er an' kiss HUH-er on de back of de neck. She'd act angry. 'HUH-orace, stop tha'!'"

There was sudden inflection in his voice as he repeated what his mother had said.

"But she smiled an' Ah knew she lakhed it." He paused as if thinking. "Papa lahked HUH-orses, too. HUH-ee promised me a pony fuh muh birt'day."

There was a soft sigh.

"Dat was de las' t'ing HUH-ee said tuh me."

"You don't remember anything about the accident?" Anna hated asking him. She despised her curiosity but told herself perhaps it was better if she knew.

"Nuh. Ah 'member we were at de car-r-rridge. Nanny HUH-eld muh HUH-and. Ah waited for Mama and HUH-er to get intuh de car-r-riage an' Papa said, "Dat's a good boy, Davy." Again, David's voice rose and fell, changing to a normal intonation as he repeated his father's words. "Yuh a li'l gennulman, an' a gennulman needs HUH-is own HUh-orse. What if Ah get yuh one for yur birt-day?"

David's arms tightened around Anna.

"Den we got intuh de car-r-riage, an' ever'one went away…'cept me."

Something struck Anna's hand. She looked down at the single tear sliding across her fingers.

"Oh, David, I'm so sorry…" Now it was her turn to wipe tears off his cheeks.

"Next' t'ing Ah 'member, muh HUH-ead HUH-urt

an' Ah cried…Ah knuh Ah did but Ah couldn't hear it. Ah opened muh eyes an' saw Elly and she spoke tuh me but Ah couldn't HUH-ear her, so Ah cried some more. Later, she wrote on muh slate an' explained. Ah still tried tuh ta'k but Ah couldn't HUH-ear muh own voice an' soon Ah forgot words, lahk Ah'm forgettin' Mama an' Papa. Dey neffer HUH-ad a portrait painted an' now Ah can't 'member HUH-ow dey look."

Pulling her toward him, David kissed Anna's forehead.

"Yuh made de words come back, Ah-na. Ah wish yuh could make Mama an' Papa come back."

"I wish I could, too." Anna sat up, eyes meeting his. "Be sure of this, David. Your father was right about one thing. You *are* a gentleman."

Chapter 33

"Yuh unnerstan' why Ah mus' duh dis?" David regarded both Eleanor and Anna with more than a little exasperation. "Why yuh be dif'cult?"

At breakfast, he informed them he was riding to the village, and if there were any horses to be shod, or Cook needed any staples for the kitchen, he would do those chores also.

"No," Eleanor spoke up. "I don't understand. Robert tends the horses, and while we may need items for the pantry, if there's any chance Desmond may come out the winner in this trial, I certainly am not going to provide him with food. Let him buy his own!"

"Ah don' care if Desmond starves," David replied. "Dis is for me." He turned to Anna. "Yuh unnerstand?"

"I believe I do," Anna answered. As Eleanor began another protest, she explained, "I think what David means is that he has to prove he can go to the village alone…"

"He's been to the village many times," Eleanor interrupted. "While he wasn't truly *alone*, I often gave him permission to set off by himself and visit the smithy and Albert and James. Why does he have to do it again? Now?"

"…he has to go alone," Anna repeated, patiently. "To make certain he can use his new skill in communicating with people more or less strangers, without you or me nearby to rescue him if he has problems." She looked up at David. "You want to test yourself, don't you? To see exactly how you handle yourself?"

He nodded. "Dis make me se'f-'ficient, Elly. Don' yuh see?"

"Of course I do, David," his sister admitted with a defeated sigh. "I suppose I'm simply afraid to let you…"

"Ah ride in de woods alone. Gone from morn' to noon." His fingers moved defiantly, then stilled.

"You're right," Eleanor surrendered. "You and Horse have been over most of this section of the shire on both sides of the highroad. Alone." She gave an ironic little laugh. "You're no different than you were on those occasions, except now, you can talk. I should've been more frightened for you before, I guess."

"Good." He patted her shoulder and smiled. "Now then…duh yuh haff list?"

Anna noted he made a distinct effort not to huff his "h." "Have" came out almost naturally. He'd also conquered the "R" problem.

"Of course I do," Eleanor answered. "I was merely being difficult. It's in the library on the desk. I'll get it."

She hurried down the hall.

"Glad yuh unnerstan'." David looked at Anna.

"I won't lie and say I'm not anxious," Anna replied. She placed a hand on David's arm, saying, without Signing. "Is it all right if I worry? A tiny bit?"

"Why?" His fingers moved in a way she could only described as *laughing*…at her worry. "Not goin' tuh be…" He frowned and spelled out w-a-y-l-a-i-d. "…by highwaymen. None uh dose here." Again the "h" was normally accented. He looked toward the library. "Shall

Ah carry one uh Papa's pistols?" He aimed a forefinger, squinted along it and tapped his thumb against his knuckle as if releasing the trigger. "Make yuh happy?"

"I think that would make me worry more," Anna admitted. "Do you know how to fire a gun?"

David shook his head, shrugging. "Easy. Point an' fire." Again, his fingers pantomimed the movement.

"Here it is." Eleanor's return forestalled Anna's reply. She held out a small sheet of paper on which several words were visible. "Give it to Mr. Greeley, and—"

"Know what tuh duh, Elly." David's tone might be flat but it held obvious impatience.

"Of course you do," Eleanor answered. "How many times have you gone with me?"

"'Zactly." Plucking the list from his sister's hand, David folded it and tucked it into the hip pocket of his riding breeches. He bowed to her and Anna and aimed himself for the closest door exiting onto the back of the house and the way to the stables.

"I'll worry about him every minute until he returns," Eleanor whispered.

"If it's any consolation," Anna said. "So shall I."

She couldn't interpret the look Eleanor turned on her.

After a moment, she said, "When this business is over, you and I must have a talk."

A brief *zing* of fear slid through Anna.

"Very well." What else could she say? She didn't ask the subject. She was afraid she knew.

"I thought to do some reading while I waited," Eleanor went on. "If you care to join me…" She turned away.

"Thank you. I would," Anna frowned at this abrupt change of subject. *First, she makes that cryptic remark, now invites me to sit with her?* "I need to write my father. I'm afraid I've neglected letting him know I arrived safely. I got so involved with David's lessons."

Eleanor stopped, looking back over her shoulder. "Yes, you've definitely been very busy. With David's…lessons."

The *zing* turned into a cold stab. Anna decided it would be best if she didn't answer.

"There's plenty of writing paper in the library," Eleanor continued. "You may sit at the desk and catch up on your correspondence while I read."

She continued down the hall.

"Thank you." Anna followed, forcing out the dire thoughts crowding into her mind.

****

It was a beautiful day to ride, David thought. Briefly, he wished Anna was with him. Elly, also. *Too bad we don't have other riding horses.* He'd like to ride through the woods with his sister and his woman trotting beside him.

A grin tilted his lips. He supposed Anna would object to being called 'his woman.'

What should I call her? My angel? My heart?

There were plenty of words in Papa's book to describe the woman a man loved, but from their context, David decided none of those were appropriate for Anna. Oh, well. Sooner or later, the correct one would come along.

In the meantime…

Perhaps when this is over, if I'm still Baron Mayfield, I can buy Elly and Anna horses. I don't even

251

know if Anna can ride. If I'm one of Mr. Brown's grooms, perhaps he'll let her ride his horses occasionally, if I do a good job for him. David shook his head. *None of that. I'm going to win this case, and then…*

He allowed himself a moment of fancy. His fist colliding with Cousin Desmond's head and his cousin tumbling bum-over-heels into the dust, perhaps coming to rest in a mud puddle or a pile of horse dung.

That happy thought stayed with him until he arrived at the outskirts of Mayfield Village.

First off, he decided to deliver Eleanor's list. He made his way to Greeley's Mercantile. It was still early morning, but a good many people were already out and about. A couple recognized and nodded to him but didn't speak, and David returned their gestures as silently.

In front of the store, a youngster of around ten lounged against the wall. David recognized him as Mr. Greeley's youngest, Robert, nicknamed Robin.

Arms crossed over his chest, eyes shut, Robin appeared to be dozing in the morning sun. He wasn't barefoot as most of the village children at this time of year. Instead, he wore scuffed but well-made boots, and stockings tucked under the kneebands of his breeches. As David dismounted, he roused, and fairly leaped forward, hands reaching for the reins.

Slowly, his fingers said, *Hold your horse, sir?*

Apparently, Mr. Greeley had relayed his knowledge of Signing to his offspring.

With a nod, David released the reins into his hands. Robin looked past him, saying something. David turned in time to see a short, slender, white-haired gentleman coming hurriedly toward them. He was dressed drably, in dark knee breeches, stockings, and buckled shoes. A tight-fitting weskit with at least two dozen buttons was visible in the front of his morning coat, some of them hidden by the single layer of neckcloth wrapped around his throat and flapping down his chest. Between buttons and swath of linen bounced a small cross on a silver chain.

David waited for him to pass. Instead the gentleman stopped and spoke.

"Your Lordship? It *is* Baron Mayfield, isn't it?"

Recognition set in. Understanding of what he'd said came a moment later. David smiled.

"Good mornin', Rev'ern Morse." He made certain he didn't growl his "r," and also didn't Sign since he was certain the minister couldn't read Signing anyway. He hadn't been to any of Anna's classes.

The minister's reaction was comical. He stopped short, taking a step backward as if David had aimed a fist at his chin. His mouth dropped open.

"Sweet mercy! Did you speak or are my ears playing tricks on me?"

Stifling a laugh, David nodded. Robin wasn't so well-mannered.

"That he did, Reverend. My da says His Lordship can talk as good as us'n now he's got a teacher."

"Teacher? What's this?" The pastor looked back to David.

"Miss Ah-na Leighton," David explained. "Teacher of deaf."

"She's pretty, my da says," Robin supplied. He juggled the reins, carefully Signing out those words for David's benefit. The pastor frowned at the movement of the boy's hands.

David nodded his agreement to that, then put his

hand over the boy's fingers to forestall any further compliments. He didn't want anyone else speaking of Anna in such a way. He looked back at Morse.

"It's a miracle." The pastor touched his cross.

"Nuh mir-cle," David disagreed, shaking his head. "Ah-na."

"Ah, but some divine power must've sent her to you," Morse argued. He placed a hand on David's shoulder. "Oh, my boy, you don't know how many nights I prayed for something like this to happen."

David thought about that a moment. Before his accident, he'd been too small to grasp the concept of a divine entity. Afterward, seeing him fidget while being forced to sit in his prison of silence during those interminable sermons, Eleanor discontinued going to church altogether rather than leave him at home while she attended. A couple of times curiosity sent him attempting to read the family Bible, though most of the words were too difficult or archaic to comprehend. He'd grasped the story of Adam and Eve and the Serpent, but the rest was beyond him, though he liked the engravings and illustrations, especially one of an angel appearing before a young boy.

Perhaps the pastor's right. Perhaps Someone did send Anna to me. David decided that after this business with Desmond, he would speak to Morse in more detail about that.

"Ah-na teaches me," he told the reverend. As always when he spoke of Anna, his fingers moved slower, more gently, as if he were caressing her body. "She is…wunnerful."

Caution prevented him from speaking of their true relationship. He had a definite feeling the pastor might not appreciate that. David was still surprised Eleanor was so tolerant. He wondered if the Bible mentioned anything about his relationship to Anna, and if so, exactly what it said. Perhaps he'd ask the reverend about that, too.

"I daresay, if she can performed such a miracle as helping the deaf speak," Morse returned.

"She taught me Signin'." David held up his hands.

Behind him, Robin Signed, *I can do that, too*, and the pastor looked even more surprised. "Robert? Are you speaking to Lord David? Where did you learn to…"

"Ah-na," David explained. "She had class for people in village. Tuh he'p me."

"And I missed it?" Reverend Morse was appalled. "It must have been while I was away."

David gave him an inquisitive look. After Eleanor stopped attending church, Reverend Morse had attempted a couple of visits to Mayfield Manor, only to be politely but gently rebuffed. After the third time, he'd stopped coming.

"I've been visiting my sister for a few weeks. She's been ill."

"A' right now, Ah hope?" That was the proper thing to ask, David thought. He delved deep into his memory, drawing on conversations he'd heard his parents make to their friends concerning family.

"Oh, yes, complete recovery." Morse looked around. "Where is Lady Eleanor? Could I possibly hope you and she might be returning to worship again?"

"Muh sister home. Ah no longer need her tuh chap'rone," David answered. That made Morse laugh. "Ah speak tuh her 'bout church."

He decided he wouldn't mention the trouble with

Desmond. If things didn't go well, the Reverend Morse would have his cousin to contend with soon enough. He doubted if Desmond would be eager to see the inside of a house of worship.

"Excuse...mus' duh errand for sister." He gestured to the mercantile's entrance.

"Oh, of course." Morse gave a departing bow. "I'll call at the manor soon, if I may. I'd like to meet your miracle worker."

Instead of answering, David merely bowed and walked to the store's door. Behind him, the reverend spoke a moment more to Robin, then hurried on.

Inside, David was met by Mr. Greeley, who enthusiastically Signed a greeting. *See? I haven't forgotten.*

"Ah speak now, too." David answered as he Signed those words also.

While Greeley was recovering from that, being as flabbergasted as Reverend Morse, he pulled the list from his pocket.

"From muh sister." He handed it to Mr. Greeley. "Deliver as usual."

Greeley nodded and David made his departure, signing *Goodbye* in answer to the store owner's own gestures.

Outside, David sighed, feeling his body relax. Until that moment, he hadn't realized he was tense, that he'd actually been on edge. He took back Run's reins from Robin, then dug into his pocket, producing several of those treats he always carried for the horse. They were made of strawberries, dried and crushed by Cook, then rolled into little red balls. He offered them to Robin.

"Thanks." The boy scooped them off David's palm,

tossing one into his mouth, then signing his gratitude.

With a wave of his hand, David led Run down the village's main street.

I'll stop by the smithy, see Al and Jem.

He hadn't seen his friends since the day the smith called their lessons to an end and, though he was happy in Anna's company, he missed being in the company of young men his own age, even if some people might've considered the smith's sons unacceptable companions for a baron.

Maybe I can make another horseshoe.

As far as he was concerned, meeting the Reverend Morse and then delivering Eleanor's list successfully completed his mission.

Elly worried for nothing. He decided he didn't understand sisters.

He found Al and Jem at the forge. Al was stripped to breeches, the smith's heavy leather apron shielding his bare chest from flying sparks. His face and body were shiny with sweat forced from his pores by the forge's heat. Under the eave of the little single-stall shop, Jem sat on a nearby stool, mending a harness.

"Well, now! Look here!" Al called out as David and Run came into sight. He dropped the hammer on the anvil, fingers Signing a greeting. "It's been a long time since you've darkened our doorway."

"Tha's 'cause Ah've been busy." David waited for their obvious reaction.

"Would you listen to that?" Jem barely gave him time to finish speaking. "When did you become such a chatterbox? Did you hear, Al? He's actually talkin'!"

"Who wrought this miracle?" Albert demanded, looking quite like the Reverend Morse had when he used that same word.

"Ah-na," David indiscreetly threw caution to the winds. "Muh beautiful, beloved, angel Ah-na."

"Beloved? Angel? Oh-ho!" Albert's eyes narrowed. Swiping a forearm across his forehead, he came around the anvil. ""Jem…could it be…" He glanced back at his brother. "His Lordship's discovered things every other noblemen we've heard 'bout already knows?"

"Well now." Jem abandoned the harness and stepped to his brother's side. They both stared speculatively at David.

"What else should Ah call de woman who brought me out uh darknes'?" Realizing he'd said the wrong thing, David affected that innocent look so far fooling Eleanor, Shelton, and on occasion, Anna.

"You're right." Al considered that. "If I'd been cut off from the world like you've been, I guess I'd call her an angel, too."

"Well now, Davy, what can we do for you?" Jem asked. He looked past David at Run. "Horse needin' new shoes, does he?"

"Nuh." David shook his head, silently thankful he'd managed to distract both brothers from probing further into his lyrical description of Anna. "Wanted tuh see muh chums."

"An' we're right glad you did," Jem replied.

"Where's your da?" David glanced around, noting the smith hadn't come from the back of the shop to greet him.

"I told Da to rest a bit today," Al explained. "Farmer brought in a rambunctious colt t'other day. Ne'er been shod afore. Kicked Da."

"He not hurt?" David looked anxious. He'd never

been kicked by Run or any of the coach horses, but he'd seen one of Mr. Brown's grooms injured by Charger. The man's leg was broken and he'd been bedridden, then walking with a crutch for months before he was healed again. He had a bit of a limp ever afterward, too.

"Na…Da's quick on his feet. Dodged so's only got a graze, but I told him I'd take over today an' he could rest. Decided I'm not leavin' after all. Goin' t' stay here an' work with Da an' Jem."

"Been walking out with one of Greeley's daughters," Jem confided, putting a hand to his mouth as if telling a secret.

"Truly?" David looked delighted.

"Probably be wedding bells soon," Jem went on as his brother swatted at him. "Whirlwind romance…on Al's side. Lass won't let him even kiss her."

"Nuh…" David hesitated, then decided to ask it. "Nuh grindin' corn?"

"Look, I'm sorry 'bout that," Al truly appeared repentant. "But your teacher's such a toothsome lass, an'…well…I'm knowing you're a virgin lad, Davy, so I wrongly assumed…"

David waved away his apology and held out his hand. "Happy for yuh, Al."

"Got t' get back t' work." Al caught David's hand, gave it a hearty shake, then turned back to the anvil.

"Yeah, me, too." Jem went back inside the shop.

"Use another pair o' hands?" David asked.

"If'n you want t' help repair some harness…sure," Jem replied.

Tying Run to the hitching post, David took off his coat, unwound his neckpiece, and tossed both over the first plank of the corral fence. Rolling up his sleeves, the twenty-seventh Baron Mayfield pulled a stool alongside Jem's and picked up the piece of harness needing restoration.

Chapter 34

Anna and Eleanor greeted him as he rode Run into the front courtyard.

"Where have you been?" Anna demanded. "Eleanor was getting ready to send Shelton after you."

"Visited Al an' Jem," David replied. He was abruptly aware of the sweat stains on the bosom of his shirt as well as the fact that his neckpiece wasn't as neat it had been when he left the manor. "Sat, talked, patched a harness."

"David," Eleanor reprimanded. She touched his neckcloth, frowning at the loose way it was now tied. "A baron doesn't repair harness."

"Dis baron does." David swung off Run's back, pulling the reins over the horse's head. "Ah delivered your list, saw Rev'ern' Morse…"

"Reverend Morse?" Eleanor interrupted. "What did he have to say? About you speaking?"

"Ah-na's a mir-cle worker. He want tuh meet her. When will dinner be ready? Ah'm hungry." Not giving either woman chance to say more, he led Run around the house to the stables.

****

"I'm glad things went well today," Anna said.

They were at dinner and it was the most lively and noisy one so far.

David raised his water glass. "Here's hopin' tuh-day's uh por-tent of t'ings to come t'morrow."

"What time should we leave in the morning?" Anna asked Eleanor. She began to butter her roll.

"The papers said we should be present by nine o'clock," Eleanor replied. "I suppose we should leave around six."

"Don' lahk eatin' so early," David put in. He broke off a piece of roll and began to sop his gravy.

"I daresay none of us may want to eat tomorrow," Eleanor replied. "I know my appetite is already waning."

"Mus' keep up stren'th." David stuffed the soggy piece of bread into his mouth, chewing and swallowing. He raised a hand, making a movement as if stabbing something. "Saint David bravin' dragon Desmon' need 'trition."

Anna laughed, thinking it was a good sign that David could joke. She looked at Eleanor again, thankful she was still speaking to her. "Will your barrister be meeting us there? You haven't mentioned him."

""Barrister?" Eleanor looked as if she didn't know the meaning of the word.

"Yes." Anna's next words were a little cautious. "You *have* retained legal representation, haven't you?" She glanced at David. "Surely, you're not going into court alone?"

"Of course we're not." Avoiding her gaze, Eleanor got very busy fiddling with her napkin, pulling it off her lap, folding, then unfolding it and abruptly pressing it to her mouth. Momentarily, she looked pale. "My goodness." She yawned, fingertips to her lips. "I can't believe how weary I am. I suppose if we're getting up so early tomorrow, we should all retire early tonight, so I believe I'll lead the way. Goodnight."

With that, she stood, laid down her napkin, and walked from the room.

Anna watched her leave, then got to her feet, also. "I suppose we should follow your sister's example."

David took a final swallow of water before standing. He offered Anna his arm. She wrapped her own around it and allowed him to escort her from the room.

In the hallway, she Signed, *I don't think you should come to my room tonight.*

No? David's eyes twinkled with mischief. *Can't we make love to bring me luck tomorrow?*

You won't need luck, she told him.

Then may I love you simply because I wish to?

That made her laugh, then sign seriously, *Truly, David, I think we should sleep alone tonight.*

Bowing, he accepted that, but swept her into an embrace. *Then I'll at least escort you to your bedchamber door.*

Scooping Anna into his arms, he carried her up the stairs.

****

Two hours later, as Shelton was in the process of locking up for the night, Eleanor appeared at the top of the stairs. She was in her nightclothes, dressing gown tightly buttoned.

"Shelton?"

"Here, my lady." The old man slid the lock on the front door into place and turned. "Did you need something?"

"I have a missive which must go to my barrister in Harris Crossing. Tonight," She held up a rather bulky packet. "Have Edward saddle Horse and deliver it for me."

"Horse, m'am?" Shelton frowned. "His Lordship won't like a footman taking his horse."

"His Lordship won't know unless someone tells him," Eleanor replied. She came down the stairs and thrust the packet into the butler's hands. "This has to be delivered tonight."

"As you will, my lady. I'll see to it right away." With a bow, Shelton hurried to the backstairs leading to the servant's quarters.

Eleanor stood a moment longer, watching him disappear into the hall's darkness before she went back up the stairs.

Chapter 35

"What do you say when addressing the judge?" Anna asked.

"Your Honor, or Muh Lord Justice," David answered promptly.

"Remember, be polite," Eleanor cautioned. She was dressed in bonnet and traveling coat, ready to leave. She continued giving instructions as she looped and folded David's neckpiece. Eleanor had tucked up his collar so she could wrap the length of linen around his neck. "No matter what."

He was dressed in his best clothing, an up-to-date suit fashioned for his last birthday. His coat was dark blue, of the new cut, front a bit high above the waistline so the bottom edge of his vest was visible. That garment was of pale gray satin with yellow and royal blue brocaded trim. The ruffles on his shirt cuffs peeked past the braid on the straight edges of his coat sleeves. Pale gray suede gloves encased his hands.

Gently, he pushed her away, pulling his coat closed and straightening the collar.

The front door was open. Through it, they saw the coach approach. A sleepy-looking Robert, today in his capacity as driver, pulled the horses to a halt in the front yard.

Both animals and conveyance gleamed in the sun. The groom had worked for hours the day before, polishing the harness, as well as the coach itself, scraping mud from the wheels and smartening the leather trim. The coach horses were curried and combed so their coats shone like polished onyx.

"Time tuh go." David looked at the two women. "Ah-na…Elly?"

"You go ahead," Anna said. "I need to speak to Shelton a moment."

Nodding, David offered his sister his arm and they went through the door.

"What is it, miss?" Shelton asked.

Anna opened her reticule, bringing out three small packets. Shelton started as he saw them, remembering the items Edward had taken to Harris Crossing for Lady Eleanor the night before.

He was grateful David hadn't decided to pay a visit to the stable this morning to see his horse. There might've been a bit of a row when he discovered Run had been ridden. Though Robert stayed awake into the wee hours to rub down the gelding when Edward returned, the horse still showed evidence of having been ridden hard and fast.

"As soon as we leave, I want you to take these to the village." She placed the letters in the butler's hands. "Deliver one to the Reverend Morse, One to Al at the smithy, and one to Mr. Greeley."

"What are—"

"No time to explain," Anna said as Eleanor called from the carriage for her to hurry. "Tell them it's very important."

Snapping closed the reticule, she whirled and ran out the door. Edward assisted her into the coach, then slammed the door and climbed onto his seat at the back.

With a snap of the whip, Robert turned the coach and the horses started down the carriage road.

Shelton looked at the three letters he held.

"Jane," he called. "I've an errand to run. I'll be in the village for a bit."

Chapter 36

The county seat was in Harris Crossing, a three-hour journey from Mayfield Village. Anna and Eleanor were silent during the trip, both keeping their gazes steadfastly on the countryside speeding past the coach windows.

David appeared unconcerned. In fact, he seemed to be dozing, slouched against the seat opposite his sister and Anna, legs stretched before him, arms crossed over his chest. Eleanor had insisted he wear a hat, though he protested that. It lay beside him on the seat, a fine example of the local hatter's art, fashioned from gray beaver pelt imported from the recently liberated colony of New York.

****

No one might be speaking, but everyone's thoughts were a frantic jumble.

David has to win this case, thought Eleanor. *Too much and too many are counting on him. The judge has to recognize how able he is. Granted his reading skills aren't the best, but there are a good many gentlemen who hardly ever read, so that doesn't matter. Surely His Honor will see that, and after he declares his verdict and David's title is secure...* She glanced out of the corner of her eye at Anna. *Then there's another problem to settle...*

****

Oh, my darling, Anna looked fondly at the young

man pretending to sleep. *You have to win. So many people need you. Though it means I'll lose you, you have to be declared Baron Mayfield. At least, then I can leave you knowing I've succeeded in what I was hired to do.*

****

As for David, his thoughts were much less complicated. *I'm going to win this case. Then I'm going to beat Desmond within an inch of his life, and then…I'm going to marry Anna.*

****

The courthouse was an imposing structure, marble and granite, in a style always managing to fit in no matter the architectural changes coming and going over the years. It housed the upper court as well as the lower magistrate court where all criminal trials began and many civil proceedings were held.

Outside, there were people milling around, some waiting for their cases to be called, others merely spectators. All looked curious as the Mayfield coach pulled up. Seeing the crest on the doors, they crowded around a bit, then moved back as Edward jumped from his perch, demanding, "Here now, move away so His Lordship and party can disembark!"

That brought some grumbling and commentary, but they obeyed. David got out, assisting Eleanor, then Anna. He turned to Anna but, before she could say or do anything, Eleanor seized his arm and pulled him to the steps. Giving Anna a backward glance, he allowed himself to be led away, and she trailed behind.

Edward climbed back onto the coach and Robert drove it around to the livery stable where it would stay until time to return.

If *we return,* Eleanor thought, with a pessimistic

stab as she glanced back at the disappearing coach. *Will Desmond allow us to go back to the manor if he wins?* She had a feeling he might strand them in Harris Crossing simply because he'd have the right to do so.

Inside, there were many rooms where simultaneous trials were being held. As outside, people of all classes lined the halls, upper society beside the lower, all with bailiffs keeping them orderly and confined within the area of the courtroom to which they would go when called.

Benches were positioned against the walls with men and women as well as a few children crowded upon them. Several of the women held infants and occasionally one would whimper and cry, probably from a wet nappie or hunger because those in attendance couldn't leave until the case in which they were involved was completed. Bared bosoms were in evidence, with nipples thrust into eager little mouths, stopping tears.

As David glanced at one such mother nursing her infant, Eleanor caught his arm, jerking him around so violently he stumbled as she steered him away from the sight.

"Don't stare." Her fingers ordered.

Edward appeared in the doorway, looking over the heads of the crowd. He saw David. Pushing some aside, skirting others, he made his way to his master's side.

Find out where we must go. Signing, David leaned toward him. Abruptly, he had a sudden shyness of speaking in public, with so much confusion, so many strangers' ears listening.

Nodding, Edward sought out a bailiff, speaking earnestly to him. The man nodded, and consulted a book he carried, opening it and running his finger down a list of names. "Walters versus Woods, Hearing to Determine Competency and Re-Awarding of Title?"

David nodded, placing a hand on Eleanor's arm as she started to protest the wording.

The bailiff gestured, and they followed him to the end of the hall where an empty bench stood by a closed door.

"Be seated here, sir. It appears your case will be the next to be heard."

"When will that be?" Anna asked.

The bailiff shrugged. "Whenever a verdict's declared on the current one or the judge calls an adjournment for the day, miss. I can't say."

With that, he walked to the other side of the door, tucked the book under his arm, and stood. Edward sighed and took up a position at the end of the bench, stiff as a sentry on guard duty. David seated himself while Eleanor and Anna did the same.

"Lady Eleanor? I got here as soon as I could."

They looked up as a gentleman stopped before Eleanor. He was as well-dressed as David but a great deal older than either he or Eleanor. He was panting slightly though attempting to stifle it.

"Mr. Abbott." Eleanor acknowledged him. To Anna, she explained, "Our barrister. This is Miss Anna Leighton." She introduced Anna, who nodded as Mr. Abbott acknowledged her with a similar gesture. "She's taught David how to Sign…"

He bowed and looked at David as he straightened. "Is this Lord Mayfield?"

"Ah am."

David's answer surprised the barrister, though he recovered quickly.

"…as well as speak," Eleanor continued.

"You've changed quite a bit since I last saw you, my lord," Abbott said. "I believe you were four at the time."

"Sorry," David looked apologetic. "Ah don' 'member."

"No matter. Lady Eleanor, may I speak with you a moment?" He held out his hand.

Taking it, Eleanor allowed herself to be pulled from the bench. They walked a few feet away, speaking in low tones, Abbott's head inclined toward Eleanor's. Once or twice he looked David's way, then said something quickly.

Eleanor and Abbott returned to the bench.

"Your Lordship, I have to confess I'm completely unprepared to present your case. Her Ladyship waited until yesterday to notify me as well as send me the papers served upon you."

David shot Eleanor a shocked glance to which she turned away, dropping her gaze.

The barrister went on, "I immediately tried to get a continuance, coming this morning to the courthouse and discovering who would try the case, then going to the judge's home. A most disturbing occurrence, as you may imagine. His Honor was not pleased to have his breakfast interrupted. I believe that is the reason he refused my request."

"Elly?" David's tone was accusing.

"I'm sorry, David," Eleanor said. "I know I should've notified Mr. Abbott directly but …at first I kept putting it off, telling myself the problem would go away, that Desmond would drop his charges. Then Anna came, and I was certain we wouldn't need a barrister. After Desmond's visit, my mind was in such turmoil, I swear the last thing I was thinking about was that Mr. Abbott hadn't been informed. In truth, I'd actually given up hope."

She lowered her gaze, avoiding her brother's accusing look.

"Yesterday, when Anna questioned me, I realized I shouldn't have delayed, that we needed representation, no matter what happened, that I was foolish to give up, as long as there was one iota of a chance…" She took a deep breath. "After everyone went to bed, I sent Edward to Mr. Abbott's home with the papers. Better late than never, I suppose."

She gave David a hopeful, and very tentative, half-smile.

David didn't answer.

"I roused my clerk," Abbott said. "In the little time we had, I've found as many legal arguments as possible, as well as a few cases to cite, but I've no idea if it's going to be enough, and for that I offer my sincere apologies."

"Ah mustn't lose dis case, Mr. Abbott." David shot Eleanor a venomous glance. "No t'anks tuh muh sister."

Eleanor looked crushed. She appeared on the verge of tears. Impulsively, Anna put her arm around her. She was surprised when Eleanor leaned against her.

"I'll admit when I read the papers your cousin filed, I truly believed you had no case," Abbott continued. "Now, however…it's startling, actually hearing you speak."

"Ev'ryone says dat," David replied. "Ah wish *Ah* could hear me."

"Yes, well…" Abbott appeared embarrassed by this frank statement. He hurried on. "Here's what I propose: After the preliminaries, your cousin's barrister will lay out the facts, perhaps call a few witnesses to testify to your condition. Then I'll present your case and have you testify and speak for yourself...literally. I'm hoping once His Honor hears you, he'll simply dismiss the case then and there."

"One can hope," David answered.

"Now we must simply sit and wait to be called," Abbott finished. He looked around. "I see neither Mr. Walters nor his barrister are here yet."

"Thank God," Anna muttered.

He stepped to the end of the bench and seated himself. Edward glanced at him and back at David but didn't speak.

A man pushed through the crowd, coming determinedly toward them. David looked up, saw him, and nudged Abbott, nodding at the man.

"No," Abbott said. "That isn't your cousin's barrister."

"Lord Mayfield?" The man stopped in front of Abbott. He was short, plump, and very out of breath.

Puffing rapidly as he waited for Abbott's answer, he took off his spectacles, steamed over by the sweat streaming down his cheeks. Rubbing them against his sleeve, he slipped them back on with one hand, the other being encumbered with a small, black portmanteau-like case.

"This is Lord Mayfield," Abbott said, gesturing to David.

David got to his feet, nodding to the man.

"Dr. Philip Pennington." The man hurried on, "I've been instructed by the court to examine His Lordship and certify that he is, indeed, deaf."

"What?" That brought Eleanor out of her shameful

daze. "That's absurd. Why would he feign such a condition?"

"Nevertheless, miss…"

"Your Ladyship." She snapped her title. "Lady Eleanor Woods."

"Your Ladyship." He bobbed his head in a quick bow. "In a case such as this, it's within the purview of the presiding judge to order such an examination, and His Honor has done so."

"Quite so." Abbott abruptly sounded very businesslike. "Would you like to conduct this examination now, Doctor? Where?"

"There's an anteroom just there." The doctor indicated a door across from the one leading into the courtroom.

By this time, David, showing his usual aversions to physicians, was shaking his head and showing some agitation, as well as signs of the temper he'd kept under control up to this point. Anna touched his shoulder, trying to quiet him.

"Go with Dr. Pennington, Your Lordship," Abbott told David, seeing the frantic headshakes. "Cooperate, but don't speak to the doctor."

He got a confused frown from David, though he obediently stood, looked at the doctor, and then stalked toward the door.

Dr. Pennington followed. He spoke to the bailiff, who went with them also.

The wood of the door wasn't thick. In a short time, sounds issued forth…the blast of a trumpet, the shrill tweet of a whistle, and at last, a sudden report as of a pistol being fired.

At this last, Eleanor jumped, as did several others

nearby. "What in the world? Was that a gunshot?"

Anna patted her hand.

Soon David, the bailiff, and the doctor returned. The bailiff resumed his place by the door.

David looked a bit flustered. He carried his coat over his arm. Pulling it on, he threw himself onto the bench beside Eleanor. His waistcoat was buttoned wrong and his neckcloth untied.

"Thank you." Pennington bowed. "I'll write up my report and submit it to His Honor forthwith." He hurried down another hall to a different part of the courthouse.

Eleanor began to reclose David's vest.

David jerked away from her, pushing away her hands. Eleanor shrank back as if he'd struck her. Taking a deep breath, he began to rebutton the vest, lips compressed into a straight line. When it was closed to his satisfaction, he very deliberately and calmly stood, walked past Eleanor to where Anna sat, pulled the linen from around his neck and held it out to her.

Eleanor drew in a soft, sobbing breath.

Standing, Anna took the neckcloth from David, wound it around his neck, folded and tied it, and sat down again. David sat beside her, as far from Eleanor as he could get.

In a moment, there was a flurry of sound down the hall and two men burst through the crowd. David stiffened. So did Eleanor as they recognized Desmond. David half-rose. Anna placed a hand on his arm. He dropped back onto the bench.

Desmond and the other man stopped, looked from them to the bench opposite, then sat there. David's cousin was dressed once more in the height of fashion. The other man was more solemnly attired. Anna supposed him to be Desmond's barrister. They spoke quietly together for several moments before Desmond raised his head, his eyes meeting Eleanor's.

"I daresay it's a good thing looks can't kill," he drawled. "Otherwise my dear cousin might be up on murder charges directly."

David's gaze fastened on Desmond's mouth. Anna's hand tightened on his arm.

"Well, Cousin." Desmond looked David up and down with a supercilious sneer. "I see you've the dummy dressed in his Sunday best. Do you truly think that's going to help? Though I will admit if clothes did indeed make the man, one would believe him the most intelligent creature on the planet."

He settled back onto the bench, both hands closing over the head of his walking stick.

David's hand closed into a fist, lips flattening into a straight line. Anna's grip was so tight now, her hand ached. Abruptly, he relaxed, his own hand patting hers before dropping to the bench.

"How long is this going to take, anyway?" Desmond demanded of the bailiff.

The bailiff leaned toward the door as if listening. "I believe the proceedings inside are coming to an end, sir."

As he finished speaking, the doors burst open, held by the sergeant-at-arms. He stepped aside and a flood of people poured out. The two in the lead were slapping each other on the shoulders and offering congratulations as were those around them. They continued down the hall. The last ones out of the courtroom were a man and woman. The man shook his head.

"How did it go?" the bailiff asked. He seemed to know the man.

"Lost," he muttered. "Now I've got to pay that scoundrel four months' stable fees because he kept my strayed horse that long before notifying me he'd found it." He shrugged. "Just don't seem fair!"

He and the woman hurried on.

"Sirs?" The bailiff looked from Desmond to David. "You may enter now."

Getting to his feet, David went inside, followed by Abbott. Eleanor and Anna trailed behind, being careful to walk fast enough not to be near Desmond and his barrister.

"You'll be here, sir." The bailiff indicated two chairs behind a wooden railing on the left. As David and Abbott took seats, he motioned to another set on the right. "And you here, sir."

On the right was another railing with two chairs behind it. Desmond and his barrister sat in them.

Looking around, Anna settled herself in the first row of seats behind David and Abbott, beside Eleanor, who huddled into the chair as if attempting to make herself as small as possible. Behind them were more chairs.

On the far side of the room stood a high desk on a dais and before it a table with three chairs. Because there was no jury, there was no prisoner's dock nor a witness box. To the right of the high desk was a door. Next to the door was the red, white, and blue Union flag with St. Andrew's cross counterchanged with St. Patrick's cross and the cross of St. George over all.

The bailiff called through the doors, "The rest of you may come in now."

Immediately, there was a scramble of feet and a stampede of people rushed in. They clambered over each other, seating themselves in the rows of chairs a few spaces behind those in which Anna and Eleanor sat. All were strangers, idle townspeople out for a morning's entertainment at the expense of those involved in a case, as well as the merely curious as to the goings-on of a small town's legal system. There were quizzical stares at both David and Desmond, jostlings and elbow jabs, as they muttered among themselves and each other, asking who the two men were and what was going to happen.

The bailiff pulled the doors shut. The sergeant-at-arms took his place before them.

Abbott turned to David. He had time for only one sentence as the door to the right of the dais opened. "Remember, don't speak until I call you as a witness."

"All will be silent!" the bailiff shouted, ordering, "All rise."

Everyone fell silent, scrambling to their feet, with the exception of David, who didn't move until he realized everyone around him had gotten up. Belatedly, he stood also.

Through the door, three bewigged men in black robes entered. Since there was no jury in a magistrate's court, most cases were merely heard by a judge or three lay judges. This particular case was being heard by a justice who required a bench of two lay magistrates. Each man, called a winger, carried several thick volumes. The third, the court scribe, held several quills and an inkpot. Selecting chairs and sitting, they placed the books upon the table. Behind them came a fourth man, also black-robed. None wore the court dress of a black silk damask robe, however.

The justice climbed to the high desk and settled himself.

The bailiff went through the opening in the railing,

turned, and intoned, "Hear ye, hear ye, this court is now convened with the Right Honorable Justice Sir Hubert Clive presiding. All present attend with courtesy and respect or leave now. God save the King."

David would later learn Sir Hubert was considered a Justice of the Peace and a professional magistrate as opposed to a lay magistrate who was chosen from the citizenry but wasn't necessarily titled.

Studying the papers before him, the Honorable Sir Hubert seized his gavel, rapping it sharply against its base. "Bailiff will read the charges brought in this case."

He sounded completely bored, as if he had no care one way or the other what was said or who was in the right.

Anna felt her heart sink. A queasiness coiled in the pit of her stomach.

Between Abbott's lack of preparation because of Eleanor's dereliction, and the judge's unconcerned attitude, this might not be as easy or as simple as they had thought.

Chapter 37

"This is a competency hearing, my lord," the bailiff referred to the book he held. "Charges brought by Desmond Walters, cousin to His Lordship, David Woods, Baron Mayfield, in which he states His Lordship is not competent to bear the title twenty-seventh Baron Mayfield due to a mental infirmity making it impossible for him to continue the line of inheritance."

There was a long silence.

As David scowled, Anna realized the bailiff had spoken too swiftly, face partially hidden by the book he held upraised, and he hadn't understood all that was said. Touching his arm, she quickly signed an explanation when David turned toward her. His expression cleared, and he nodded, looking toward the judge again.

"The barristers will introduce themselves and their clients," Justice Clive ordered.

The clerk opened a book, dipped a quill into the inkpot, and began to write. The scratching of the pen made an odd counterpoint to the judge's words.

Abbott and the other man got to their feet. The judge looked from one to the other.

"Charles Grant, Your Honor," Desmond's companion announced. "Barrister for Desmond Walters, petitioner." He nodded at Desmond, who inclined his head in a falsely gracious manner.

"I'm William Abbott, Your Honor," Abbott said.

"Barrister representing Baron Mayfield." He indicated David, who was again scowling fiercely because Abbott was turned away from him. "This is Baron Mayfield."

Anna hitched her chair closer to David's. It made a scruffing noise against the floor. The judge looked past David to her.

"Be still, young lady."

"I-I'm sorry, sir," she stammered. "I was simply trying to get close enough to His Lordship to explain what's happening."

"Explain? I thought His Lordship is deaf."

"He is, sir, but I can Sign to him and…"

"I see. Very well, but no more chair scraping."

"No, sir." Quickly, Anna told David what Abbott had said. Behind her, curious eyes followed the movement of her fingers, necks craning to watch.

"Now then…" Justice Clive settled himself, looking from one side of the courtroom to the other. "Petitioner's barrister will begin. Mr. Grant?"

"Thank you, my lord." Grant got to his feet, came around the railing, and stopped before the magistrates' bench. He bowed. "Sirs."

They nodded in return.

"David Woods, the present Baron Mayfield, has been deaf since the age of five."

He waved a hand in David's direction, giving a grand and dramatic gesture making David, as well as Eleanor, stiffen.

"His sister, named his guardian in their father's will, has secluded him at Mayfield Manor, the country estate, ever since. He can't read or write. He's never been to University, never had a Grand Tour," Grant declaimed. He sounded more as if he were making an oration than a legal statement. "Indeed, he's never been in the company of his peers. He's not been introduced into Society, nor courted any young woman with the intent to marry and continue the family name. At Baron Mayfield's death, my client, Desmond Walters is next in line to inherit. With the reaching of His Lordship's majority in several months and no attempt having been made by either the Baron or his sister to secure him a marriage…indeed, there being little use for such an occurrence in his present and permanent condition, Mr. Walters is petitioning the court to declare David Woods incompetent by way of mental disability and to award the title and all inheritances to him so he may bring about the continuance of the family name."

He paused, taking a deep breath before continuing, "We will produce expert testimony proving these charges, sir."

"And you shall get your chance, Mr. Grant," Justice Clive rumbled. He had a deep voice, almost like the growl of a watchdog, with the appearance to match, a very intimidating man. "As soon as Mr. Abbott gives his answer to these charges."

He looked from Desmond's side of the courtroom to David's.

"Mr. Abbott?"

"Thank you, Your Honor." As Grant went back to his client, Abbott rose and presented himself to the court. He performed the same bows to both justice and lay magistrates, was recognized, and paused, clearing his throat.

Behind Anna, there was a shuffling, as if the spectators were straightening eagerly in anticipation of what he was about to say.

Those cruel people. She was appalled. *They're here merely for the drama. Can't they understand what's at stake? That it isn't simply a day's entertainment?*

"My lords…" In contrast to Grant's slightly bombastic tones, Abbott's words were calm and almost conversational. "It's true His Lordship is deaf. It's untrue he can neither read nor write, for he was in the process of learning his letters when his accident occurred. I daresay, at this time, his reading and writing levels are probably on a par with a good many nobles who care more for hunting and gaming than education."

There was a lilt of laughter through the spectators at that. Justice Clive tapped the gavel once against the desk and the laughter subsided.

"Lady Eleanor has since hired a tutor from the acclaimed McAdam Academy for the Deaf to teach His Lordship Signing."

At that, Desmond glanced at Anna, scowling fiercely.

"It's also untrue that he's been secluded from society. Lord David may not be as polite as some, but he's aware of manners and etiquette and no doubt could mingle in Society with barely a ripple, considering the lack of refinement of some of our nobility."

At that, there was a loud snort, and another ripple of laughter, quickly cut off as the Justice raised his gavel.

"In fact, once his training is complete, it is his expectation that he will take his place in the *ton* and go about procuring a wife to bring about that hoped-for continuation of his family line."

David turned to Anna and smiled. Her answering expression was rather shaky.

"In summation, Your Honors, this request filed by

Mr. Walters is completely untrue and unnecessary, and we ask that the petition be dismissed."

There was a silence as Justice Clive considered this.

"I'm afraid I need more evidence than your mere say-so, Mr. Abbott," the justice answered. "Hearing will continue."

"As you will, My Lord." Abbott's expression showed he'd expected that answer. "We will so prove the charges false."

He bowed and took up a position similar to Grant's, standing by the railing where David sat. Desmond followed his movements the way a cat might watch a bird he was stalking.

"Good enough." Clive's gavel again struck its base. "Mr. Grant, you've witnesses? Call your first."

The clerk paused in his writing, looking up.

"Thank you, Your Honor." Grant looked at the bailiff. The clerk began to write again. "I wish to call Lady Eleanor Woods."

"What?" Eleanor didn't raise her voice, but the way her body jerked and the sharpness of her whisper bespoke her shock.

A mutter ran through the crowd in reaction.

"Lady Eleanor Woods will rise," the bailiff called out.

Reluctantly, Eleanor stood. With gloved hands clasped together at her bosom, she appeared more like a prisoner in the dock than a witness.

The bailiff approached, picking up one of the books on the desk. He held it out. As hesitantly as if thrusting her hand into an open flame, Eleanor placed her hand upon it.

"Do you swear or affirm to tell the truth, the whole

truth, and only the truth, to all questions put to you in this matter knowing that not to do so can be considered an act of perjury which is a crime?"

"I do." Eleanor accepted the Bible, kissed it, and returned it to the bailiff.

"Please state your full name and title," he instructed.

"Eleanor Sarah Augusta Woods, Lady Eleanor Woods."

The bailiff returned to his place.

Grant rose and placed himself before Eleanor, who regarded him as if he'd transformed into a snake. She was visibly trembling. Behind them, David's hands clenched into fists, his animosity toward his sister forgotten in her distress.

"Lady Eleanor, your brother has been deaf since he was five, stemming from a carriage accident in which your parents died?" Grant asked.

Eleanor nodded.

"Witness must speak aloud," the bailiff reminded her.

"Yes..." Eleanor swallowed, coughed, and swallowed again. "That's correct."

"He's how old now?"

"Tw-twenty."

"In all that time, has he been given any schooling?"

"N-no...I mean, he had just begun learning his letters and to read when...when he was injured."

"But since that time, there have been no governesses or tutors?"

"Miss Leighton has been his tutor." Eleanor looked at Anna.

"For how long?" Grant asked.

"Only...a few weeks." Eleanor's voice got even

quieter.

"But other than Miss Leighton's…uh…instruction…" Grant's pause made Anna's teaching sound very dubious indeed. "There's been no entry into university or even talk of such?"

She shook her head, then remembered to speak up. "No."

"Has he ever been to a ball, a house party, or received any of the usual invitations from people of his rank?"

"No."

The word was spoken so reluctantly even His Honor frowned.

"Thank you, Your Ladyship." Grant walked away to stand near the railing separating him from his client. "No further questions."

Eleanor looked as if about to protest. Justice Clive spoke up, "Mr. Abbott? You wish to question this witness?"

"I do, Your Honor." Abbott turned to Eleanor. "Your Ladyship, is your brother illiterate?"

"Of course not!" she flared. "David can read."

She bestowed a fond look upon him. By now, seeing her fright at testifying, David had overcome his previous anger toward her. He returned her gaze, smiling slightly. Eleanor took heart from that.

"He has his own books and has access to any in our father's library."

"Is he completely without friends?"

"David has several friends in the village," Eleanor answered. "The blacksmith's sons, all of the mercantile owner's children, Mr. Brown…"

"That's Mr. Absalom Brown, owner of Brown's

Stables and Stud Farm?"

"The same. He's also David's riding teacher."

"If David has that many friends and acquaintances, then surely he has some knowledge of manners."

"David's manners may not be as refined as someone living in London," Eleanor retorted. "However, we aren't completely cut off from civilization though we live in the country. I've personally instructed him in both manners and etiquette."

She shot Desmond a glance full of hatred. Their cousin stared back at her nonchalantly, but a slight tightening of his lips indicated he hadn't anticipated what she was saying.

"He knows which forks to use and wouldn't be out of place if we were at a ball or a dinner party."

"Thank you, Lady Eleanor." Abbott bowed and returned to his place.

Eleanor started to sit.

"A moment, Your Honor." Grant practically bounded forward. "May I redirect a question to the witness?"

Clive gestured his permission.

"You say your brother wouldn't be out of place at a dinner party…"

"I did."

"But what about a ball? He can't hear. How could he dance with anyone?"

"He…" Eleanor paused. "He couldn't."

"So he would be a mere spectator, standing on the sidelines watching, as couples moved about the floor soundlessly."

"I…you might say that," Eleanor hedged.

"My dear Lady Eleanor, I believe I just did." Grant

turned away with a smirk.

Desmond allowed himself a wide grin.

"No further questions, thank you, my lord."

Eleanor dropped into her chair so heavily it groaned. Anna caught her hand. Their fingers tightened around each other. Releasing Anna's hand, Eleanor dug into her reticule, bringing out a tiny linen handkerchief. She pressed it against her mouth.

"I'd like to call Dr. Philip Pennington," Grant said.

"Dr. Philip Pennington, please step forward," the bailiff intoned.

There was a brief silence as Pennington extracted himself from the crowd and they made room for him to approach the railing. He handed Grant several sheets of paper. The scratching of the scribe's quill filled the silence. The bailiff went through the swearing-in, the doctor stated his name and qualifications, and Grant started his questioning.

"You were requested by this court to examine Baron Woods?"

"I was."

"What are your qualifications in that area, Doctor?"

"I'm a general practitioner and have been in practice in Harris Crossing for fifteen years now. I've been requested for examinations several times by Justice Clive as well as other judges."

"You performed the requested examination today?"

"I did, shortly before we were admitted into the courtroom."

"Your Honor, I'd like to submit Dr. Pennington's written report of that examination, dictated earlier. To be labeled Petitioner's Exhibit A." Grant walked over to the bench, handing the papers to the clerk, who accepted them and wrote something on the top of the left corner of the first page and set them aside.

Grant walked back to the doctor.

"Please give your findings, sir?"

"First off, let me say, I found His Lordship recalcitrant and uncooperative."

"In what way? Was he violent?"

"Not violent but very slow to respond. As soon as it was communicated to him what I was to do—"

"Communicated?" Grant interrupted. "How was that done, Doctor?"

"The young lady…" Pennington nodded at Anna. "She…I believe the term is *Signed*…to him. He shook his head, and she appeared to argue with him before he calmed. He went with me to an anteroom where I carried out the exam, but he did so with great reluctance."

"What type of examination was done?"

"I gave a cursory physical one…listened to his heart and lungs, et cetera. I discovered a small scar on his neck, just below his left ear. Well healed. Souvenir of that carriage accident, I surmised."

Scar? Anna glanced at David. She'd seen no scar, so it must be at a point where his collar and neckcloth hid it. When they were alone together, she'd not been interested in scars. That thought brought a slight flush to her cheeks.

Pennington was still talking. "I then proceeded to test his hearing."

"And that was done how?"

"I examined his ears, of course. Then I stood behind him and spoke. He didn't respond."

"Could he have been faking? Merely ignoring what you said and pretending not to hear?"

"That's possible, but I doubt it. I had a hunter's trumpet and blew that." The doctor smiled. "As you know, they're tremendously loud. He didn't move. I also blew a pennywhistle. Not a flinch. As a last test, I blindfolded His Lordship, and fired a pistol into a sand bucket, directly by his side. He didn't react at all."

"Your conclusion, Doctor?"

"That Lord David Woods is completely and incurably deaf."

"Were there any witnesses to this examination, Dr. Pennington?"

"The bailiff was in attendance, as is usual in such cases."

"Thank you, Doctor." Grant bowed. "No more questions."

"Mr. Abbott?" Justice Clive spoke.

"No questions, Your Honor," Abbott answered. "We'll concede Lord David is deaf as the doctor diagnosed, and has been for fifteen years."

At that, there was a buzz throughout the spectators. *Wot's he mean? Don't that prove wot they's sayin'? Seems like they've lost this case.* The words spun through the crowd.

Anna asked herself the same thing.

"Your Honor, I'd like to call Miss Anna Leighton as my next witness," said Desmond's barrister.

Oh, no... Anna's legs were shaking so badly, she had to grasp the rail to keep from falling back into her seat. She went through the swearing-in no better than Eleanor had, stood waiting for Grant's first question, fearing David might react or that she would give the wrong answer.

"You were hired by Lady Eleanor to teach her

brother Signing?"

"I was."

"You seem young to be a teacher of such a serious subject, Miss Leighton."

"I'm twenty-two."

"Nevertheless, that's fairly young. What are your qualifications?"

"I was an assistant teacher at the McAdam Academy for the Deaf for two years, then was promoted to fulltime teacher two years ago."

"Did you apply for the position with Lady Eleanor?"

"No, sir. Dr. McAdam, owner of the Academy, recommended me."

"I see. So you accepted and set about teaching Lord David how to Sign?"

"Yes, sir."

"Was he an eager student?"

Anna hesitated, then decided she'd better tell the truth. "Not at first."

"Oh?"

"He thought I was a doctor of some kind and wanted nothing to do with me."

"You know this because…"

"Lady Eleanor told me. She said his show of temper meant he thought I was another doctor going to tell her he's incurable."

"Show of temper?"

"He…smashed a vase…to show his displeasure." Oh, how she hated saying that.

David turned away as if to show his own embarrassment. Immediately, he looked back so he wouldn't miss anything said.

"You witnessed that?"

"Yes." She'd heard it, wasn't that the same as witnessing it? Eleanor and David both admitted his doing it.

"So he has fits of violence." Not giving her time to speak, Grant turned to the bench. "My lord…I will admit that this bit of testimony is hearsay, a repeating of someone's opinion by a second person to a third party. It may be unusual, since I called this witness, but may I request it be stricken from the record, except for the fact Miss Leighton witnessed His Lordship's display of temper?"

"So be it." Justice Clive looked over the desk at the clerk. "Scratch out that portion of the testimony."

There was a nod. The quill was dipped into the ink. Black lines obscured Anna's words.

"His objections notwithstanding, you did teach His Lordship?"

"Oh, yes. Once he discovered what I wished to do, he was eager to learn."

"And he now can Sign quite effectively?"

"Very." She glanced at David.

He gave her an encouraging smile.

Irrelevantly, she wondered if he was tiring of looking back and forth between her and the barrister.

"Are you telling the truth, Miss Leighton?"

"I beg your pardon?"

"Why? Are you hard of hearing, also? I asked, *Are you telling the truth?* I submit you're lying about your pupil's ability because you're aware of what is involved in this case."

"I assure you, sir, I am very aware of what's involved, but I wouldn't lie." It was Anna's fear realized, but she was still outraged that her veracity was questioned.

"Oh, no? Say hypothetically the Baron wins this case and you continue to be his tutor. What happens then?"

"Well…as soon as he's reached his full potential in Signing and I have nothing more to teach him, I'll have completed my assignment, and…" She paused. "I'll leave. I'll go back to the academy."

David stiffened. He shook his head. Out of the corner of her eye, Anna saw Abbott place a hand on his shoulder.

"You'll leave? I rather doubt that." Grant's tone turned sinister.

"What do you mean?"

"Aren't you lying to ensure His Lordship keeps his title and fortune? Haven't you formed a relationship more than student and pupil with the Baron? Don't you intend to have a permanent place in his life from now on?"

"How dare you insinuate that—"

"I wasn't insinuating, Miss Leighton. I believe I was being very plain in stating it."

A low growl made her look around.

David sprang to his feet, pushing her aside. Anna fell into her chair as David shoved past her, aiming for the opening in the rail. Immediately, Mr. Abbott was there, blocking his way.

The spectators began cheering and hooting. This was more like it, the drama with perhaps some of the real violence they wanted to see.

Justice Clive slammed his gavel against the block, calling for order.

Under Abbott's restraining hands, David calmed.

He returned to his seat, shooting Grant a look that made the barrister cringe slightly.

Order was restored.

"Miss Leighton, instruct His Lordship that he must not disrupt testimony again, or…disability or not, I'll cite him for contempt of court."

Anna rapidly Signed, turning David's head so he could see her whispered, "Please, David, that won't help."

He nodded, looked at the judge, and nodded again.

"Your Honor, may I request Miss Leighton's testimony be marked as extremely prejudicial and suspected for truth and also a notation be made of His Lordship's reaction?"

"It will be so done." Clive answered.

The clerk scribbled hastily.

"Have you any more witnesses?" Clive asked Grant.

"Only one more, sir, and then I believe our case will be ready for your deliberation."

"Then proceed."

"As my final witness…" Grant looked directly at David who glared back at him. "I call Lord David Woods."

Chapter 38

"Miss Leighton, you will interpret for His Lordship so there will be no chance he misunderstands," Lord Clive instructed.

"Your Honor, if I may…" Grant spoke up.

"What is it, Mr. Grant?" The justice glared at the barrister.

"In view of Miss Leighton's involvement with His Lordship…"

"You've proved nothing to that effect," Lord Clive interrupted.

Secretly, Anna blessed him for that.

"Nevertheless, Your Honor, I feel it would be better if a neutral party were to Sign for His Lordship."

"A neutral party? Mr. Grant, I'm afraid there aren't that many people walking the streets of Harris Crossing who have the knowledge of Signing."

"Me, I can!" someone shouted.

"Who said that?" The judge looked across the courtroom.

"I did, Yer Honor." From the crowd, a sandy head emerged. Al, with Jem in tow, stepped into the aisle.

"Who are you, sir?"

"Albert Ashley, sir…my da's th' smith for Mayfield Village. I can sign an' I'll speak true whate'er Lord Davy says." He glanced at Anna, saying in an undertone, "Got your message. Came as fast as me an' th' pastor could.

Mr. Greeley couldn't make it. One o' his childer got hurt an' he had to go for th' doctor.''

Looking back, Anna saw a man in clerical garments hovering in the aisle. She smiled her thanks.

"My Lord, if this man is from the village under His Lordship's property rights, he surely won't be impartial," Grant argued. "I've asked Mr. Joseph Watson, founder of the Watson School for the Deaf, to act as interpreter."

"A better choice, I must admit." Clive looked at Al. "Be seated, sir. Let Mr. Watson come forth."

Mr. Watson was duly called. Waiting for Anna to step aside, he took his place beside David, who turned so he could see both him and Grant. Watson signed a greeting, which David returned.

"I've heard of you, Mr. Watson," Clive said. "I believe you also taught Dr. McAdam, who runs the Academy where Miss Leighton is employed?"

"That's correct, Your Honor," Watson replied.

"Then those are credentials enough. Bailiff, swear in His Lordship."

The bailiff brought the Bible. Watson Signed the question of the oath. David nodded, kissed the Bible and returned it. Grant attacked before the bailiff was back to his place.

"Please identify yourself by your name and title."

Watson's fingers flashed.

David shot Anna a questioning glance. He appeared to have nearly reached his limit of restraint, his face dark with anger as well as something she could only interpret as impatience. Fearing what might soon be coming, Anna nodded encouragement and forced herself to smile.

I am David Woods, David's fingers moved as

quickly as Watson's had, causing that gentleman to nod in approval. *Twenty-seventh Baron Mayfield.*

Verbally, Watson relayed the message. Now it was the justice who nodded. David kept his attention on Grant.

"You have been deaf since you were five?"

Watson Signed the question. David didn't move. He simply stared at Grant.

Oh, no. The distress to Anna's stomach returned, this time with an extra pang of fear. *David, this is no time to be stubborn.* She raised her own hands, preparing to tell David exactly that.

"He's mulish." Desmond spoke up, his voice clear and plainly understood.

"The petitioner will remain silent," Clive said.

"Your Honor, instruct the witness to answer," Grant requested.

"Repeat the question to His Lordship," Clive ordered.

Before Watson could move, David's fingers flashed a question of their own.

Why do I have to answer that? You know who I am. Why do I have to Sign?

Watson repeated his words aloud, then told David, *They wish to see how well you can Sign. To make certain you can be understood.* He also spoke those words as he Signed them.

Why doesn't someone simply ask me? David looked around, including His Honor, then the entire courtroom in the sweep of his arm. *Why can't I speak?*

As Watson repeated that last question, Grant laughed.

"Please, Your Honor. With all the other things

we've been told, are we now to believe he can actually speak?"

Anna braced herself as David took a deep breath. He didn't look at Watson's hands but stared directly at the barrister. His own hands dropped to his sides.

"Yes, yuh bleedin' sod. Becuz Ah can."

There was a stunned silence. From the section where Jem, Al, and the pastor stood, came a call.

"Attaboy, Davy! Tell 'em!"

That was greeted with a titter of laughs, quickly dying down as the judge pounded the desk.

"Wh-what did you say?" Grant stared at David, eyes wide.

On the other side of the railing, Desmond was equally goggle-eyed with shock, mouth open. He took a deep breath. "Can't be. I've never heard him speak. It can't be."

His face went abruptly white as he realized nothing was going as he expected.

"Yuh heard me," David snapped. A sarcastic smile twisted his lips. "Are yuh deaf? Mus' Ah repeat muhse'f?"

"Lord Woods…" Clive's soft-spoken interruption went unheeded.

Watson touched David's hand, pointing to the judge. David turned to him.

"Am I correct in saying you can hear?"

"Nuh, Yuh Honor." David gave a rapid headshake, brushing one hand across his right ear. "Ah truly can't hear a soun'." He reached across Watson and caught Anna's hand. "But Ah-na he'ped me speak. She taught me lip readin'."

"David already knew how, a little bit," Anna put in.

"Lip reading?" The judge looked thoughtful. "I've heard of that. Using the shape of the lips during speech to determine word meaning." He looked at David, mouthing, *You speak very well.*

"T'ank yuh," David answered, proving he understand every word the justice spoke. "Ah know Ah don' speak good as some, but Ah hope to get better. Anna taught me much."

"What else has she taught you?"

David was momentarily distracted by Grant walking behind the railing and dropping into a chair beside Desmond, who began to berate him in a low whisper.

"You should've called me as a witness, you fool! I knew not doing so was a mistake."

The barrister shook his head and ignored his client, watching David, who looked back at the judge.

"Ah-na he'p me read. We play piano…" He raised two fingers, miming tapping the keys as he had when he picked out the tune. Glancing again at Anna, he smiled. "She taught me tuh dance."

"Dance?" Clive looked disbelieving. "But that requires listening to music…"

"David's a very good dancer, Your Honor." Anna spoke up.

"Show me." Clive demanded. He waved a hand at the space before the bench. "Miss Leighton, give me an example of His Lordship's dancing skills."

"Yes, sir." Taking David's hand, Anna led him around the railing.

"We're goin' tuh dance?" He sounded dubious. "Here?"

She nodded. Stopping in front of the magistrates' bench, she positioned David facing her. His hand went around her waist as she tightly clasped the other.

"Ready?"

He nodded and took a step forward. Anna began to hum, loudly enough for all to hear, simply so there would be some rhythm for the spectators to listen to. She let David lead her through eight sets. Lips moving as he counted the beats of the steps, he gently whirled and turned her so they traversed the small space twice before she stopped humming. Squeezing his arm gently, she pushed his hand from her waist. David stopped.

From the spectators, there came a smattering of applause as David bowed over Anna's hand, then released it.

"Remarkable." Justice Clive murmured.

"Your Honor," Grant was on his feet. "I object to—"

"Silence, Mr. Grant." Clive picked up his gavel. "I'm calling a recess, during which I'll deliberate this case."

"But Your Honor," Grant's protest was as near to a wail as an adult man could make without sounding childish. "I haven't finished my questioning of the witness. We haven't made our summations."

"I believe we need no more testimony from this witness, Mr. Grant. As for summations, let me help you. The summation is as follows: Lord David Woods is deaf due to a childhood accident, as verified by Dr. Pennington's examination. He has a teacher who has now enabled him not only to sign but to speak. Do I have the facts correct? Mr. Grant? Mr. Abbott?" Clive looked from one barrister to the other.

Both men nodded, Grant in apparent defeat. Desmond glared.

"There's no need for further to be said. The clerk will enter that as both sides' summary." Clive got to his feet and climbed down the steps.

To the clerk, he said, "Bring the minutes of the proceedings." He looked out at the courtroom, where a few spectators were inching toward the sergeant-at-arms and the closed doors he guarded. "Everyone will remain while I review the facts of this case." He gave Desmond a significant look. "I don't believe this will take long."

With that, he walked out, followed by the clerk. The bailiff closed the door behind them.

Chapter 39

Like an audience after a play, the spectators chatted among themselves. Asking permission from the sergeant-at-arms, Al and Jem, with Pastor Morse in tow, darted across the aisle to speak to David.

"Wish you could've flattened that gent with a good right one," Al said, giving Desmond and Grant both grim looks. "That cousin o' yours, too."

"Now, Albert, violence never solved anything," the Reverend Morse reminded.

"Mayhap not, but it sure makes a body feel better on occasion," Jem replied.

David glanced across at Desmond, who had left his place and was pacing back and forth on the other side of the railing, swinging his walking stick. He nudged Anna, who had returned to her seat after Mr. Watson left them with a gracious bow.

David gestured at his cousin. "Looks worried. Good."

Before Anna could reply, the courtroom door opened. Al, his brother, and the pastor scurried back to their places.

"My God," Abbott murmured. "He's only been gone five minutes."

"All rise," the bailiff spoke.

Desmond stopped his frantic pacing. His expression was blank as the others got to their feet. The clerk

303

appeared, returning to his place at the table, setting down the book containing the minutes. Then he seated himself.

Justice Clive came through the door and ascended to his chair behind the high desk.

"You may be seated," the bailiff said.

Desmond rounded the railing, taking his place beside Grant.

Clive rapped his gavel. "I have made my decision in this case."

"All be silent to hear the Right Honorable Justice Sir Hubert Clive's verdict in the case of Walters versus Woods," the bailiff intoned.

Dead silence fell upon the courtroom. No one moved. It seemed none breathed.

"When I first received notice of this case," Clive began, his voice carrying to every corner of the room. "I thought it an easily decidable one. A man deaf since childhood, untaught, cut off from the world, against a man who was educated, cultured, and concerned with the survival of his family name."

By Anna's side, David's fingers twitched. She looked down.

Desmond only concerned with survival of his next card game.

Stifling a smile, she placed her hand over his.

"Once the trial began, I still felt the same way," the justice went on. "But when testimony began, I discovered how wrong I was, as well as what an error it is to make even the briefest judgment beforehand."

He paused, looking first at Desmond, who had leaned forward, one hand clutching the rail, the other tightening around his walking stick until the knuckles were white. Clive's gaze swung to David, who was as tense, though he appeared placid enough, probably because he was unable to hear the whispers circling behind him.

"After reviewing the minutes of this trial, considering the ramifications of the possible decisions I might make, as well as the effect they will have upon the participants, I feel there is only one verdict I can be morally justified in handing down in this case."

There was another pause.

Anna wondered if His Honor wasn't a bit of a showman, playing the spectators as an actor might, leading them toward a brilliant and dramatic finale. She was certain if she looked behind her she'd find more than a few sitting on the edges of their seats.

Clive raised his gavel. Every one tensed. Several leaned forward, hands clutching their seatmates' shoulders.

Tell us! she wanted to scream.

Only her hold on David's hand kept her from doing exactly that. Next to her, Eleanor drew in a deep breath. The color was slowly leaching out of her face.

"In the case of Walters versus Woods, I find in favor of…" His Honor took a deep breath. "David Woods."

"What?" Desmond leaped to his feet. "You'll let that idiot keep the title…and the money…"

"Your Honor." Grant was beside him, interrupting Desmond's harangue. "That previous bit of theatrics notwithstanding…"

"That bit of theatrics is what lost you the case, Mr. Grant," His Honor answered, drily. "The title of Baron Mayfield will stay in the possession of David Woods, who is as competent as I am, as will all fortunes and properties."

"It isn't fair!" Desmond spluttered. "Why should that simpleton be allowed…"

"You'll be quiet, Mr. Walters," Clive admonished. "Else I'll have the bailiff remand you for contempt. I've made my decision and it stands and is now entered into the court records. Case dismissed!"

The gavel slammed against the desk, and the courtroom broke into chaos.

Jem and Al rushed to David, pounding him on the shoulders. Pastor Morse was close behind, hands clasped, muttering a prayer going unheard in the cheers issuing from the spectators. David hugged Anna, then seized Eleanor and kissed her cheek. He shook Mr. Abbott's hand while across from them, Desmond watched with hatred blazing in his eyes.

Grant tried to speak to him, but Desmond thrust him away, pushing past the barrister to the doors. He was nearly swept aside as the crowd rushed to David, strangers reaching for him, offering their congratulations, both for the verdict and also for a good afternoon's entertainment. Desmond struggled through the crowd. Flinging the sergeant-at-arms out of the way, he wrenched the doors open and dashed into the corridor.

"Ah-na…we won." David's announcement, joy-filled in spite of his lack of inflection, floated over the noise.

"No, David." Anna told him. "*You* won."

She didn't get a chance to say any more, as David seized her in an embrace and spun her around. Then he kissed her.

A second cheer broke out, the sound sweeping through the courtroom. Today had been better than any traveling mummers' show.

"Hey, now, would you look at that?" Al spoke into the silence following. "Looks like Davy's as normal as a man can be."

David released Anna long enough to swat at his friend and laugh.

****

It was nearly half an hour later before the uproar died down and the crowd dispersed. Fortunately, David's case was the last of the day, so the bailiff didn't have to hurry them from the courtroom. He and the sergeant-at-arms stood to one side, discussing the case, and watching the spectators as they trickled out, talking among themselves. The two officers of the court gleefully reviewed with obvious enjoyment bits of testimony and things the judges and barristers had said.

David, Anna, and Eleanor, along with Mr. Abbott, still sat in their places.

Divested of his robes, Lord Justice Clive gave the garments into his valet's custody and joined them.

"I wish to be advised of your progress, my lord," he said, shaking David's hand. "I want to know how much this young lady can teach you before she decides her task is done."

"I'll send you reports, Your Honor," Anna promised. "Be assured."

"You know…" The judge looked thoughtful. "I don't try many criminal cases. Most of mine are civil, though sometimes those can get fairly dramatic, and occasionally violent, depending on what's at stake. Often I've great difficulty making a decision, and frequently, even after a verdict has been given, I question whether I was right or wrong, but today…" He smiled, and his entire demeanor changed. "This is one of those times when I know I made the right choice and have no doubt about it."

With a bow, he left them.

"I must say this was the easiest case I've ever had," Abbott said. "Especially considering I was so ill-prepared."

"As for that," Eleanor turned to David. "David, can you forgive me? Please? I don't know why I did it. I guess unconsciously I was running away, not wanting to face the reality of your losing everything."

"'Neffer run away…face it head on,'" David quoted. "Ah 'member Papa sayin' that." He hugged Eleanor, then pulled her through the door and into the hall. "Let's go home."

Edward was gone from his place beside the bench.

"I took the liberty of telling your man to fetch your carriage, sir," the bailiff explained.

"T'ank yuh," David offered an arm to Eleanor, and the other to Anna. "Shall we?"

Abbott accompanied them to the door. As they went down the steps, he bade them farewell and started down the street. At the corner, he paused as the coach passed, a smiling Robert guiding the horses and a grinning Edward perched on his seat at the back.

"'Bout your reports tuh His Honor," David told Anna. He brushed a kiss against her cheek. "Yuh realize your task neffer be done?"

She didn't answer.

David stepped into the street, releasing Anna to raise a hand in greeting to Robert. Behind him came the sound of hoofbeats, a horse being ridden fast. Anna looked back.

"David!"

He didn't hear her cry, didn't react until Desmond's cane came down on his shoulders. Staggering in pain and confusion, David spun and saw his cousin mounted on a horse that reared as heels dug into its ribs.

"I'll be damned if I'm going to let some dummy do me out of all that money!" Desmond looked murderous. Eyes narrowed, face red with fury, he raised the cane again, striking David on the side of the neck. "I'll kill you first!"

David stumbled backward, putting up his hands, attempting to ward off another blow.

"Hey! He's attacking His Lordship." One of the spectators, standing to one side speaking to a friend, looked up as the cane descended a third time.

He and his companion rushed to David's aid.

There was momentary pandemonium. The horse neighed wildly, Eleanor was screaming, Anna crying. Attracted by the man's shouts, others on the street crowded around. Robert pulled the horses to a halt to prevent running over the two women huddled in front of him. Sliding from his seat, Edward ran to David, trying to get between his master and Desmond's deadly cane as it continued to rise and fall, striking David about the shoulders with deadly accuracy.

"Someone stop him!" The shout came from the crowd. "Get a constable!"

The cane struck the footman across the back. Edward went down. David made a desperate lunge, catching his cousin by the leg, dragging him from the saddle as the horse reared again.

Desmond regained his balance. He gripped the cane in both hands as he and David faced each other. With all his anger behind it, he swung the cane twice. One blow struck David's neck, the second his temple.

A searing jolt of red pain ripped through David's head. Everything was enveloped in a black cloud...

Chapter 40

David awoke in a deep, dark chaos more frightening than any nightmare he could ever have dreamed.

He knew he lay in a bed, but it wasn't his own, of that he was certain. It was too soft, and it creaked as he moved. The sheets were coarse and limp. The nightshirt he wore also felt wrong…too big and heavy…

The vision of Desmond's face flared before him, red and angry, eyes slitted…the cane rising and falling…

There was a low rumbling, a violent explosion blasted into his brain. It swirled and spun, cutting through the darkness, making brilliant red sunbursts behind his eyes. He had a momentary vision of a giant stalking across a field, the ground shaking and collapsing with each massive footfall. Sharp raps like the strikes of Al's hammer chopped through his consciousness, a murderous smith beating on his skull…his brain shattering into fragments. He'd swear he felt bits of it crumble and dissolve.

It hurt…like the stab of a thick, dull blade.

The carriage…

David was thrown into the center of that long-ago tragedy…the horses running away…the axle breaking…Mama, Papa, Nanny…a splintering and crashing, bodies being thrown about, David himself sailing through the air…a tree looming ahead of him as he struck it headfirst, then slid down…the bark cuting into his neck, gouging out a groove of flesh…

Slapping his hands over his ears, he screamed and rolled onto his side, covering his head with his arms.

There was tapping…grating…a screech…high-pitched trilling…more chaos inside his head…the pandemonium of Hell attacking from all sides.

He began to sob.

The bed tilted, and someone seized his hands, ripping them from his damaged ears.

"David…oh, David, at last you're awake."

David opened his eyes.

"Ah-na?"

*Anna…Anna…Anna…*her name echoed inside his head, burning and burrowing like a murderous beetle chewing its way into his brain. That hurt, too…but not so violently this time.

"Anna…" He spoke her name again, feeling the world calm and become sane, and something else…

"I was so worried." She stooped to kiss him.

David wiped his eyes. He cupped Anna's face in his hands, smearing his tears upon her cheeks, then said the words neither he nor anyone else ever expected.

"Ah-na…Ah can hear you."

Chapter 41

"It's my theory those multiple blows to your neck, landing directly on the scar left by your original injury, restored your hearing," Dr. Pennington said.

Amazing how being able to hear can change one's attitude, David thought. Toward Dr. Pennington and toward physicians in general.

Unconscious and bleeding, both Edward and David had been carried to the doctor's surgery not far away. After giving them emergency care, Pennington dismissed the footman but declared David needed to be kept under observation until he regained consciousness. He was moved to the doctor's home, where he lay unconscious for several days. A frantic Anna and Eleanor were offered rooms in Justice Clive's home, returning to Pennington's every day to take turns sitting by David's bedside.

"I imagine you're going to have a ringing in your ears for a good many months to come," the doctor continued as David shook his head, a gesture he did quite regularly and unconsciously when the sounds he now hearing became almost too much to bear.

Where previously he'd heard nothing at all, now David suffered a surfeit of sound. The shutting of a door was like the most violent clap of thunder, that act of Nature being almost unbearable. A dog's bark, the rattle of a carriage wheel, footsteps on carpeted floors—things those with hearing took for granted—caused him, not having experienced those sensations in fifteen years, near-excruciating pain.

He was inundated by those devastatingly terrible and at the same time delightfully welcome sounds. Even the clink of a teacup against a saucer made him wince while at the same time making him ecstatic with joy.

Often Eleanor would find him sitting in a chair by the window, drumming his fingers upon the sill and looking up at her with the delighted expression of a happy child. When he was brought tea, he'd repeatedly tap the bowl of his spoon against the cup's rim, listening to the musical tinkle. Once Anna found him laughing while listening to the flesh-cringing *skrill* of fingertips being dragged down a dry windowpane.

"It's childish, I know, but I want to hear it all," he told her, brushing his hand across the bed quilt and cocking his head to one side to catch the soft whisk of the threads giving under his touch.

Now that he could hear, David's inflection returned. His speech was improving day by day, sounding more and more natural.

Eleanor had brought to the house one of the specialists who had previously examined David. After the usual exclamations of surprise at finding the man he'd declared incurably deaf now not only able to hear but also speaking, he assured David his speech would soon be indistinguishable from anyone's.

"Even when it hurts, I want to hear it. I want to revel in every sound in the world…from the smallest squeak of a shoe to the most devastating, house-shaking thunderclap." He caught her hands. "Eleanor tells me the sea makes a monstrous noise. When I'm well, let's travel to Cornwall and listen to the waves as they strike the cliffs."

"When you're well, David, you can travel everywhere you wish," Anna replied. *But I won't be going with you.*

David, too happy in his newly recovered hearing, didn't catch the careful way her answer was worded.

****

It was several days more before David asked about Desmond. On a visit from Justice Clive, who'd taken an interest in David since he was now having his sister and sweetheart as his houseguests, he finally broached the subject.

"What's happened to my cousin?"

"You pulled him from his horse," the judge told him. "He struck you again as you both went down. That made you lose consciousness."

"Please tell me I didn't kill him," David exclaimed. The look he gave Clive held true fear. "Your Honor, I don't want to hang. I've too much to live for now."

"Don't worry," Clive assured him. "It's your cousin who's cooling his heels in gaol. He continued beating you after you lost consciousness. I must say you put up a valiant fight, my boy. Your coachman and my bailiff hauled him off you and dragged him away to a cell."

He laughed slightly as he sipped the tea Mrs. Pennington had served them. Glancing around, he pulled a small hip flask from his pocket, opened it, and poured a healthy dollop into the liquid. Holding it up, he glanced at David.

"Please." David held out his own cup.

The judge poured an equal amount into his cup, then capped the flask and put it away. "I like tea, but the good doctor's wife makes it a bit weak."

"This certainly isn't." David swallowed and took a deep breath. "What is that liquid called, sir?"

"Scotch whisky," the judge answered and winked. "Twelve-year-old. I always keep some handy for emergencies…and drinking Mrs. Pennington's tea is such an occasion."

"Scotch whisky…" David looked thoughtful. "I'll have to remember that. I'm certain there's nothing like that in Mayfield Manor's cellars."

"I'll give you the name of my supplier," Clive offered. He took another sip from his cup, then said. "Where was I…oh, yes…I was certain we were going to have to arrest your man. He was all for killing Mr. Walters then and there.

"I take it he didn't, either?"

"No, sadly."

"What'll happen to Desmond?"

"He's been charged with assault with intent to do bodily harm to your footman, as well as your attempted murder. Your sister filed the complaint since you were in no shape to do so. They've postponed the trial until you're fully able to attend and testify."

"Wish I didn't have to," David mumbled. "The less I see of my cousin, the better."

"I imagine Mr. Walters is going to be going away to one of our fine prisons for some time to come, so you needn't worry about seeing him any time soon."

"Will you be presiding over the trial, Your Honor?" David tilted his cup and drank the last of its contents. "Might I have some more of that whisky, sir?"

"Perhaps we'd best go slow on that since I sense you've not had any before," Clive suggested. He lifted the teapot, filling David's cup. "Let's stick to the regular beverage for now. Indeed no," he answered David's question. "That's one trial where I'm certain I couldn't hand down a fair verdict. No, Your Lordship, I've done what's called *recusing* myself, meaning…" He laughed. "I know too much about the defendant to deal with him impartially. One of my fellow justices will settle Mr. Walters' hash."

****

In the Pennington parlor, Anna and Eleanor faced each other over another tea table.

"Now that David's inheritance is no longer in jeopardy, I believe you and I have some business to settle," Eleanor said, sipping her tea.

"Not necessarily," Anna answered. She'd been dreading this moment, but now that it was here, she felt strangely relieved. She set down her cup. "My work at Mayfield Manor is over. David no longer needs me, so I'll be leaving…"

"But of course he needs you, my dear," Eleanor interrupted, hand hovering over the teacakes. She selected one and bit into it daintily. "Whatever makes you think otherwise?"

"I've taught David all I can," Anna answered, frowning at the calm gaze Eleanor turned upon her. "From here on, David is able to handle any problem he faces, on his own."

"Anna, I don't think you'll ever stop teaching David." Eleanor laughed and reached across the table, placing a hand over the ones in Anna's lap. "You have to stay."

"I don't understand. Don't you want me to leave?"

"Whatever makes you think that?" Eleanor looked

as surprised as if Anna had suddenly startling cackling like a hen.

"Why…perhaps the fact that David's a baron and I'm not even of the nobility…and we've…he's…formed an attachment…"

"What does that matter?" Eleanor's laugh was tantamount to saying, *You silly girl.* "Though I'd say it's *more* than an attachment." She brushed away that argument with a wave of the hand holding the remains of the cake. Crumbs scattered. "Since the moment you arrived, you've never treated David with pity but as if he were as normal as everyone else. Now he is. Besides, you can make him do things when I never could. Didn't I tell you I wanted you to be part of our family? I couldn't ask for a better sister-in-law, Anna."

"But I thought…"

"Quit thinking," Eleanor ordered. "I'm proud to know you, Anna. As for not being noble… I daresay you won't embarrass me when we're at a dinner or a house party. Truth be told, it's probably David who'll do that. I doubt if he's ever going to outgrow speaking his mind."

"Eleanor…I…" A tear rolled down Anna's cheek, and she began to sob, very quietly.

"Anna, what's the matter?" Eleanor left her chair, dropping onto the couch beside Anna.

"I'm so happy…I was so worried…"

"I suppose I'm not very good at saying things," Eleanor apologized. "Too long keeping everything bottled inside." She offered a napkin from the tea service. "Better not let David see those tears. He'll call you *silly*."

"I remember." Once again, Anna could see David as he hugged Eleanor because she was crying, then told her women were silly to cry when they were happy. "Why don't we speak of something else?"

"Such as your wedding?" Eleanor laughed then, aloud. "I thought you'd never ask. I was thinking we could have it in the garden here. The flowers should be in full bloom in a few weeks. Oh, we must notify your father. Did you ever get that letter sent? I'm truly anxious to meet the man who raised such a strong daughter."

Chapter 42

Once again David stood in Harris Crossing's courthouse, awaiting the entrance of the court magistrate. David didn't want to be there. He never wanted to see the inside of a courtroom again, yet here he was, waiting patiently for his cousin's trial to begin.

It had been explained to him by Mr. Abbott that this was merely a hearing, to determine if a crime had been committed, and if so to remand his cousin to the Crown Court for trial. David didn't care what it was called. He simply didn't like being present.

The courtroom closely resembled that other one in which he'd been more or less the accused, but it held a few differences. Instead of the judge's high desk, there was only a table for the three lay magistrates. On either side of the table were two doors instead of the single one through which Justice Clive had entered in David's case.

To the right of the desk was a gallery in which witnesses sat, David, Anna, and Eleanor on the front row, with Mr. Abbott beside him, though he wasn't involved in this case. Eleanor had asked him to attend more for moral support than anything else, David imagined. On the second row sat Edward, fully recovered, and the bailiff, along with Robert and the two men who'd come to David's aid.

There were no seats behind the railing separating the spectators from the courtroom area. Any curiosity-seekers wishing entertainment in this venue had to stand. As expected, it was filled nearly to capacity with both those who'd been on the street when Desmond attacked David and others who had heard of the somewhat sensational happenings and wanted to be on hand to see how the trial unfolded.

As before, there was no box where a jury of Desmond's peers would decide his fate. Sardonically, David wondered if that meant they were unable to find a dozen schemers, gamblers, and liars to stand in judgment on his cousin.

Behind them all, the sergeant-at-arms guarded the outer doors.

The door to the left of the desk opened. A guard, stiff in his dark blue uniform, led in a shuffling, manacled Desmond. He was dressed as nattily as usual and appeared to have shaved and indulged in a normal morning *toilette.* The only thing out of place were the heavy iron manacles upon his wrists, incongruous against the ruffles protruding from his coat sleeves.

Desmond stepped into the prisoner's box. The guard shut the door and produced a key, unlocking the manacles and dropping them to the floor outside the box. They made an ominous metal clank as the links settled. The guard stationed himself beside the door.

Desmond glanced in David's direction. Briefly, their eyes met. His cousin was the first to look away.

The other door opened. Unlike before, only two lay judges entered with their books. A third man, the court clerk, carried paper, quills, and ink. Behind them came the chairman, the lead magistrate, though all three would determine the verdict in the case. The chairman would simply speak for the group, three *good and lawful men* chosen for their character to be guardians of the peace in their county.

"This court is now in session, the Honorable James Headley, presiding as chairman."

There was no solicitor for the defendant or a Crown Prosecutor. Those would be in attendance at the trial, if there was one.

"All rise." A new bailiff spoke. David wondered if the old bailiff felt odd, hearing someone else say the words he generally called out.

As everyone got to their feet, the magistrates settled themselves, and the bailiff continued, "This court is called to order in the case of the Crown against Desmond Walters, charged with assault with intent to do bodily harm of one Edward Withers and attempted murder against one David Woods, Lord Mayfield. Draw near and give heed. God save the King."

Again, Desmond's gaze flicked to his cousin. David met it with an unblinking stare before looking back at the magistrates again.

You damned son of a bitch. David had learned quite a few curses from Al and Jem during his convalescence.

Anna leaned toward him. "Are you certain you want to go through with this?"

"It's the best way," he answered and stood, resting his hands against the gallery rail. "Your Worships, before this hearing begins, may I speak?"

"Who are you, sir?" The chairman looked his way.

"My name is David Woods. I suppose you might say I'm one of the victims in this case."

"You're definitely the victim," Eleanor muttered.

"What is it you wish to say, Mister…" One of the wingers whispered something to the chairman. "Your

Lordship?"

"I'd like to request the charges against my cousin be dropped."

That caused a mild uproar from the spectators. Desmond stared at David in disbelief. The chairman rapped his gavel.

"Order. Silence." He gave David a startled stare. "Your Lordship, this man…" The gavel waved in Desmond's direction. "This man is charged with attempting to beat you to death, of knocking you senseless and continuing to do so after you lost consciousness, and you wish to have him released? Without punishment?"

"That's correct, Your Worship."

"May I ask why you'd want such a thing?"

From the spectators came loud murmurs repeating the same words. The chairman tapped the gavel again. The mutterings died away.

"Certainly, sir." David paused briefly as if collecting his thoughts. "I had a good deal of time to think while I was recuperating. You see, the Woods have always been a fairly staid family. We've lived quietly and never gone in for sensationalism. My cousin is part of that family, and I don't particularly want him to be the first blot on our escutcheon."

There were more mutterings, someone asking what a *'scutcheon* was. This time, the chairman ignored the disruption.

"Therefore," David continued, "I'm respectfully requesting the charges against my cousin be dismissed, since I, as the victim, didn't file them. It was my sister doing so."

"Nevertheless…" Mr. Headley paused. "You'd

simply have us set him free, to perhaps try to harm you again?"

"No, sir. I'd ask that you release him with a *proviso,* which, if he doesn't obey, would result in his being re-arrested and brought to trial."

"That sounds intriguing, Lord Mayfield." Headley looked thoughtful. "Are you perhaps reading for the law?"

"I'm afraid not, sir." David glanced at Abbott. "My family's barrister advised me on this."

"I see…what is this *proviso*?"

"That upon leaving this courthouse, my cousin sells to me his current manor house, Wellesley, with all its properties and holdings, and takes the money and forthwith leaves England forever."

Desmond started at that, shaking his head violently. He was ignored by both David and the judge.

"May I remind you that if he's remanded for trial and found guilty, the same could occur—without any money changing hands?" the chairman said. "He could possibly be sentenced to ten years' hard labor and transported to Australia to serve his sentence."

"Which would result in the notoriety I wish to have my family avoid."

"This is most unusual." Headley looked thoughtful. "I don't know if there is a precedence for this or even if it can be done." He looked past David to Edward. "Also, there's Mr. Withers to consider. He was attacked also, and has filed a complaint, and is also named in the charges."

"I understand, Your Worship, and have spoken to Mr. Withers concerning this. He agrees with me that, if the case proceeds, he will refuse to testify, as will I, and

I believe, without our testimony as the aggrieved, even if others step forward, the case may be a bit weak."

"We'll need to discuss this." The gavel struck the table. "There will be an hour's recess."

He and the others rose, gathered their books, and with the clerk trailing behind, left the court.

It was over two hours before they returned.

"Surprisingly enough," Headley announced, when order had been restored and they were once more seated, "we were actually able to find another case which ran along similar lines. I must say this is a most unusual legal occurrence, but citing the previous case, which will be noted and entered into the minutes of this hearing, we order the charges against the accused dismissed. Also he will be released from custody with the stipulation that Lord David's *proviso* is put into effect. If, within two months, Desmond Walters is still found to be residing within the English boundaries and not on a ship bound for some other country, he will be summarily re-arrested…"

"And at that time, Mr. Withers and I will gladly sign a complaint, Your Worship," David finished for him.

"Guard, release the prisoner from the dock."

The gavel struck the desk, the sound like a thunderclap.

The guard opened the door to the prisoner's box, stepping back so a slightly dazed Desmond could exit. David had supposed the spectators would leave quickly, disappointed there'd been no dramatic testimony, but no one made an attempt to go to the outer doors, even as the sergeant-at-arms unlocked them.

What are they waiting for? Do they hope he'll attack me again?

David looked at Abbott and nodded, and he and the barrister left the witness gallery, coming around the railing into the courtroom proper. Recovered now and with a bit of a swagger, Desmond met them halfway. Out of the corner of his eye, David saw Anna and Eleanor, following close behind, stop.

"I suppose you expect me to be grateful I'm not about to become a transportee." Desmond's greeting was both an attack and an insult.

"Of course I don't," David responded. "You're a selfish, greedy, lying swine, and as such you don't have the integrity to be thankful for anything."

"At least we understand each other," Desmond sneered. "God, I never thought I'd actually have an intelligent conversation with you."

"You're going to have more than that," David told him. "In Mr. Abbott's office."

"You mean you were serious about that?" Desmond was astounded.

"Very much so. We're leaving here in a group and going directly to the chambers of Abbott and Waverly, Barristers, where a Bill of Sale is awaiting your signature—"

"See here." Desmond attempted a blustering tone. "If you think I'm signing away Wellesley—"

"Shut up."

That startled Desmond so much he actually did.

"I'm well aware the manor's in jeopardy and a gentleman has been holding markers that would have enabled him to gain possession of it if I hadn't bought them from him." David's voice held an undertone of threat, his gaze turning so cold Desmond took a step backward. "I wish this to be an aboveboard transaction, however. You'll sign those papers, Cousin, after which I'll write out a draft for the sale and you'll cash it at my bank. Then, I'm very graciously giving you the loan of my coach and driver to take you to the nearest port, where I believe the *Clementine Joy,* a Baltimore clipper, is even now preparing to set sail for Boston, Massachusetts."

"I…" Briefly, Desmond's gaze flicked away. He sighed, as if realizing he was trapped and only a term on a faraway island continent awaited him if he refused to cooperate. "Very well."

His eyes met David's, his tone becoming abruptly ingratiating. "I hope you understand, Cousin, I was only thinking of the family name and keeping it alive. That's why I did what I did."

"Of course I understand, Cousin," David replied easily, though his smile appeared somewhat sinister. "Just as I hope you realize I'm only thinking of the family name as I do this."

With that, he pulled back his arm and, throwing all the weight of his twelve and a half stone body behind it, struck Desmond on the jaw.

Epilogue

"We're going to be leaving in an hour," David told Alleyne and Elizabeth. "I want you two to go upstairs and assist Nanny with the packing."

"But Papa, she doesn't need our help." The Honorable Alleyn Harold Aubrey Woods replied.

"Yes, Papa," the Honorable Elizabeth Anna Maisie added. "She shooed us out of the nursery because she could do better with us out of sight."

The twins were twelve now, both as like their father as a boy and girl could be. *Too much like him*, their mother said when they got into mischief, which was too often to count.

"No argument. Upstairs." The parental forefinger gestured to the stairs.

Turning his back on his offspring, David looked into the music room where his wife was pushing the bench under the piano. Anna held a dustcover in her hands. She shook it open, flinging it into the air where it billowed as it settled over the piano. She walked around it, smoothing the edges and straightening it over the closed instrument.

It had been thirteen years since that dramatic scene in the courtroom. Two months later, David and Anna were married in Mayfield Manor's garden with the Reverend Morse presiding and with their servants and immediate family, as well as the inhabitants of Mayfield

Village, in attendance. Eleanor was Anna's maid of honor, while Al, uncomfortable in his Sunday best, was David's best man.

A year later, to Eleanor's relief as well as Anna's, the twins made their appearance, being born exactly nine months and two days after the wedding.

And now they were on their way to London for the winter. Eleanor had gone ahead to open the townhouse and see to the airing out. They would stay there while Anna taught several school sessions at the McAdam Academy, ending the first month of autumn, after which they'd spend Christmas at Wellesley, then return to Mayfield Manor until spring.

Shortly after the wedding, David had decided to brave London Society. The Woods townhouse, vacant since the death of Lord Harold and Lady Beatrice, was re-opened. As soon as it was noted new faces were on the scene, David received an invitation from the Lady Patronesses of Almack's Assembly Rooms where the Countess of Jersey, having heard of his dramatic recovery and how he'd gotten even with his cousin, made him a gift of one of the non-transferable vouchers, allowing him and Anna access to their Wednesday night balls.

Lord David Woods, twenty-seventh Baron Mayfield, had been accepted by true London society.

Not staying to confirm whether his children obeyed, David tiptoed into the music room. As Anna straightened and stepped away from the covered piano, he put his hands over her eyes.

"Guess who?"

Behind him, Elizabeth giggled, the sound cut off as Alleyne clapped a hand over her mouth.

"It can't be my husband." Anna stood still. "He's busy attempting to make our unruly offspring pack for our trip to London."

"Was he the slightly frazzled gentleman I saw arguing with those two adorable children?" He sighed. "I agree. It isn't that poor sod."

"In that case, it must be my secret lover, come for a goodbye kiss before we leave."

"He wants more than a kiss." Removing his hands from her eyes, David spun Anna around and kissed her on the lips. As he straightened, he whispered, "Are the children still watching?"

Anna glanced toward the door. "They're still in attendance."

"Disobedient creatures. In that case, I suppose I'll have to continue our conversation this way." He raised his hands, fingers moving rapidly. *It pays to Sign. Glad I kept it up.*

Is that what you wanted to tell me? Anna asked.

No, my dear. We have an hour before we leave, and as your husband and not-so-secret lover, I wish to take you upstairs and give you my amorous attention.

David...

All right, if you wish me to be extremely frank, let's go knock boots...grind a few ears of corn. As a matter of fact, I've a tremendous yearning to plant a seed today. He waggled his eyebrows at her with a comical leer, then kissed her again, this time with quite a bit of tongue added.

Are you serious? Anna pulled away slightly. He tightened his grip around her waist, holding her against his chest. *David, the twins are twelve...*

Which means it's time for another chick in the nest

to replace our two rapidly growing brats. Wouldn't you like to have another baby? Perhaps we might have another set of twins.

What would the children think? She frowned. *If we have another baby at our ages?*

That their parents love each other? We're not in our dotage, you know, he answered. *After all, I'm only two and thirty while you're...* He hesitated. *All right, so you're more than that...*

Anna didn't like being reminded she was two years older than David. She grimaced at him.

Anyway, in a few months, they'll both be at an age to have a certain Talk. In fact, Alleyn's already asked me a couple of pointed questions which I deftly sidestepped with a promise that on his thirteenth birthday all would be revealed.

David moved closer so their bodies touched. He began to sway back and forth, certain parts of his anatomy brushing corresponding points of Anna's.

I thought you might speak to Elizabeth while I enlighten her brother.

All I ask is that you don't use those terms Al and Jem taught you.

My dear! David brushed a kiss against her temple. *Those are for your ears alone. I intend to describe relations between the sexes in the most lyrical terms possible. I'll inform our son how love between a man and a woman can be the most enlightening, passionate, and wondrous sensation in the history of the senses, that...*

Enough. Saying it in plain terms with an emphasis on caring will be sufficient.

As you will, my love. He bowed his head obediently, then gave her an impish stare. *In the meantime...?*

With that, David scooped Anna into his arms and walked out of the music room, nearly running to the stairs leading to the bedchambers.

Neither saw the twins crouching beside the grandfather clock standing to one side of the music room door.

"Why is it they always go upstairs when Papa starts that funny business with his fingers?" Elizabeth asked. "I know he's talking to Mama, but I wish I knew what he says."

Both twins were well aware of the story of how their father met their mother…because he'd lost his hearing after a terrible accident that killed their paternal grandparents and Mama had been hired to teach him to speak with his fingers. Without going into Desmond's part in the tale, David had told them his hearing was restored after he and Anna fell in love.

"*I* know," Alleyn declared. "Remember how you laughed at me when I asked Shelton to teach me to Sign? It's come in handy. I know everything Papa says to Mama." He didn't add he didn't understand most of it, however.

"Papa might not like it if he knew," Elizabeth warned.

"Well, he won't know, unless someone tells him…and you'd better not," Alleyne declared. "Anyway, I imagine Papa and Mama are going to have one of those long talks like they always do when they shut themselves in their bedroom, so I suppose we'd better go up and help Nanny as he said."

Taking his sister's hand, he pulled her up the stairs.

****

"Now then…" David set Anna on her feet.

"This would be more romantic if you'd come through the window." Anna glanced toward the tightly closed trio in the master bedroom.

"Only at night, when everyone's abed and there are no witnesses," David promised. He kissed her, reaching behind her to fumble with the buttons on her gown. "When we get to London, let's give a party. I've a sudden desire to have lots of laughter and music as I whirl you around the dance floor."

"I'm sure Eleanor and Father would like that," Anna replied. "It's going to be good to see them again."

With Anna and David married, Eleanor had taken up residence in Wellesley, from which she traveled to London every year to spend summer months with her brother and his family. After meeting Eleanor at the wedding, Anna's father abruptly began courting her, informing his daughter he didn't care how it looked or whether people gossiped. They were married a year later.

"As if you don't see both several times a month," David replied. "Does it still make you uncomfortable, knowing my sister married your father?"

"Not as much as it did originally," Anna answered, laughing as she remembered her embarrassment. "The main irritation is explaining how my sister-in-law is also my stepmother and my father my brother-in-law, and the children…whether they are my nieces and nephews or my half-brothers and sisters."

"All of the above…and let whoever asks untangle it." David brushed off any problems of kinship.

"Speaking of Wellesley…" Anna turned so he had better access to the buttons.

"Were we?" Deftly, David got her gown open to her waist. He kissed her shoulder, running his tongue around the angle of her shoulder blade.

Anna shivered. "Have you heard anything about Desmond lately?"

"My Boston solicitor…I suppose I should say *lawyer*, since that's what they're called in America…writes me he's been working at that printing firm for over seven years now. Who'd have imagined my dandified cousin would be at home up to his elbows in printer's ink…and enjoying it?" David dropped the gown to the floor and tackled Anna's lacings with the ferocity of a kitten with a ball of yarn. He glanced down at his wife's bare buttocks visible under the corset's edge. "You aren't wearing those pantalette thingies? Good. Apparently Desmond's also courting the owner's daughter, so he's still scheming, I'm afraid."

The corset followed the gown. Anna reached for a garter.

"Leave the stockings on," he ordered. "They're arousing."

"As long as he never bothers us again." Anna released the garter, managing not to shudder as she thought of how Desmond could've badly injured David or even killed him, to say nothing of poor Edward. "You were more than generous in the way you repaid him for that murderous act."

"The man restored my hearing." David gave her a sardonic look. He caught her hands, then stepped back, looking her up and down. "Now there's a pretty sight." He leaned forward and kissed her again. "It was the least I could do, for now I can tell you how much I love you and hear myself say it."

Putting his arms around her, he carried her to the bed, gently laying her on the bare mattress that had been stripped of sheets in preparation for the family's departure. David stepped back and pulled off his coat, flinging it to the floor. With comic and exaggerated haste, he unwrapped his neckcloth, tossing it aside carelessly, then slid down his braces and pulled his shirt over his head.

"Somehow, it was much more romantic when you couldn't speak," Anna said. She lay back, arms going over her head in a sensual stretch. "Mmm. Have I ever told you how much I like watching you undress?"

"Quiet, you shameless hussy." Boots were toed off and sent flying, followed by stockings. "Don't want your husband to hear."

David's fingers went to the buttons at the front panel of his trousers.

Pushing them down and stripping them off, he continued, "When I think of all I gained, from the moment I rode into the courtyard and saw you standing before the manor door… Do you know, the last time we were at Almack's, right in the middle of the quadrille, I wanted to stop, fling my arms wide, and shout to everyone within earshot, *I love this woman!*"

"I'm glad you didn't. I'd have been embarrassed no end. Even worse than that time you swatted at a fly and that countess declared you'd insulted her. That took a bit of fast explanation."

"You're right." David sighed. "It's getting to be a bit of a bore, being referred to as the Miracle Baron."

"Come here, you equally shameless man." Anna held out her arms. "Did we come up here to talk? I think there's been enough of that."

David climbed onto the bed, settling himself beside her. Clasping her naked body against his, he nibbled along her neck to her breast, planting a kiss on a nipple looking abruptly pert on a woman having nursed two infants.

"That's because I know you much prefer I say it this way." Cradling Anna's hand in his left, he kissed her palm. With his right hand, David signed, *Anna...* He touched his heart and then his forehead as he had that very first day.

I love you.

Author's Notes

While the descriptions of trial proceedings, magistrates, courts, and sentencing, etc., are in general accurate, some author's license has been used in order to create a more dramatic story.

A word about the author…

Toni V. Sweeney has lived 30 years in the South, a score in the Middle West, and a decade on the Pacific Coast, and now she's trying for her second 30 on the Great Plains.

Since the publication of her first novel in 1989, Toni has written 92 novels, with 89 of them being published. This includes several series.

Thank you for purchasing
this publication of The Wild Rose Press, Inc.

For questions or more information
contact us at
info@thewildrosepress.com.

The Wild Rose Press, Inc.

www.ingramcontent.com/pod-product-compliance
Lightning Source LLC
Chambersburg PA
CBHW051134030726
47504CB00004B/870